≡ HEROINES OF WWII ≡

A Rose for the Resistance

ANGELA K. COUCH

BARBOUR
PUBLISHING

A Rose for the Resistance ©2022 by Angela K. Couch

Print ISBN 978-1-63609-207-2

eBook Edition:
Adobe Digital Edition (.epub) 978-1-63609-209-6

All scripture quotations, unless otherwise noted, are taken from the King James Version of the Bible.

This book is a work of fiction. Names, characters, places, and incidents are either products of the author's imagination or used fictitiously. Any similarity to actual people, organizations, and/or events is purely coincidental.

Cover Photos:
Model image: © Stephen Mulcahey / Trevillion Images;
Background image: © Igor Marx / Shutterstock

Published by Barbour Publishing, Inc., 1810 Barbour Drive, Uhrichsville, Ohio 44683, www.barbourbooks.com

Our mission is to inspire the world with the life-changing message of the Bible.

Member of the
Evangelical Christian
Publishers Association

Printed in the United States of America.

withdrawn

A lovely romance and a touching story of a wounded family. Set amid the bleakness of Nazi-occupied Normandy, *A Rose for the Resistance* raises thoughtful questions about loyalty and courage and trust. Rosalie and Franz both find strength in dire circumstances, and their love grows from impossible to inevitable. You will lose yourself in this beautiful and suspenseful story!

—Sarah Sundin,
Best-selling and award-winning author of *Until Leaves Fall in Paris*

A Rose for the Resistance is a compelling historical romance, rendered upon the atmospheric canvas of the French resistance and the rising tension of the count-down to the invasion of Normandy. Braiding together the stories of a French woman drawn into the fight to free her country from occupation and a German soldier who finds himself on a journey he never expected, Angela Couch crafts a heart-tugging tale sure to keep readers eagerly turning pages. For fans of WWII fiction, this is one for the keeper shelf!

—Amanda Barratt,
Christy Award-winning author of *The White Rose Resists*

The French paid the price "with the blood of their men and the tears of their women." Writing like this, which etched into my heart, drew me deep into the lives of two grief-stricken people struggling to overcome their fears to protect the ones they love. Though set amidst the chaos of World War II, the story focuses a soft light upon growing faith, challenging family relationships, and enduring trust. Angela Couch's novel is an emotional escape into a tension-filled era.

—Johnnie Alexander,
Best-selling and award-winning author of *Where Treasure Hides*
and *The Cryptographer's Dilemma*.

Wow! *A Rose for the Resistance* is a story that will capture you from the start and not let you go. The way Angela has of telling a story and drawing you into the time and place is beautiful. I couldn't read it fast enough. Fabulous storytelling, lovely word choice, and realistic characters. I highly recommend this book.

—Liz Tolsma,
Best-selling author of *A Picture of Hope*

DEDICATION

To those who sacrifice for freedom.

———————— ≈ ————————

ACKNOWLEDGMENTS

A huge thanks to all those who have helped bring this story to life. To Jonathan—there is no way I could write, homeschool, and keep up with five young children without an incredibly supportive husband! Thank you for giving me wings. To my kids, who play together and take care of each other while Mommy is writing. To my critique partners, beta readers, and editors for making my work shine. And to the Lord for all His tender mercies that made this possible.

ⵣ CHAPTER 1 ⵣ

Normandy, France – June 1940

"*Aie-aie-aie!*" A drop of blood dripped from Rosalie Barrieau's finger as she jerked back. The dead thorn remained in place, mocking her effort. Ignoring the sting, she leaned in and clipped the lifeless stem from a rose growing over the arbor that led to acres of gardens—young plants, green with vigor in the warmth of spring. The rainbow of irises, rhododendrons, and geraniums had begun to fade, but poppies would open soon under pink hedges of tamarisk. And roses. The roses were a little late this year, but soon they would bloom, and she would keep them perfect until Papa returned.

"There you are!"

Rosalie spun to see Lucas Fournier's hurried approach up the lane. She flashed a smile at the tall, dark-haired man who had somehow gone from a childhood friend to the desire of her heart. "Where else would I be?"

His face showed no amusement. "In the village hearing the latest from the front, or at least inside with the radio on."

Her gut twisted, both at his chastisement and the reasons she hid in the gardens. "I don't know if I want to hear what's going on out there." Every evening for the past month—since the Germans had invaded their borders—her mother and younger brother would sit close to the radio, and they would all listen to the latest reports about the war. And every night the nightmares would come, tormenting her with worry for her father and others who had gone to fight the Germans. Lucas would also soon leave. He'd said so enough times, and grew more adamant each day.

"It's important, Rosalie." Lucas gripped her arm.

She usually loved his touch, but there was a bite to his hold. "I know it is! I know." Rosalie pulled away and folded her arms across her stomach. She ignored the dark strands of hair that had come loose from her bun and fell across her face. "But there's nothing I can do. They are far from here, and I have no control over what happens."

He reached for her again, this time more gently. She fell into his arms and buried her face in his chest. The war surging toward Paris could not be ignored, but at least there was security in his embrace. "Tell me."

The rhythm of his heart raced beneath her ear. His grip tightened. "We've surrendered."

"What?" She jerked back enough to see his face "What do you mean? Who surrendered?"

"Prime Minister Reynaud is stepping down and giving the government over to that fool Pétain." Lucas huffed out a breath and a curse. "He's agreeing to an armistice with the Germans."

Her chest refused to take in air. "An armistice?"

His brown eyes swam with both frustration and fear. "I should have gone. I should have been part of the fight."

"So you could have also surrendered?" She felt the bitterness build on the back of her tongue, but she could do nothing but swallow it. "What does an armistice mean for us, or for my papa? Or yours?" They had left around the same time, both veterans of the last war, both pledging to protect France from another invasion.

Lucas shook his head and pressed a kiss to her hairline. "I don't know, but I for one will not stop fighting no matter what Pétain and his advisors say. How can we roll over like obedient dogs trying to placate our new masters?"

"Oh, Lucas." She tightened her grip around him and felt him do the same. She'd heard too many stories from the last war, only twenty-two years earlier—almost the span of her own life. Papa had fought in that war too but preferred not to speak of it though he still wore scars on his hands. And Maman. . . Her scars seemed deeper. Perhaps from the loss of her three brothers, all killed in battle. Rosalie only had one sibling, and though he could be infuriating sometimes, she couldn't imagine losing him. Or Papa. Or Lucas.

She felt his mouth warm on her head again and closed her eyes. Was it a crime to enjoy this simple moment? Were they expected to stop living and feeling? She dared a glance at his face, then his mouth. What would a real kiss feel like? She'd begun to imagine a future with this man. Marriage. Children. A life built together.

He met her gaze for a moment, then glanced at her lips. He inched closer, until his breath caressed her skin. She leaned into him, and their lips brushed—

"Lucas!" Marcel's call jerked them apart.

"I need to go," he whispered. "He's waiting for me."

Curse her little brother. Though Marcel was almost eight years younger, Lucas had taken him under his wing. She released Lucas. "I'm sorry you had to come find me. You're right, I shouldn't be trying to ignore what's coming." Yet she still wanted to hide amongst Papa's flowers and pretend he would soon be home. Maybe he would be. With an armistice, would there be any reason to keep French prisoners? Perhaps Germans only wanted control of the government and life could continue with some normality as it had in Austria.

Lucas squeezed her fingers, and then she watched his departure. She sighed and allowed her eyelids to slide shut. June sun warmed her skin, and the aroma of hundreds of flowers and rich soil teased her senses. If only she could push aside the growing gloom settling over her and her beloved France.

———— ≈ ————

Not even a week passed before the Nazis arrived in Caen, a city a few hours east of Sainte-Mère-Église, and continued their march westward along the Normandy coast. Every hour coming closer.

"We're leaving."

At her mother's announcement, Rosalie dropped her spade and followed Maman's hasty retreat toward the stone and plaster cottage Papa had inherited from his parents. "What do you mean, leaving? We can't leave the gardens." Everything Papa loved would be overgrown with weeds by the end of summer. Yes, others had fled south as the Germans approached, but they had less to lose.

Inside, Maman hurried about, packing photographs and trinkets that might be considered valuable. "We will go to the village and stay with the Fourniers until we know what the Germans expect of us. We must not be alone. *Oui*, this will be safer." She bundled the valuables, silverware, jewelry, and a gold watch that had belonged to her Grandfather Barrieau into a handkerchief and then into a leather bag. She thrust it at Rosalie. "Bury this somewhere safe and cover the area so no one will suspect."

Rosalie hurried with the task, returning minutes later to find her mother loading Marcel with bundles. "We must go, we must go."

"Are they so close?" Rosalie took a pillowcase already stuffed with clothes.

"Past Blosville." Marcel headed out the door.

Maman waved at them to go quickly. "We have little time."

The village buzzed with folks gathered in the streets or hurrying from house to house. Shopkeepers locked their doors despite the hands on the clock not quite reaching the noon hour. *Père* Roulland hurried from the church, his long black robe billowing behind him as he jogged across the street to Alexandar Renaud, the mayor. Sweat beaded on his brow while he spoke with Monsieur Dumont, one of the wealthier citizens. The prefect *de police* was also headed in that direction when he looked their way and paused. He changed his course.

"Madame Barrieau."

Maman shoved another bundle at Rosalie. "Head toward the Fourniers' home. I will meet you there."

Marcel started with an objection, but Rosalie grabbed his sleeve and pulled him after her. Aline Fournier met them with hasty kisses and beckoned them to help her hide more of their possessions. China and paintings were tucked away behind cabinets and under the stairs. Lucas appeared for only a few minutes to press a kiss to his mother's cheeks and gather a canvas sack from his room.

Rosalie followed him to the back door. "Lucas?"

"I can't." His jaw stiffened, but his eyes held moisture. "Please understand."

Her breath hitched in her throat. "What are you planning?"

He shook his head and pressed his lips to her forehead. "We must not give up." His second kiss brushed her mouth all too briefly.

"Lucas."

He left, leaving Rosalie's stomach knotted. When Maman returned, all color had faded from her face.

"Are they here?"

Maman stared at Rosalie, her eyes wide and glassy.

"Maman?"

The church bells rang.

Rosalie hurried to the parlor window that faced the main street through their village and drew back the lace curtains. The rumble of heavy vehicles mingled with the thud of boots. Hundreds of boots. Heavy boots. German boots. Gray-clad soldiers pounded out the advance through the heart of Sainte-Mère-Église.

Lucas's mother stepped beside her, hand fluttering in a hurried cross from head to breastbone to shoulders. "More than twenty years have passed, and they look the same. I hate them the same."

Rosalie glanced back at her mother, who sank to a rocking chair. Marcel was absent, and now that she thought of it, she hadn't seen him since Lucas left. Rosalie withdrew from the window.

"Where are you going, *ma fille*?" Aline asked, hindering her from slipping out unnoticed.

"I need a drink." Though that was the furthest thing from her mind. Hopefully, she would find Marcel in the kitchen, though she doubted he had any more of an appetite than she. No, he'd likely followed Lucas. He wanted too badly to be like Papa. "I shouldn't be long."

The kitchen sat empty but for Aline Fournier's overfed cat. The yellow feline came to her expectantly, a guttural meow begging for a morsel to eat. Aline had probably forgotten her beloved pet in the franticness of the morning.

"*Je suis désolé*." Rosalie whispered her apologies to the cat. She snatched a worn gray scarf from a hook near the back door and slipped into the alley. She would find both Lucas and Marcel and bring them back before they did something stupid. Why hadn't she kept them from leaving in the first place, had an argument for Lucas, paid more attention to her brother? She twisted the scarf over her head and around her neck as she went, ignoring the warmth of the day. The need to hide felt more pressing.

Up ahead came a muffled shout in German—not that she'd have understood, even if the words were clearer. Rosalie knew very little German and had no desire to increase that knowledge, refused to have anything to do with the Nazis. She would keep her distance and hope they did the same until, by some miracle, France won back her freedom. Surely England would help them as they had in the last war. Surely the world would not sit idly by and allow Germany to tromp over half of Europe.

She slowed as she approached the main street and the flow of uniformed men. Her heart pounded against her ribs. *Be wary of soldiers. Never go out alone.* Maman's words spoken over and over in the past week nagged her, layering dread upon fear.

Rifle fire punctuated Rosalie's thoughts and jerked her head toward the north. The look in Lucas's eyes when he'd left sent a weight to the pit of her stomach and sped her feet back the way she'd come, past the house and on toward the church. Never mind that she ran toward the barrage. If anything happened to Marcel or Lucas. . .

Out of breath, Rosalie slowed and pushed herself over a stone fence separating her from the churchyard. The great stone walls and bell tower of the centuries-old church rose high, guiding her path. Faces stared out nearby windows, staring forward, trying, just as she was, to see what was happening on the street past the wall of trees. A thunderous boom dropped Rosalie to her knees on the cobblestones, and pain shot up her legs as smoke and dust billowed upward above the branches.

Boots scurried and someone shouted.

More gunfire. Lighter feet skittered in her direction, and she ducked behind a bush. A form rushed past her and vaulted the fence she had passed over. She recognized the clothes and murmured a curse under her breath.

She jerked to follow Marcel, but heavier treads pounded behind her. She dropped from the wall and spun out of sight behind a bush. Three uniformed men rushed past her hiding place but paused at the fence, speaking quickly to each other. One set his hands on the fence and began to pull himself over.

"*Non.*" She stood, the need to protect Marcel outweighing any immediate thoughts of her own safety. Their guns swung to her.

"*Wer bist du?*" one of them hollered, prodding her with his weapon.

Sweat tickled her back and neck as she held her palms toward them. "I—I don't understand what you are saying. I did nothing."

The largest of the soldiers gave an order, and another grabbed her arm and yanked her forward. His hands moved to her sides and slid down the length of her body to the hem of her dress just below her knees. Rosalie set her jaw. *Don't flinch. Don't flinch.*

"I have nothing," she managed, though they likely didn't understand French any better than she understood German.

The leader seemed to smirk and motioned his men back to the stone wall. With a single word, he sent them over it—in the path Marcel had escaped. The German officer stepped close and leaned toward Rosalie with hot breath. His accent was strong, but his French was almost perfect. "We *will* find your little friend, mademoiselle."

She froze in place while the man patted her cheek with his meaty palm and strode away, back toward the street. A tremulant breath did little for her air-starved lungs. She had to find her brother; she had to keep him safe. She set a hand on the wall to climb over, but a smear of red marred the stone. Blood.

"Oh, Marcel." Rosalie pulled herself over and scampered down the alley. Possible scenarios flashed through her mind, each more horrible than the one before, few of which spared her little brother. She searched each crack and garden she passed. Had he taken refuge at Fourniers', or would he try to go home? How badly was he injured? And where was Lucas?

She glanced over her shoulder, thinking she heard footsteps. Or was it her imagination? Her pulse rushed in her ears as she gulped another breath.

"Rosa!"

The whispered call pulled her around the thin opening between a woodshed and a stone cottage. Marcel crouched against a stack of wood. A smudge of black marred his otherwise pallid face, and his dark eyes were wide with panic.

"I need help." His breath came in quick puffs and his hand gripped his shoulder. Scarlet stained his fingers.

"What happened?"

Both jerked at the shuffle of more boots down the alley, and Rosalie dodged into the crevice beside him. "Come on." She led him to the front of the structure then ducked inside. He followed and pulled the door closed, plunging them into shadows. Only cracks between the shed's wooden slats allowed her to see her brother, who leaned against a large wooden barrel. He sank to the littered floor.

Rosalie dropped beside him, remembering too late her already damaged knees. "What happened? I heard an explosion. Where's Lucas?"

Marcel drew his hand away from his torn shirt.

"You've been shot."

He shook his head. "It's from the blast. Shrapnel."

Rosalie ground her teeth and tightened her fists. "They could have killed you. They might still if they find you. What were you thinking?"

"I was just watching. I followed Lucas. He met up with Pierre Gautier. They had a grenade or dynamite. I didn't see."

A bead of sweat tickled her spine. Rosalie gulped, not wanting to hear more, but needing to. "What happened to Lucas?"

Tears pooled in Marcel's eyes. "They shot him. Pierre too." He pressed his fist into his face and his shoulders shook.

Rosalie's teeth ached from the pressure of holding a sudden deluge of emotion from overwhelming her. She smoothed her hand over Marcel's head and pressed her forehead to his. A trickle of moisture rolled down her cheek. *No, no, no. This can't be real, can't be happening. Not Lucas.* She'd seen him only minutes ago. He'd kissed her. She couldn't lose him.

Marcel's voice broke through her shock. "Lucas was a hero."

Was? Bitterness of loss refused to accept the sentiment as she choked on the need to sob. "He was a fool."

"You want us to do nothing? Papa would—"

"Papa is not here." But how she ached for his strong arms now.

"Because he is fighting the Germans!"

"Non! He's not fighting anymore. They've all surrendered. Given up. And we must too if we are to survive. No more fighting. They're here, and there is nothing to be done." In the silence that followed, she could make out the continued march of their enemy and the hum of tanks over cobblestone. Lucas was dead. Her head knew it, but her heart screamed it couldn't be so. Death was too. . .

Final.

Marcel groaned and sank lower against the barrel.

"I'll find something to help." She forced her limbs to move despite the numbness spreading through her and searched the shed. Stacks of firewood. Several barrels of who knew what. A rake and other gardening tools. A pile of trash remained where it had been swept. Had someone thought to tidy their yard for the Germans? She nudged the dried grass and leaves with her toe. An empty bottle of wine peeked from its resting place amongst the refuse, as did a book, the corners of its cover singed. Another nudge cleared the title, and she shook her head. Someone had tried to burn and then dispose of a small Bible. Probably while tipsy from the wine. With the chaos crashing upon them, she could hardly blame them on either account.

Marcel groaned, and she focused back on needs at hand. Not much she could do but press her clean handkerchief over his wound and hopefully stop the flow of blood.

Hinges creaked, and light flooded their hiding place. A German soldier's icy blue gaze took in the scene, and his rifle rose.

Marcel pulled on her arm in an attempt to stand, but she couldn't turn away from the soldier and his gun. "*Bitte.*" One of the few German words she knew squeaked from her throat. Her lungs refused air. "Please. Don't hurt my brother." Perhaps this one also spoke a little French. Perhaps he would spare them.

The soldier stepped forward, then glanced down at the scattered rubbish at his feet. He looked back to Rosalie and her brother and slowly crouched. Taking the Bible in his free hand, suddenly he appeared almost. . .uncertain? He remained unmoving for several long moments.

A hurried string of German words spilled through the opening from somewhere farther down the alley. The soldier shoved the book into her hands and straightened. "*Nein,*" he hollered out the door. He stepped out of the shed and plunged their world back into darkness. German mumblings faded, and Rosalie sank beside Marcel.

"What was that?" he questioned.

She dropped her gaze to the book in her hands. A miracle? She was raised attending church and with prayers to the saints, but was it possible God truly did exist, and that He might take an interest in someone as simple and unimportant as her? Rosalie shook the consideration from her head. Chance, perhaps. Good luck, maybe. But if there was a God who cared, why would He allow the Nazis to rain down terror upon their heads? Why would He take the boy she loved?

⅀ CHAPTER 2 ⅀

Berlin, Germany – March 1943

Here again. Franz Kafka stared at the polished oak door, dreading what awaited him on the other side, memories of the last time he'd stood there clear despite the five years that had passed. If anything, they had been etched deeper into his soul with each passing day.

"Stop worrying like an old lady." His words before he'd left his friend that night—the last time he'd seen Heinrich alive. His friend's fears had been realized. And it was Franz's fault.

"I'm glad I can fight at your side."

"Soldat Kafka, Major Rintelen will see you now."

Franz startled from his memories and jerked to his feet, the spike of pain through his hip punishing him for his haste. Two months had brought healing, but he still couldn't walk without a noticeable limp. Especially without his cane, which he had abandoned at home for this meeting, much to his mother's distress.

After so long at the front, living in every condition imaginable and frequently without a roof over his head, the posh office glared in stark contrast. Thick Persian rugs with an array of red and cream hues. Ornately carved furniture. Paintings with heavy frames. A smoking cigar on the crystal ashtray at the edge of the large desk.

Rintelen stood as Franz entered, returned his salute, and then waved him toward a chair. "I see you have returned to us in one piece."

Franz answered with a nod. It had been a near thing. Soviet mortar took a fair chunk out of his right thigh, including some bone. After fighting a bout of infection en route back to Germany, even returning had been in question. "You wished to speak with me?"

The SS officer straightened his tailored gray coat. He moved to the window and glanced at the street below. "Your mother has been concerned with your recovery and had hoped you might be allowed to remain in Berlin." He gave Franz a pointed look. "But you and I know that cannot be."

Franz schooled his expression.

"But, seeing the extent of your injury, I have arranged to have you transferred to the 709th *Bodenständige*, an infantry division designed to hold Northern France. You have served well at the front, and I am confident you will continue to do your duty."

"Of course."

"Good." Rintelen returned to the chair behind his desk but remained standing, planting his palms on the surface. "Times are even more precarious than before, the risk greater. We must leave the past where it is and focus on what lies ahead. The Third Reich has never been stronger or better positioned. It is time for you to move forward. You need not remain a mere Soldat forever. Prove yourself to your commanders and do your father's memory proud."

Franz glanced past Rintelen to the window, to the blue sky beyond. Sunlight streamed into the room, but he could feel none of its warmth. "Of course."

"Your father was a hero. He saved more than my life that day in France. He sacrificed himself for the Fatherland."

Franz held his retort. Despite the throb in his leg, he ached to stand. Because of his father's noble sacrifice at the end of the last war, he had never known his son. Had he even known he was to be a father? "I will do my best, sir." His best not to consider the past—any of it. The past five years had numbed him to most everything. Other than flashes of memories of a different life, of caring for anything, he retained little emotion. Little reason to care what became of him.

"As before, I will see that your mother is looked after in your absence."

"Thank you." She was the only reason to keep going—to know that she would be protected and cared for.

"You will have a few days to say your goodbyes before you leave for France."

"Again," Franz muttered.

"What was that?"

"Before I *return* to France. I was on the front during the invasion."

"Ah, so you were."

He'd been on one front or another since then until his tussle with a mortar shell. So much death. So much killing. His soul bore the stain. Maybe away from constant battle, he would find some semblance of peace.

Despite the growing ache in his leg, he walked home through a city he hardly recognized anymore. Shops and homes were boarded up or simply abandoned. Buildings were damaged from British and American bombers—the reward of Germany's sins.

Almost an hour later, he climbed the stairs to their second-story flat. His mother met him at the door, expectancy in her eyes—eyes now fringed with deep lines where he remembered none. Her fair hair had somehow lightened, something he hadn't noticed before. The subtle change from blond to white. "What did he say? You won't be sent back?"

Franz took her arm and led her to the sitting room. He lowered himself to the velvety green sofa and waited for her to join him. "No, not back to the front. I'm being transferred to Northern France."

"But your leg." The lines around her mouth and eyes deepened. "You've given enough."

Franz fought the laugh making his chest ache. No. Never enough. The Fatherland and the *Führer* required all—every sacrifice, everything he had. Perhaps even his life before the war was through.

He took his mother's hands. She was the one thing he refused to give. "It is you I am worried about. You should not stay here. It is not safe anymore."

She squeezed his hands and then pulled away. "Nonsense. This is our home. I will be fine—you will see. Ernst is watching over me." She smoothed the red fabric of her skirt, her fingers seeming to tremble with the motion.

"Major Rintelen?" His promise to Franz was one thing, but he had never seen his mother so. . .

"I told him I wouldn't agree until I had spoken with you and told you his—our plans." Her face infused with color as she spoke, making her appear younger than moments before. "Your father and he were friends, and it has been so very long."

"You and Rintelen."

She dipped her head in a nod. "He wishes for us to marry."

Franz stared. The man had always been there, checking in on them from Franz's earliest memories. He'd always been attentive. How had

Franz missed seeing Rintelen's intentions? Looking back, he could see that they were there all along. "That's why," he murmured.

"You understand."

"I understand enough. But is this what you want? Do you love him?"

Hesitation. And then a nod. "This will be good. I will be happy and looked after until you return. *Ja?*"

Franz nodded, though his mind rebelled. "If this is what you want." How could he argue? What could he say to convince her away from the man who had saved his life—only to thrust him into hell?

―――― ≈ ――――

Normandy, France – April 1943

Rosalie glanced up at the clock on the wall and frowned. Five minutes until nine o'clock. The local curfew recently imposed due to increased resistance activity throughout France. Where was Marcel?

She set her book and reading glasses aside and moved to the window. With her hand pressed to the cool glass pane, she peered out into the country lane. If he were even one minute late, she would strangle him.

"Any sign of your brother?" Maman asked from the table littered with seeds, packages, lists, and charts. They had spent most of the day planting seeds and transplanting small plants. Tomatoes, peppers, eggplant, and every other vegetable that needed an early start for longer and better yields. No planting flowers this year—or any year since the German occupation.

Rosalie turned back to the window and the darkness there. Oppressive, like the pressure weighing heavier on her heart with each passing year of knowing she wasn't free. In so many ways, life continued just as before. But it wasn't the same. And there was nothing she could do—not about the Germans and not about her reckless brother.

"Why don't you go to bed," Rosalie said. "I'll watch for him."

Maman's gaze flicked to the clock on the wall, concern pinching her brow. "It's that late?"

"Oui." Rosalie went to her mother and squeezed her shoulder while taking the newly written marker for cucumber from her hand. "But I am sure he is close. Probably lost track of the time." If only Marcel's recent activity was so innocent.

"I wish he wouldn't go out in the evenings."

"I know." She also hated how accustomed she'd become to her mother's lethargic voice, as though she were only half aware of their world. "Why don't I make you some tea while you prepare for bed." Rosalie patted her arm, feeling more like the mother than the daughter.

"That would be nice." Maman pushed up from her work at the table and moved toward her bedroom.

Rosalie sighed and set the kettle on the stove.

The clock struck the hour.

"I'm going to strangle him," she murmured under her breath. Rosalie jerked her shawl from the back of a chair and wrapped the wool around her shoulders against the cool of the evening. She sat on the stoop at the front of the cottage and watched down the lane for any sign of Marcel. He'd sworn he'd be home before curfew. Not that she believed him. This wasn't the first time for his tardiness.

Anxiety scratched her insides and forced her again to her feet. She paced the short stone walk, back and forth, and clenched her fists. She should be getting ready for bed. Instead, she listened to the crickets and cursed her brother's name.

The kettle's high whistle compelled her back indoors, and she forced her fears deep so Maman wouldn't see them. After setting a cup of chamomile-lavender tea on the bedside table, Rosalie gave her mother her book on propagating mushrooms and slipped back out into the night. The air was cooling quickly, and the scent of rain hung on the air. A shower would do wonders for the gardens, but she would rather not be caught in it.

"Where are you, Marcel?" It was unfair of him to torture Maman this way.

A thud spun Rosalie toward the greenhouse. The night seemed to pause, everything listening along with her. A shuffle. Footsteps? The hair prickled on the back of her neck, and a chill passed through her.

Non. She had to be imagining things. The waiting and worrying played with her senses.

Another thud, and her heart raced away with her imagination again. She couldn't tell if it was from inside the greenhouse or behind.

Rosalie glanced quickly for something to defend herself. The door and the lamps beyond beckoned her to lock herself in the cottage's safe embrace with a cup of tea and ignore whatever was out here.

"Hello?" She glanced to the cottage's soft lights, aching to retreat inside and forget what she'd heard. At least until the light of day. But instead, Rosalie sucked a lungful of air through her nose and reached for the straw broom leaning alongside the house. They couldn't afford to lose any of the seedlings and starts that would provide not only their own garden with produce throughout the summer but for the community's gardens as well, after the Nazis took the large portion they demanded.

Meow.

"Ahh." Rosalie laughed at her foolishness and set the broom back in place. Of course, it was nothing more than a cat. Probably the old gray one who kept the mice at bay. He often left "surprises" for her near the greenhouse. From the sounds of it, he had somehow gotten inside. She would have to chase him out before he knocked over any more seedlings.

Rosalie's pulse kept a healthy pace as she hurried to the greenhouse and eased the door open. "Here pussy."

Meow.

A dark blur darted across her path and into the bushes lining their yard, but the feline hadn't come from the greenhouse.

Thud.

She startled at the noise and leapt back, only to catch a dark form rising from behind the wall of glass. She screamed.

"Rosa!" The whisperer leapt from the greenhouse and slapped a palm over her mouth. "It's me."

Behind the blackened face and dark hood, she recognized Marcel's eyes. And his voice. She shoved his hand away. "What are you doing out here? You nearly scared me to death." She slapped his shoulder. "Never mind, I have been worried sick waiting for you to come home. How long have you been here?"

He latched the door to the greenhouse and jogged past her and up the path. "I told you I'd be home in time."

"Don't tell me you've been hiding out here for the past hour. It's almost nine thirty. We don't need any more trouble. And wash quickly. I don't want Maman seeing you like that."

"Like Maman will be paying attention," he muttered before dodging inside.

"Marcel—"

"I know." He groaned as he pulled off his hood and cleaned up at the kitchen sink.

Didn't he understand she was just trying to protect him? Rosalie had thought he'd accepted the need to keep his head and wait out the occupation, for her and Maman's sake if not his own. But the past few months. . .

"Did you leave any dinner?" He toweled off his brown hair that matched her own. His dark gaze scoured the kitchen, so much like Papa's did after a long day in the gardens. Marcel's eyes were just as rich brown as Papa's, with the same flecks of gold when the light hit them. So unlike her Maman's hazel eyes, swirls of greens and browns. Or Rosalie's dark blue irises she'd inherited from some distant ancestor no doubt.

"There's nothing?" Marcel pulled her from her wanderings.

"Dinner?" She planted her hands on her hips. "There is no dinner. You were not here, and Maman had no appetite. Not to mention the vegetables haven't grown big enough yet, and our pantry is all but bare. Again. I will not get paid until next week." Not that it would keep them long. Thanks to Aline Fournier she'd had employment this winter, but only a few hours once a week cleaning for Monsieur Dumont. Early spring was always the hardest, but with the ever-stricter rations enforced by the Germans, there was little food for anyone.

Marcel dropped a handful of coins on the table. Each sang a musical note.

"What is this?"

"Monsieur Dumont sent your wages."

Rosalie sank into the closest chair. "Where did you see Monsieur Dumont?"

Marcel shrugged. "Never mind that. He said you shouldn't come next week, maybe longer. He'll send word."

Strange, unless they had planned a trip somewhere, but trips were uncommon and not at all safe nowadays. Even for one of the wealthier members of the community. The Germans cared little for one's standing unless they could leverage it to their advantage. "I will go buy flour and eggs tomorrow." She fingered the coins, doing a quick count. "And maybe a little sugar or salt." Whichever she could find. Either would be a wonderful addition to their usual fare.

"Good. I have work plowing for Guillot. I will be gone most of tomorrow."

At least that was something. It was better when Marcel had work. Less time for him to get into trouble. She returned the kettle to the stove and spread a thin layer of butter on the slices of bread she had set aside for tonight. The butter had little taste with the absence of salt but had been generously provided by Guillot's wife for the promise of tomato seedlings.

People depended on the Barrieau greenhouse, just as they had before the war, only now it carried a necessity. No blankets of flowers or carefree days watching Papa tend the roses. She'd taken so much for granted.

She fixed more tea and set Marcel's meager supper out for him, and then took her own with her to find the book on pruning roses. The bushes surrounding the cottage had been neglected. Maman had ceased showing any interest in them shortly after the Germans arrived, but Rosalie wouldn't risk Papa's roses, because he'd be home someday—and there had already been too many casualties in this war.

⚏ CHAPTER 3 ⚏

Sainte-Mère-Église, France – April 1943

Franz tugged the collar of his *Zeltbahn* higher to keep water from trickling down his neck. The rain had started yesterday evening and continued steadily. Now midmorning, puddles formed, and the moisture quickly saturated any clothing not shielded by his cloak. His frown deepened. Why patrol this village when so few people were out in this weather? Even those in the French Resistance, though increasingly active this past year, were probably smart enough to stay home.

The soldier at his side looked at his watch and groaned. "Two more hours," Schneider muttered under his breath. Franz got the feeling Karl was more bored than uncomfortable. Barely eighteen, the boy was almost an anomaly in this division, which primarily consisted of older soldiers or those previously wounded. Most likely Karl Schneider had a family member with enough influence to keep him away from the front lines.

"Is that all?" *Unteroffizier* Herbert Bayerlein scoffed. He fell into the "wounded" category with Franz, but other than the obvious three missing fingers and scars on the left side of his face, Franz wasn't sure the extent of his injuries or how he'd obtained them. "What I wouldn't give for a steaming bath right now." Bayerlein halted, and Franz followed his gaze to a young woman hurrying across the street. "Though an attractive woman might warm me enough. French mademoiselles are good for that much."

The girl who had attracted their attention joined a line of people waiting for entrance to a produce market, and Franz's breath returned to normal. He hadn't realized how much tension had followed Bayerlein's comment. Karl also narrowed his eyes at their superior. Apparently,

Franz hadn't been the only one disturbed by the suggestion.

"Where are you from, Schneider?" Franz asked, ready for a change of subjects and to get his mind off the weather and the growing ache in his leg. Although his limp was less noticeable now, the cool temperature sharpened his discomfort.

"Berlin."

"Me too."

Karl cracked a smile. "We live just east of Humboldt University. My father taught there."

"Ah, we lived farther west on the edge of Reinickendorf Borough." At least they *had*. That apartment sat empty, his mother now answering to *Frau* Rintelen. They'd held the wedding the day before his return to France. He cringed every time he thought of Ernst as his stepfather. The man was deep in the Nazi party.

And you aren't?

Franz shoved the voice deep. He'd stayed alive and protected his mother. Nothing else mattered.

Bayerlein paused under an eave to light a cigarette. He leaned against the stone wall of the building and drew a deep breath.

Franz fought back a groan. "Why are we stopping?"

"Relax, Kafka, it's just for a moment. Here." He held out a cigarette, making Franz all the wearier.

"Thanks," he mumbled grudgingly. He slipped the end between his lips and dug in his pocket for a match. A minute reprieve wasn't that big of a deal. And maybe Bayerlein wasn't so bad after all. First impressions weren't always accurate.

No one had much to say while they sheltered from the downpour. The rain tatted on the rooftops, its song interrupted only by the purr of several cars and a truck passing by. The odd pedestrian hurried about his business or to join the queue at the market, hardly giving the three soldiers a second glance. Why would they, after living under German occupation for so long?

The rush of boots against the stone walk brought up Franz's head, and he saw another soldier he had only met briefly since his recent arrival. Younger than even Karl, boys like Brenner Krause were seen more and more in the *Wehrmacht* as the war dragged on and manpower stretched thinner. Not quite seventeen, Brenner shouldn't have to worry about shaving, never mind staying alive at a battlefront. He was one of the lucky ones being sent here.

"I was told to report to you, *Unteroffizier* Bayerlein."

Bayerlein nodded, but hardly looked at the boy. "Ah," he breathed, pushing away from the wall. He ground the tip of his cigarette into a moist stone and dropped the butt into a puddle. "We have work to do. Who of you speaks the best French?"

Karl shook his head, and Brenner shrugged. Franz sighed and nodded.

Bayerlein smiled and waved for them to follow.

Franz put out his cigarette but shoved the short stub into his breast pocket. Didn't take long on the front to learn to hold on to little things like that. He trailed after the other three men as they jogged across the street, with only a brief pause to allow for a large farm truck to pass by.

They were most of the way across before Franz realized their target. The young woman they saw earlier. Arms laden, she stepped from the cover of the market's eaves and turned toward the north.

"*Fräulein, halt*," Bayerlein ordered as he caught up with her. "I see you have been shopping," he said in German, patting her packages. "Show us your papers." He nodded to Franz to translate, and he did so.

She stared, eyes wide as her small hat did little to shield her from the rain.

"Your ration card," Bayerlein barked.

Franz translated again but gentler.

The girl moved to comply, but her attempt was stilted by the parcels she tried to balance. The larger of them tumbled from her arms, and she yelped.

Franz lunged, snatching the heavy parcel before it hit the ground. It appeared to be a sack of flour wrapped in paper to keep it from the rain. A worthy attempt, but not a long-term one.

"Mademoiselle." Anger tightened his jaw as he reached for another of her packages. Though Franz could not stop his superior's unnecessary demands, he could free her arms for a moment.

Her eyes narrowed, but she relented. Tucking the final box under her arm, the young woman withdrew her papers. She tried to shelter them with one hand as she passed them to the Unteroffizier.

Bayerlein smirked and feigned interest in the documents, ration card on top. "What you have looks to be much more than your allotment."

"I have my mother's and brother's as well. Here are their cards," Franz translated for her. "And as you see, we live outside of town. It is for the week."

Franz tightened a smile, wishing they could let her be on her way before her clothes soaked though. He admired the set of her jaw and the glint in her eyes—her fire had not been fully doused by the occupation. Familiarity tickled the back of his mind. He couldn't say where he'd seen her before, but he felt certain he had. But when? He'd only been here several days. Wouldn't he remember?

"Rosalie Barrieau." Bayerlein crooned the name before handing the now drenched papers back to her. She glared at him as she tucked them away.

She turned to Franz and reached for the parcels. "*S'il vous plaît.*"

He passed them to her as Bayerlein nudged his arm, sending them tumbling. The large one struck the ground with a splash and a poof of white that the rain quickly washed from the air.

"Non!" The girl grabbed for the parcels, frustration and panic twisting her expression.

She managed to get them back in her arms, but as soon as she righted herself, Bayerlein grasped her wrist. He leaned in close, his face almost touching hers.

"This, nothing. I get you more. Better. All you want." His French was stilted but far too understandable, as was his proposal.

The girl pulled back, blinking the water from her lashes. Her head shook. "Non."

"You go too far," Franz said in German, stepping to intercede.

Bayerlein kept his hold on her arm and shot a glare at Franz. "It's just some fun."

"I will report you if you do not release her."

He laughed out loud but relaxed his hold enough that she pulled away. "You think anyone would care?"

The distraction was all the girl needed to turn and run, puddles splashing to her hemline. Bayerlein cursed at Franz before stalking in the opposite direction. Karl nodded his approval, though concern showed on his face. Brenner looked uncertain, his gaze jumping between their superior and Franz. Franz understood the direction of their thoughts—he'd crossed a line and needed to tread more carefully.

———≈———

Rosalie looked at Papa through her tears while he tenderly washed the droplet of blood from her small finger. He snipped a rose from the offending bush and

28

whittled off the thorns. "Do you know why roses have thorns, my Rosa?" He pressed a kiss to her head. "To protect their beauty."

She breathed deeply as Papa brushed the plump blossom under her nose. "I don't like when they prick me."

"No, but everything has two sides to it, opposites, good and bad. Even people are like that." He tickled her chin with the rose's soft petals until she giggled.

Rosalie smiled at the memory while carefully maneuvering the shears for the sake of her hands. Every once in a while, a thorn would snag her sleeve or prick her skin, but the effort would all be worth it if Papa came home to healthy roses.

Three years without word. What if he never comes home?

"He'll come." Rosalie spoke the words out loud as she often did when fears became overwhelming. She missed him so fiercely already and refused to imagine a life without him.

Like it was without Lucas.

She blinked back the burn in her eyes and set her jaw. A deep breath pressed against constricted ribs. Three years only numbed the pain and emptiness that remained.

But things would be different with Papa. Soldiers continued to trickle home from prisoner-of-war camps, released on a trade—three French workers sent to Germany to labor in their factories and fields, for a single French soldier. Soon it would be Papa's turn.

Unless he's already dead.

A murmur of frustration pulled her thoughts from their downward spiral, and she glanced at her mother.

"*Pourquoi*, Rosalie? Why do you waste your time with those bushes? They do not feed us."

"It's just a few minutes. Papa would not want them neglected."

Maman's eyes tuned glassy, and she shook her head, as she did every time Papa was mentioned. "Do as you like," she murmured, walking past.

Marcel trotted up the walkway from the road.

"I hope you are home to help." Rosalie set the shears aside. She would come back to the roses.

"Can't." He paused at the door to the cottage and turned back. "I have errands to run. Can I borrow your bicycle?"

"How far are you going?"

"Only to Valognes. I'll be home before curfew."

She stood and dusted her knees, uneasiness swimming in her

stomach. "Where did you get the travel papers?" The Germans had check stops between most towns.

"Monsieur Dumont arranged them." He quirked a smile that almost looked genuine but averted his gaze. "He's arranged everything."

Antoine Dumont had business across the whole region so there was no reason to doubt her brother. She tried not to be bothered by him being hired when it had been weeks since she'd been asked to clean for the Dumonts. "Very well, take my bicycle. But be careful, and make sure you have all your papers on you."

"I'm not a child anymore," he mumbled on his way around the side of the house.

She sighed and picked up the shears again, needing a distraction. How she wished she could keep Marcel close and always safe. But the older he got, the more restless, and the more potential for the Nazis to set their sights on him either with suspicion or for labor.

Footsteps again approached. "Hand me the rake before you leave." She might as well take a few minutes and gather the dead briars.

"Here."

Rosalie jumped at the unfamiliar voice and brought the shears up to defend herself. She spun to the German soldier holding her rake—one from the incident in the rain. What was he doing here? How had he found her?

"I did not mean to startle you." He spoke good enough French, but his accent grated.

"What do you want?" Thankfully, Marcel was home. He would come running if she screamed. But then what? The German wore a sidearm.

The soldier glanced down, as though embarrassed, though that couldn't be. He passed her the rake. "I am sorry for how you were treated. I feared your food might have spoiled."

She stared. Half the flour had been soggy and lumpy by the time she arrived home, but they had made do just the same. With how little food they were allowed, what choice had they? Rations, no matter how spoiled, were too precious to be wasted.

"I. . ." He unhooked a pouch from his neck and held it out to her.

Her suspicions spiked. "What is that?"

The soldier lifted one shoulder. "Flour, sugar, salt. Chocolate."

Heat rushed through her, and she tightened her grip on the shears. "I don't want it."

His eyes narrowed, whether with confusion or anger, she couldn't tell. But she wouldn't sell herself for a cup of flour.

"It is a gift."

"I won't be in your debt."

He glanced to her hold on the shears and then back to her face. His own face took on a reddish hue. At least he had the decency to feel some embarrassment for his proposal. Or was he just upset that she refused him? "Nein," he murmured under his breath along with something else in German. His mouth tightened. "No."

She stepped back. "That's what I said. No."

He shook his head almost frantically. "I do not want anything from you. I only felt bad for what was done." More mumbles in German under his breath. She hated that she couldn't understand.

"What are you saying?"

He shook his head. "I was only berating myself for not foreseeing the misunderstanding. I called myself an idiot."

At least they could agree on that.

"Forgive me."

For being an idiot? She wished she were brave enough to say it out loud.

"I only meant to repair any damage we may have done by delaying you in the rain. I desire nothing in return."

Rosalie stood silent, unsure of how to respond.

Marcel appeared around the corner of the cottage with the bicycle Papa had bought when she'd begun making most of the flower and plant deliveries to the nearby towns. She wished she could wave her brother away.

"What's happened, Rosa?"

Too late. "Nothing." But the sooner the German left, the better. Already he watched her brother with too much interest. His gaze moved back to her. And again to Marcel. His eyes widening ever so little. She didn't know how involved her brother had become in the Resistance, but what if he was recognized for something he'd done?

"Your brother." The soldier turned back to her. "And your mother lives here as well."

It wasn't a question. How much did this soldier know about her and her family? Enough to discover where she lived. "Yes. My father is still being held prisoner." She tried to calm some of the accusation from her voice.

The soldier's blond eyebrows lifted, and then dropped as though with a realization of something. His face paled.

"What do you know about my father? About any of us?" Her grip again tightened on the shears. She'd never felt so bold in the presence of a German soldier before, but something about him and the information he might have gave her courage.

"Very little." He backed up, his hands rising. "I searched out your name to find you. That is all. The record shows you live with a brother and mother, and that your father. . ." He clamped his mouth closed and the muscles in his jaw flexed.

"What does it say about my father? We were informed he was taken prisoner with most of his regiment, but nothing more. I don't even know where he is confined."

"He is no longer being held."

A spark of hope died a quick death at the solemn expression on the German's face. "He's dead?"

A single nod.

Rosalie glanced at Marcel, who stood as though he'd been struck. She felt the same blow to her midsection. Her heart seized. *No, no, no!* It couldn't be so. Not Papa. "When?" Her mouth managed to form the word, but it rang in her ears as though someone spoke. Someone calm and unaffected.

"A while back—I don't remember the date written. But I can find out."

She managed a nod, not considering what else it meant, too numb to even mutter a thanks or consider if it was warranted. The soldier was one of *them*, and they had killed her father. She walked past him and took Marcel's arm, leading him into the cottage. They had to find Maman, though Rosalie wasn't sure how to tell her. . .or how to believe it herself. Not when she could see him so clearly in her mind, the few lines at his eyes crinkling with his ready smile.

"Come here, my Rosa." Papa pressed a kiss to her head, his arms tight around her, his uniform coarse against her cheek. "Today we must fight, but I will be back, and so will happier times."

⋶ CHAPTER 4 ⋶

Franz swallowed back the taste of bile. Knowing how painfully little in rations the French were allowed, he'd meant to right a wrong in making sure a family didn't starve. He hadn't meant for his offering to be considered a bribe for future favors, nor had he intended to deliver the painful news of their father's death in a POW camp. How had they not been told by the Prefect of Police?

Slinging the sack over his shoulder, Franz walked to the front of the house. He'd not leave without making his delivery. Moving slowly, he rolled over in his mind the faces of the girl and her brother. He *had* seen them before, of that he was certain. But so many years, so much suffering, pressed between him and the first time he'd stepped foot in Sainte-Mère-Église. Still, he remembered all too well the wounded boy, one he'd been searching for after an attack from the local resistance. The men responsible had been shot, but others may have been involved and the order was to find anyone connected. Franz had tracked the boy to a woodshed—for all the good it had done because of the young woman shielding him and a charred Bible prodding Franz's conscience.

Now he'd found them again.

Franz reached the front of the country home where stacked stones formed the open archway and the weathered wooden door hung on its hinges. A murmur of voices came from a room inside, but he saw no one. He stepped inside to place the sack on a small parlor table that held only a radio.

"You knew all this time?" Rosalie cried out in French from the adjoining room, a dining room or kitchen. "Why did you not tell us?"

The weight of his intrusion heavy, Franz piled the contents of the sack on the table, ready to retreat. Curiosity nagged, and he glanced at the radio. The dial had been set to the French broadcasting of the BBC. Not a surprise, but concern swelled within him. It was forbidden to listen, punishable in the extreme.

"It was my burden." Franz barely heard the reply because of the softness of the woman's voice. "You were young."

"Not so young, Maman. We needed to know." The words were punctuated with the shuffle of shoes in his direction. Too late to retreat, he straightened as Rosalie rushed into the room. She froze at the sight of him, tears wet on her cheeks. Her gaze dropped to the radio, and her blue eyes lit with panic.

Franz gave a nod and turned on his heel. He had lingered too long.

———— ≈ ————

"Come along, ma belle rose." His gravely voice drew her, and Rosalie hitched her skirts to run down to the waves as they broke upon the sand. Papa swept her up in his arms and carried her deeper into the cool water until they fell together with a huge splash. She squealed with delight as he pulled her back into his arms above the surface. Water trickling down both their heads, he pressed a warm kiss to her cheek.

Papa.

Now those same beaches were blocked by barbed wire and overlooked by heavy artillery, mines hidden in the sand that was once squishy between her toes. And Papa. . .

Papa was dead.

Seated on the stone floor of the greenhouse, hidden by shelves laden with pots and greenery, Rosalie pressed the heels of her palms into her eyes, willing them to dry, but every thought brought another memory of her father. She wanted so dearly to convince herself that it was a mistake, that he somehow survived. But her heart had already accepted the truth of it. Papa wasn't coming home.

"Rosa?" Marcel's voice. A minute later, he stepped into her sanctuary. His red-rimmed eyes met hers. "Maman's worried."

Rosalie laughed. "Did she say so?"

He shook his head. "But she's been pacing since you walked out."

Just like their mother to never say anything about anything important. She'd taught Rosalie plenty about plants and seeds, but nothing of what really mattered. Never a word about Papa these past three years, even though she'd known. She'd simply refused to speak of him, as though he'd never been a part of their lives.

More tears leaked from the corners of Rosalie's eyes. "If she wants something from me, she'll have to ask herself." Rosalie cringed at the bitterness scratching her words.

Instead of arguing for once, Marcel came and sat beside her on the stone floor. Shoulders touching, they stared forward for a long time, not a word spoken. Just the odd sniffle. Rosalie finally glanced at her brother. He'd tucked his knees up under his chin and hugged them with his arms. He suddenly looked like the boy he was. Only sixteen—almost eight years squeezed between them, though she wasn't sure why the gap. More secrets only Maman knew the answers to.

She pushed the frustration deeper inside and focused again on her brother and his brown eyes, dark like Papa's had been but holding none of the humor. Marcel was too young to be risking his life. Too young to be without a father.

Even she felt too young for that. Papa wouldn't be there to see her married or see his grandchildren. . .

Rosalie clamped her eyes closed as another bitter laugh swelled in her throat. She choked it back. She had turned twenty-four in February, and there was no end in sight to the German occupation. Even if the war ended tomorrow, Lucas was gone along with any other man worth considering. Any suitable match was gone as a prisoner of war, labor for the German war machine, or dead.

She looked at her brother. Dark hair hung shaggy around his face, a splash of freckles kissed his nose, and his brown eyes held so much hurt. What would become of him before the end of this war? Only sixteen, but young men had been taken at barely older to labor for the Germans. The Germans had no qualms publishing about younger boys being shot for helping the Resistance. Rosalie wrapped her arm around Marcel and pulled him to her. She didn't want to ruin the moment with lectures. She just wanted to hold on to what she had while she could.

≡ CHAPTER 5 ≡

Rosalie startled at a pheasant taking flight from a bush. She caught her breath and resumed spading the moist soil, preparing their garden for planting. Every footstep, every motion out of the corner of her eyes, made her jump. He knew—the German soldier had seen the radio dial set to the BBC. She cursed Marcel for it. He was the one who kept listening. She had thought keeping the volume low was enough, but a Nazi had never set foot in their home before. Her sanctuary had been breached, and now she expected soldiers to appear at any moment to arrest them for the infraction.

Men had been shot for less.

Another spade full of dark dirt did nothing to quell the anxiety growing over the past week. Why the wait? Why had they not come?

Perhaps he's not like the others.

She thrust the spade deep in the earth and shoved the thought away, refusing to believe it. He was a Nazi, and she hated him—hated that he had crumbled her last morsel of hope. This hell under the German thumb was her reality. The war would never end. Papa would never come home.

A tear tumbled to the soil, and she buried it deep. Maman and Marcel were all she had. She had to keep them safe. If the soldiers came about the radio, she would take the blame.

The mumble of voices at the road spun her in that direction. Her breath released with a gust. Behind the hedge she could make out Marcel and a man she had seen in the village only a time or two. Almost a foot taller than Marcel, he was lanky, weathered, and perhaps in his fifties. What business could her brother have with him? Employment, perhaps? She didn't want to consider the alternative.

Both men headed toward the cottage, their movements quick yet hesitant as they searched the area with their eyes. Marcel met Rosalie's gaze, and she raised her brows. He returned a half smile—a look she knew well enough. He was up to something.

Rosalie planted the blade deep and made her way to the cottage. By the time she arrived, Marcel and the man were clearing off the table.

"Ah, this is my sister, Rosalie," Marcel told the man.

He smiled kindly enough, then proceeded to unpack an assortment of electrical parts from his pockets. He glanced to Marcel. "You have the rest?"

Marcel brushed past her, snatching her arm as he went. She followed easily. As soon as they passed through the door, she ground her heels. "Who is that man, and why is he here?" She kept her voice low to keep from alarming Maman, who worked in the greenhouse and could see them clearly through the glass.

"Monsieur Couture has come to help me with something. That is all you need to know."

"So, he's with the Resistance. Marcel, how could you bring that man to our home? It's not safe!"

"Nothing is safe."

"Exactly! So why risk more? We've already lost Papa."

"At least Papa died fighting for our freedom. Instead of withering away under the Germans."

She fell back a step but shook her head. "Marcel, you are only a boy. There is nothing you can do, nothing any of us can do."

The corner of his mouth turned up, but no pleasure or mischief touched his eyes as it used to. Only sorrow and resolve. "That is where we disagree." He turned and strode toward the greenhouse. She watched silently as he spoke to Maman and shuffled a few pots until he found the one he was apparently looking for. He dumped the soil out and took a leather pouch from the bottom. So that was the noise she had heard that night. How long had he been collecting who knew what for the Resistance? She hurried back to the kitchen and Monsieur Couture.

"What are you making?" she demanded. "Weaponry? Bombs?"

He looked up, startled, and glanced to the door where her brother entered behind her.

"It is a radio, Rosa, just a radio."

Not *just* a radio—something to listen to the BBC and Charles de Gaulle's fervent pleas to look for every opportunity to fight the Germans.

This one had a handset, speakers, and circuits. "It's a two-way radio. You can't use that here. They will find it." She'd seen the truck roll down the streets of Sainte-Mère-Église, seeking out broadcasts. Only a matter of time and they would locate the transmitter.

"We don't plan to use it from here, Rosa, only to put it together. We will move from one location to another after each transmission."

"It's too much of a risk."

Both men looked at her as though she were unhinged. Of course they knew the risks. Nothing about resisting the Germans was free from danger to life and limb—but more so when one soldier already knew they might be worth watching. Perhaps that is why the soldier had not reported them—he wanted to discover how deeply they were involved with the Resistance. They were the bait.

"Marcel." She hissed his name.

He tried to ignore her for another minute before following her outside. "This is important, Rosa."

"And dangerous."

"I will be careful not to put you and Maman in danger."

"You can't protect us if they discover what you've been doing. And having that *thing* here? It's too much!"

He peered down at her, and with a start Rosalie realized her brother had surpassed her height at some point. "If the German saw anything," Marcel said calmly, "he would have already returned. You worry too much."

"You don't worry enough, and that makes me more afraid." Two days ago, she had read that close to fifty men and women were executed in Lyon for assisting the Resistance. They were not the first. The Germans were executing anyone who even appeared to rebel, without even a trial. You could be arrested for standing in the street too long!

The somberness behind his dark eyes argued. "It'll be worth the risk." He swallowed, and for a moment she saw the fear he hid behind his flippancy.

"Please," she whispered, already feeling her arguments lose any power.

His mouth pulled at one side, but not with a smile. "*Vive la France.*"

He returned to the cottage, but Rosalie couldn't. She glanced to the greenhouse and caught Maman's gaze through the glass. Did she know how involved her son was? Would she do anything? Or just stand back as she had with Papa and let Marcel leave, let him commit suicide—that's what this was.

Returning to the garden, Rosalie threw her frustration and fears into the soil, turning under autumn's decay and reviving the dark soil. If only it were so easy to return France to her independence.

So busy with her work, she didn't notice anyone approaching until a shadow fell over the ground. The form of a Nazi soldier. Breath escaped slowly through her closed lips, and she straightened. *If You are there, God, preserve us.*

"I brought the information as promised," the soldier said, the same one from before. He had seemed kind enough, but that did little to ease her fear.

"What?" She glanced at the cottage to make sure Marcel and Couture were out of sight.

The soldier reached into his uniform's pocket and withdrew a paper. "About your father."

She felt the air seep from her lungs as she returned her gaze to him.

His blue eyes held what might be mistaken as concern. He looked to his notes. "The report was given to the Prefect of Police on June 15th, 1940." He spoke gently, his accent softening. "It stated that Charles Barrieau was taken as a prisoner of war and died shortly afterward from wounds received in battle."

Oh, Papa. She pressed her lips together and held out her trembling hand for the paper, something tangible. Her heart still struggled to grasp this reality. The breeze toyed with the note as she looked over the sprawl of words. German words. How appropriate. She crumpled it in her palm and let it fall.

"He's dead."

"I'm sorry."

Rosalie gripped the spade, struggling with the urge to strike the German soldier where he stood in his gray uniform, representing all the suffering, death, and fear inflicted on her family and country. How dare he stand there with his Aryan looks, the perfect German specimen, and pretend he felt any sorrow for what his people had done?

Perhaps he saw the rage in her eyes, for he took a step back. A retreat. Nothing more was said before he walked back to the road and toward the village. Good riddance. Rosalie released a breath, and with it, the enormity of the tension that had been building. That soldier had come too close to the cottage and to her brother. She would warn Marcel's friend not to leave until it was safer.

Rosalie took one step in that direction and then turned back to the crumpled paper, white against the black soil. She picked it up. Even written in German, this was all the information she had of her father and his death.

Marcel and Monsieur Couture were in the kitchen, and she paused only long enough to tell them of the soldier's presence in the area before slipping upstairs to her room. The Bible sat beside her bed, hardly touched since being found three years earlier. She smoothed her hand over the marred cover. With each day it became harder and harder to believe in God and His care. How could she trust someone who seemed so distant when they needed Him most? Perhaps He had helped them that day in the woodshed when it seemed hope was lost, but why hadn't He looked after Papa as well?

"I don't know what to believe," she whispered. "Or how." She slipped the paper inside the Bible and walked away.

≣ CHAPTER 6 ≣

All the way back to the large manor set up as barracks, Franz could not put Rosalie Barrieau from his mind. The dark lashes that flickered over her dark blue eyes—eyes that held so much distrust. Rightly so, but he still wished he could banish the fear from them. Guilt slithered through him. Perhaps he had not killed her father, but he was far from innocent of the suffering this war caused.

As Franz approached the two-and-a-half-story brick manor with its black roof and white shutters, Karl pushed away from the stone wall and started toward him. Brenner followed in his wake as always. "Where have you been?" Karl asked, pushing his hands into his pockets. In their uniforms it was often easy to forget how young these boys were, but occasionally, it showed in their wide eyes.

"Stretching my legs."

"Major Kaiser sent for you."

Franz halted as every muscle tensed. "What?" As a lowly soldier, he didn't even report to the major directly. What would have caused him to take notice of Franz? "Why?"

"We weren't told."

Franz continued inside, with Karl tagging along. If he was to meet with the major, he needed full uniform and polished boots. This wasn't the eastern front, and a higher standard was expected.

"Everyone is quite upset about *Leutnant* Maier's murder."

At the common wash station, Franz cleaned his hands and splashed water on his face. The Leutnant had been shot a week earlier, point-blank in the heart, on the street after curfew. Because the perpetrator had been discovered in the act and killed immediately, no greater retribution on the civilians had been taken, but everyone was certain this was the work of the growing Resistance. He had heard of such incidents being frequent enough in the larger towns and cities, but tensions were growing in France as rumors circulated about the possibility of an Allied invasion.

At his cot, he sat and took a rag to his boots. Franz couldn't fault the French for any actions they took against them with the continued deterioration of conditions here. Rations barely enough to keep a man alive. Workers sent to Germany by the hundreds. Others compelled to slave away on their own lands for the support of the Führer and his war.

But what did any of this have to do with him? He was a simple soldier and knew well his place. Fully dispensable.

"*Viel Glück!*" Brenner called out after Franz, wishing him luck as he started out the door.

"*Danke.*" He probably needed it.

The walk to the town hall that they now used as the local headquarters passed too quickly, and Franz found himself facing the major he had seen only once in the two weeks he'd been in Sainte-Mère-Église.

"Sit down, Kafka." Though probably still in his forties, Major Kaiser's hair was both sparse on the top of his head and fringed with gray. "We have had increasing difficulty with the underground or so-called Resistance. The *Maquis*, as they sometimes call themselves."

Franz raised his brow at that. In French, the word meant *bush* or *shrubland*, if he remembered correctly. The name fit, since much of the Resistance had taken to the bush country to hide from Nazi justice and to better use their guerrilla tactics.

"We will no longer tolerate them. We shall root them out and eliminate them, one by one if necessary."

Franz fought the urge to shift in the leather upholstered chair, which would have been comfortable if not for the company and direction of discussion. What did any of this have to do with him, other than following orders passed down through the lines of command?

"You were in the first push across Belgium and France and speak their language fluently." He motioned to Franz's left side. "You were even wounded for the glory of the Fatherland. Your records highly recommend you despite your lack of rank, including special notation from Major Rintelen of the SS."

Understanding dawned like a pile of bricks to his gut.

"I see no reason why you shouldn't be promoted to Leutnant."

"Major Kaiser. . ." *I don't want it.* It was one thing to follow an order and otherwise keep your head down, another to hand orders out and see them done. But this wasn't about him anymore. Rintelen couldn't let Franz remain in the shadows as he craved—not now that they were connected by his mother. It wasn't enough that the great Major Rintelen's stepson serve the Wehrmacht without rank.

Major Kaiser continued talking, and Franz forced himself to listen. "With your understanding of French, I want one of your focuses to be smoking out leaders of the underground and anyone, *anyone,* associated with them. Use whatever means necessary. We shall make an example of them."

"*Jawohl.*" The well-rehearsed answer. *Yes sir.*

"When *Hauptmann* Meyer returns from Paris, you will work under his direction, but for now start with locating and destroying their radios. We have been too generous. With the Channel only miles to our north and England just beyond those waters, too many hold out hope of some great rescue. Cut them off from that hope. Squelch it."

"Jawohl." Franz was very aware of the danger of a radio and the dreaded BBC.

"Good." The major sat back with a self-satisfied smirk. And why shouldn't he be pleased with himself? He had done a favor for a well-respected SS officer in Berlin and replaced his Leutnant in one easy move. Major Kaiser pushed a folder across his desk and motioned Franz to take it. "Those are the men under you and a list of your basic duties. As an officer you will have your own accommodations and more liberties than you previously enjoyed."

Franz nodded, grateful for that at least.

"*Obergefreiter* Schulze has your uniform and will show you to your new quarters. You are free to go, Leutnant Kafka."

"Danke, Major Kaiser." Franz stood and took the file. In the hall, a thick-girthed man—looking more like a desk clerk than a soldier—bid Franz to follow him to the small hotel down the street from the manor. An ornate stair led to the second floor. The Obergefreiter unlocked a door and nodded for him to enter.

"You will be very comfortable here, no doubt." The man either wore a permanent glower or took no pleasure in the task, probably disagreeing with the major's pick of soldiers to promote. Franz didn't blame him, especially considering how new he was to the regiment.

The room wasn't overly large but hosted a desk and leather-backed chair. Maybe his new rank wouldn't be so bad after all. Two more chairs with tall backs and ornate vined designs flanked a small table across the room from a velvet sofa. A double-sized bed hogged the far wall that might allow a man a decent night's sleep—especially considering he would no longer have to endure the snores of the other men. Might be easy to get used to privacy and some peace and quiet after years of crowded barracks.

His gaze snagged on an officer's uniform laid out on the bed, and his chest tightened. All this could never be worth the price required of him—he was already certain of that.

"Do you require anything else, Leutnant?"

Franz startled with the realization he was being addressed "Nein. Danke." He waited for the man to leave before giving the room a more thorough look. A bottle of beer had been left behind, whether as a gift or from the last resident, he wasn't sure. The handful of pencils and stack of paper at the desk interested him more. He hadn't drawn much of anything in years, but it was a hobby he had once enjoyed. A lifetime ago.

He turned away and changed into his new uniform, much less worn than his current one. Not a perfect fit, but the shorter length in the leg would be hidden by the height of his boots. If only he could hide the insignia on his shoulder and sleeve as he stepped out into the glare of sunlight. Franz could feel the heavy gazes of the other men when he returned to his old barracks to gather his few belongings.

"So, it's true then," Bayerlein spat as he plowed through the open doorway. He swore.

Franz didn't spare the man a glance and stuffed another undershirt into his bag.

"Why? Give me one reason why Major Kaiser or anyone would promote you over me. You, a common soldier with a bad leg and no drive to—"

"Watch yourself, Unteroffizier," Karl said from the doorway, "He's *your* superior now." Though he said it with a straight face, his words belied a grin.

Bayerlein cursed under his breath and twisted to Karl. "But I'm still yours." He jabbed a finger at him then strode away, his boots echoing down the hall.

Karl's smile broke free. "Word spread like shrapnel from a mortar shell."

"Guess there's nothing for it, then," Franz mumbled.

46

Brenner slipped into the room and offered a quick salute. "You're not happy about a huge promotion?"

"Doesn't matter either way." Franz hefted his bag to his shoulder. *I'll do what I'm told. Just as I always do.*

☰ CHAPTER 7 ☰

May 1943

"Tartine is my favorite because you can make of it anything you want," Papa had always said. *"There are no limits to what you can add, the flavors you can combine."* Jam or other preserves, tomatoes, green onion, cheeses, a myriad of herbs. . . This morning Rosalie felt limited as she nibbled her toasted bread, a thin smear of butter the only dressing. They were blessed to have the butter, traded from one of the local farms in return for some vegetable starts. Another neighbor had traded six eggs in return for tomato plants. With rations barely enough to keep one from starving, trading and the black market had become their only means of survival.

"I have few pots left." Maman set her teacup aside and pushed away from the table. "You must insist people bring their pots back after they plant."

"Yes, Maman." Rosalie took the last swallow of her tea, a peppermint blend from the gardens. They were no longer able to purchase black or green teas, but at least they had something to flavor their water.

Maman left without another word, but Rosalie knew she would be in the greenhouse preparing the last of the seedlings for sale. Their own had already been planted in the gardens. The remainder of the meal was spent listening to the rumble of the BBC while Marcel and Monsieur Couture leaned close, no doubt waiting for any word, any encouragement from the French leadership in England. She paid some attention for news of the war, but it all sounded rather bleak, and she often wished she could simply ignore it.

"Come, Marcel, we'd best get back to work." Monsieur Couture rose and stretched his arms. "I must leave for home before noon."

Marcel followed him across the kitchen to the cellar and down the stairs to their makeshift workshop. It was a small improvement from the kitchen table but helped Rosalie breathe easier should the Germans return.

To the drone of the radio, she finished her bread, her thoughts wandering to the soldier who had brought news of her father and replaced their spoiled supplies. He seemed different from the other soldiers who had taken control of their village and their lives, but she could not trust that. Nor the kindness in those pale blue eyes.

Rosalie shook her head to rid herself of the image and was aided by a tapping at the door. She glanced at the open cellar and hurried out of the kitchen to the front window, folding the curtain aside just enough to see who stood waiting. Her pulse returned to normal, and she slipped outside to welcome Aline Fournier with kisses to her cheeks.

"You shouldn't have come," Rosalie told her, holding her hands. "I told you I would bring your plants soon."

"I know, but I needed a reason to leave the house."

"I suppose so. And the weather is mild." Rosalie locked arms with her and walked to the greenhouse. Maman gave a short greeting from where she transplanted the small sprouts. Rosalie would have considered the brevity rude, but Aline seemed to understand. She patted Rosalie's arm as though to calm her, the gesture more motherly than any Rosalie had received from her own mother in a long time. Aline had always been more of a mother—should have been her mother by marriage. Now Lucas's death and tears shed for him were what bonded them together. Rosalie sighed. She had dwindling patience for her own mother's distance, as though she believed herself the only one suffering from the loss of Papa. Rosalie may as well have lost both her parents.

"Be patient, child," Aline whispered. "Be patient with her."

"I don't know that I can. Maybe before I knew Papa was gone." Rosalie shook her head. "But now I feel so. . ."

"Alone?"

The single word penetrated deep, boring into her soul, prodding the hurt and exhaustion buried there. Rosalie nodded but tried to keep any emotion contained while she gathered the handful of small pots she had set aside. She probably would have delivered them in another day or two, though more and more she wanted to avoid the village and its wasp's nest of Nazis.

She led Aline from the greenhouse and her mother's presence. "Would you like some tea? It won't take long to prepare some."

"Non, I cannot stay though I wish I could." She squeezed Rosalie's hand. "I can't always stomach those *tisanes* of yours. Sometimes they are incredibly good, mind you, but how I long for a heavy brew of black tea. The time will come for tea and parties and visiting for hours with no concerns for tomorrow."

Rosalie remained silent. That day would never come. She felt it, knew it. This was the reality of life now—oppressive and shadowed, the needs of tomorrow always hanging over their heads.

"Oh, don't despair, child. France has survived too much to fall now. I've seen her rise from the ashes before. I was about your age too. How bleak those days were."

"It's hard to see much further than the end of the summer at this point. We plant and nourish and then harvest with prayers for enough to eat over winter. Each year gets harder."

"Hold to those prayers. God hasn't deserted us."

Rosalie questioned that but held her tongue. The Nazis were draining the life from their country, their freedoms were revoked, her father and this woman's only son were dead—what was left to hope for?

"You'll see." Aline patted her arm again, then took the plants and set them in her basket. She headed toward the road.

Rosalie watched her go. "I wish I could," she whispered. See anything beyond the work of survival.

She drew water for the new plants in the garden and weeded a while before returning to the cottage—past the roses, half-pruned, dead stems among the living, neglected since she'd learned of her father's death. Breakfast dishes remained untouched on the table, and Rosalie gathered them into the washbasin while the kettle heated on the stove.

Other than the soft din of voices from the cellar, the house sat quiet while she wiped the table and started on the dishes. At the sound of feet on the stairs, Rosalie dropped the cloth into the washbasin and turned to her brother as his head appeared. "Why?" she murmured. Why their house? Why risk themselves this way? Rosalie folded her arms over her stomach while Marcel dusted off his pants. The tiny room built under the house for storing vegetables and wine was dirty, moist, and draped in cobwebs—though fewer now thanks to her brother and his older friend who had been down there most of a week. Monsieur Couture had even spent the night twice due to the danger of traveling after curfew.

"It's finished."

"The radio?"

He nodded. "We will attempt to broadcast tonight."

Hadn't Marcel paid any attention to her? "Non." Anger spiked with her frustration. "Not here. You promised."

He rolled his eyes. "This is just a trial. We'll move it before our next broadcast."

"That's not good enough. I want it gone tonight. You can test it somewhere else."

"That isn't for you to decide." He glared, his jaw stiffening. "You act like you are in charge of everything that goes on around here."

"Marcel—"

"This is more important than your fears."

Rosalie fell back a step, a swirl of feelings making her nauseous. Hurt. Anger. Mostly fear—he was right about that much. "My fears are warranted. You know what would happen if they found that here." They'd already lost Papa. Wasn't that enough of a sacrifice?

Marcel shook his head and walked past her to wash his hands at the basin. "People like you are the reason the Nazis took France to begin with. You're afraid of standing up and fighting. Afraid of risking your life, so you hide and give it away." He stepped close, his face coming within inches of hers, while his voice dropped to a hoarse whisper. "Don't you get it, Rosa? It doesn't matter what you do, how docile and weak you pretend to be, it won't save you. If they don't kill you, they will work or starve you to death." He pulled back. "Well, not me. I'll take some of them down with me."

Marcel turned on his heel and started to the door. Rosalie wanted to ask where he was going, but she'd probably lost the right to be curious too. Or to be worried about him. She hurried to finish the dishes, irritable that she had extras from an unwanted guest and angry that men like Monsieur Couture had made Marcel lose all sense.

If they don't kill you, they will work or starve you to death.

The truth of his words pressed upon her, along with the hopelessness building in the weeks since word of Papa's death.

The front door slammed, and Marcel appeared, diving for the cellar door, slapping it closed. "Germans!"

"Where?" Rosalie dropped the rag and hurried to help Marcel pull the rug over the trapdoor and their guest. The two-way radio—they'd all be shot if it was found.

"Coming up the walk." Marcel worked to catch his breath. "Keep your head."

They shifted the table and chairs to add another layer of protection. A knock thundered on the door.

Rosalie took a step to answer it as Marcel came behind her.

The door slammed open, and two uniforms entered followed by a third. *Him*, she recognized. "Forgive our intrusion, mademoiselle," the German said, moving toward her. She'd noticed his limp before, but it seemed more pronounced today. As did his uniform—that of an officer.

"*Qu'est-ce*—" Her voice caught, and she cleared her throat. "*Qu'est-ce que vous voulez?*" But she already knew what they wanted. Their radio. They had been listening to the BBC. Since his last visit, she had tried to make a habit of turning the dial whenever she walked past, but had she done so this morning? Would it make a difference, since he already knew?

The officer moved to the kitchen and the table, and she met him there, half a pace ahead. Her fingers brushed the dial, spinning it from the offending channel. The corner of his mouth twitched, and his gaze snagged hers. "I'm afraid we have orders to confiscate all radios, mademoiselle. I'm sure you agree it is for the best."

Rosalie glanced at Marcel, whose face had turned red. His fists clenched at his sides.

The German officer lifted the radio and subtly gave the dial another half turn before handing it to one of the other soldiers. Marcel twitched like he wanted to attack, and Rosalie grabbed his arm. "Non," she whispered. "Let it go."

The officer gave an order in German to his men. He lingered a moment longer, looking around the kitchen with his ever-assessing eye. He took a step farther to the edge of the rug and slid his boot along the fringe, smoothing out a crease. If she didn't know better, she'd wonder if he could see right through it to the hidden cellar.

As though also knowing her thoughts, he gave a half smile, tapped the brim of his cap, and left.

Marcel jerked away, and Rosalie followed him into the adjoining room and sank onto the sofa. She watched the officer through the open door as he joined his men at the road. He glanced back and met her gaze before Marcel slammed the door closed.

Marcel cursed. "Some day I'll kill him."

"Hush. What if they hear you?" Not that they could through the closed door, but her nerves burned with unspent anxiety. His words soured in Rosalie's stomach. Her brother was no longer a little boy. Despite her attempts to shield him from the war, he'd become a man so filled with hate she hardly recognized him. And yet larger concerns hung over her, threatening their survival. "He knows, Marcel."

"What are you talking about?"

"The officer. He's been here before. He knew we were listening to the BBC. He knows we covered the cellar, that we moved the table and rug."

Marcel looked as though he would scoff, but then his face fell. "How?" His brow furled. "And why? Why would he walk away?"

"I don't know."

A tapping on the floor moved Marcel to the door to make sure the Germans had left. Rosalie hurried to the corner of the rug. Marcel nodded, and she rolled it from the cellar door.

Monsieur Couture climbed out, his focus on Rosalie. "What is this you are saying about one of the Germans? He has been here before? He suspects something?"

"He must. I just don't know why he hasn't acted."

"Then we must move the radio as soon as possible. Today."

Marcel stepped in. "But we were going to attempt a broadcast first."

"We mustn't risk it. Today we will move it. We will take it to Monsieur Dumont. He isn't far and will keep it safe until we are ready."

"We can't move it in the middle of the day," Marcel protested. "It's too dangerous."

"Dangerous, oui, but no more so than leaving it here or traveling at night when every movement is suspect." He looked at Rosalie and nodded. "She will take it."

"What?" Marcel burst out.

"Non!" Rosalie agreed.

"It will be best. Fewer will suspect her." Monsieur Couture looked around the room and picked up a large basket. "We will put the radio in the bottom, with plants on top for delivery. Prepare it now, and I will tell you where to go before you leave."

"I—I know where Monsieur Dumont lives. That isn't the problem." Rosalie wiped moist palms on her skirt as her pulse sped. The risk was incomprehensible.

"Then I will," Marcel said. "I can make the delivery just as easily."

"Non." Rosalie bit her lip. She couldn't let Marcel risk himself, especially since he'd likely attract more notice than a woman, one seen often enough with her plant deliveries. "I will. I'll do it."

Monsieur Couture raised a heavy brow. "Good. Let us prepare now."

Marcel followed him back to the cellar. "And what about this German, if he suspects us, if he's watching?"

"We must be just as watchful. I will keep my distance for a time—until the threat is past."

"I want to take care of it." Marcel crossed his arms over his chest.

A chill crept over Rosalie's spine at the growl in her brother's voice. "Take care of what?"

Both men looked at her, eyes solemn. Neither said a word. They didn't have to.

⚡ CHAPTER 8 ⚡

Nausea churned in Rosalie's stomach as she pedaled her bicycle toward Sainte-Mère-Église. Every rut and stone jostled the wooden box she had strapped onto the back. She glanced at her load to see the flutter of tiny green leaves. Beneath the assortment of potted herbs, hidden under a cloth, sat the radio. And the charred Bible.

"Why are you taking that old thing?" Marcel had questioned.

She didn't have an answer, at least not one she felt she could share, but the Bible had saved her once. Perhaps it would work its magic again.

That wasn't the Bible.

Rosalie didn't dwell on the soft whisper that stole into her thoughts. She didn't understand God or how He worked, but the Bible was tangible, something she could see and touch.

On the edge of the village, she passed a group of soldiers marching in the opposite direction and straightened on her seat. Sun glinted off the rifles they carried and the black of their shined boots. Her throat tightened, and her heart raced. Several watched her for a moment before returning their gazes to the road ahead of them.

The streets bustled with activity, the line at the market three times what it had been upon her last visit, mostly women, clothes hanging off their skinny frames. So many days wasted standing in lines for handfuls of flour or a thin strip of meat. How much harder was life in the larger towns and cities? She'd heard enough rumors of life in Paris. Unbearable.

Another squadron of Germans had a large cart laden with an assortment of radios they appeared to be collecting from every home. Not just theirs. Strangely, that brought a degree of peace.

"Rosalie!" a voice boomed.

She cringed, wanting to keep pedaling and ignore Claude Fournier, but his call had already garnered the interest of one of the Germans. Her foot slipped to the ground, and she turned to Lucas's father. He'd returned a year earlier after two years as a prisoner of war. At the time, his return had sprung hope within Rosalie for her father's sake.

"*Bonjour*, Rosalie." He pulled his hat back from his brow. "How is your family?"

"Well enough." Until she was caught with this radio.

"My wife told me about your father. A sorry business, especially to not hear about it for so long. Like coming home and learning of Lucas." He cast a glare toward the Germans and spat.

Thankfully, the soldiers were faced away. "It has been hard for all of us, but I have to go."

His eyes narrowed. "Where are you off to in such a hurry?"

"Monsieur Dumont is expecting me," she lied. "Your wife was the one who found me employment with him."

"Ah, yes, I suppose she mentioned that." He looked to the loaded box behind her, his gaze not quite focusing—just as Maman's often did, making Rosalie wonder what demons or secrets he also hid. Perhaps he only thought of Lucas. Her own thoughts wandered there often enough when she saw his parents, a distraction she could not afford today.

"*Au revoir.*" She offered a small smile and pushed away, not looking back as the street passed under her tires. Almost there. She struggled not to pedal faster—a sure way to attract more attention. A breath of relief came when she saw the Dumont estate nestled within the stone wall. She slid off her bicycle and slipped through the open gate, passing under the cover of the magnificent trees in full leaf. Usually, she found the grand house's gray stone walls forbidding, but now they beckoned with promise of refuge. Vines grew halfway up the walls, and shutters hung open except for one window on the ground floor. All the other windows glinted in the sunlight.

"*Plus jamais ça,*" she murmured, unstrapping the box of plants from the back of the bicycle. "Never again." She glanced around to make sure no one watched then walked quickly up the pathway past gardens overrun with weed and briars. She'd been here at her father's side when he'd planted these beds for Dumont and had cared for them herself over the years. The neglect sat heavy in her heart and hazed her vision.

"*Can't we stop yet, Papa?*" *She had probably asked that question a hundred times already that afternoon, but her eight-year-old arms had carried at least that many pots of flowers and seedlings from the cart still laden with dozens more.*

"Not yet, my Rosa. The plants are thirsty, and we must get them into the ground before we give them the drink they crave. We can go a little longer."

"I'm so tired," she complained, sinking to the stone path, a pot of clematis on her lap.

Papa relieved her burden and patted her head, "Take a moment," he said, returning to the hole he had prepared for the plant along the wall.

"Don't you ever get tired?"

He glanced back, his dark gaze finding hers, his smile soft. "Tired, oui. But that is a part of life we cannot escape. We have a higher purpose, though, that gets us through. Not only is our work giving us money so Maman can make us wonderful dinners and sew those pretty dresses for you, but we are adding beauty to others' lives and leaving our mark on this world."

Rosalie turned from the gardens, bracing the box against her hip while she knocked. A minute passed and she heard nothing. "So help me, someone had better be home." The thought of returning with the radio set fire to her nerves. She knocked with more force.

"Bonjour," Yvonne Dumont called, rounding the corner of the house. She dusted an oversized apron, her gloves wearing the stain of dirt—something Rosalie had never seen close to the younger woman, never mind adorning her. She was only a year younger than Marcel and had always been pampered, even as others in the village struggled. Perhaps the Dumonts were finally feeling the brunt of the occupation.

Guilt twinged her conscience when a smile bloomed on the girl's face.

"Père said you would not be returning."

"I'm only here to deliver something to him." Rosalie kept her voice low. "Is he at home?"

"Plants? For Père?" Yvonne raised a fine brow. Her light brown hair hung loose around her shoulders with only the sides pulled back. "He's out, I believe." Her gaze lowered to the box, and her eyes widened. "Are those for us?"

"I suppose." Rosalie tightened her grip on the box. Oh, what was she to do now? Could she leave the radio with the plants? Trust Yvonne with it? Should she wait?

"Usually Marcel comes." The girl bit the side of her lip, disappointment in her eyes.

"Very often?"

"Weekly, at least." Her cheeks brightened with a blush.

Rosalie raised her brows. "What all does he do for your father?"

Yvonne shrugged and stepped closer to examine the herbs. "Odd jobs. Work in the yard. Chop firewood." Her fingers brushed the oregano. "Will you help me plant them? We've been trying to get along as best we can without much help, but I'm afraid I'll accidently kill them."

Rosalie glanced around. "Could we go inside first?" The street wasn't busy here, but the item she carried could get her shot.

"You want to take the plants inside the house?"

"Yes. And I need to see your father. Will he be away long?"

"I'm not sure, but I suppose you can wait. . .inside." She led Rosalie into a parlor that seemed at odds with itself. The carpets and curtains were elegant, but the furniture lacked the same expensive appearance, the Germans having removed all the best of the sofas and tables. Rosalie had learned through Aline Fournier that the Nazis had also wanted to house some of their officers here, but the Dumonts had feigned a bout of influenza. Rosalie couldn't imagine having soldiers in her own home, with nowhere to escape.

A pair of piercing blue eyes flashed through her memory, along with the dread that accompanied the German officer's presence. Twice he had stepped into her home, those blue eyes seeing far too much.

Yvonne motioned to a pale green sofa, its wooden feet scratched and worn. "Do make yourself comfortable. I would happily stay and talk your ear off, but rugs are waiting for me outside. Père reminds me we have lost our servants, not our sense of cleanliness." Her face fell. "Or propriety, which means I've already shared too much."

Rosalie might have smiled, but for the danger of her task. "Our secret."

The younger girl nodded and left Rosalie alone in the large room. She took a deep breath and looked at the box she clutched. Forcing herself to release her grip, she set the box beside her. The Germans were out there, not in here. Safety. Or at least as much as occupied France could afford.

As the minutes ticked away on the clock near the door, Rosalie examined the room. To reconcile Monsieur Dumont as a part of the Resistance was difficult. He had poor health, though she wasn't sure what ailed him, and with his wife already deceased, he had a daughter to think of. A son as well, but he was older, and most likely called away at the beginning of the war like so many others.

She glanced at the clock, watching for a while as the thinnest hand made its journey around and around and around and around. The minute hand moved slower.

Where was that man?

She moved to the window and peered past velvet curtains. Hardly a soul on the street.

"You have something for me?"

Rosalie yelped and spun to face the man standing in the doorway. "Monsieur Dumont! I was told you were away."

"Non." His bushy eyebrows peeked over his spectacles before he removed them. His gaunt cheeks made his eyes appear unnaturally large. "I was merely busy in another part of the house. I heard Yvonne bring you in." Despite his gray hair and thin frame, he stood regally, his prolonged pause demanding attention.

"I've waited for more than half an hour."

"The work I have is very important."

"And what I've brought is important too." She hurried to her box, ready to be done with her mission and return home. She'd had enough.

"Plants?"

"Of course not." Rosalie set them aside on a small end table so she wouldn't soil the sofa. The Bible came next, and she tucked it under her arm. She held the box out to him. "It was no longer safe in our home."

"The radio. They have finished it?"

"I believe so. They wanted to test it tonight, but we seem to have attracted a little attention from the Germans."

His eyes widened, and he hurried to take the box and dig past the fabric she had buried it in. "What kind of attention? Is your brother suspected? Why did he not come?"

She shook her head. "They felt it safer for me to bring it."

"You have joined our cause?"

"No," Rosalie said sharply. Probably too sharply judging from the man's expression. "I'm sorry. While I hope as much as anyone that France will again be free, I don't believe anything I do could make a difference. Not against an army."

"So instead, you refuse to try?"

"What can I possibly do? One misstep and the Germans shoot you, and for what good? It's a waste of life. Haven't enough people died?"

"Too many. And more will die so long as the Nazis are in power. But what about life?" He shook his head. "This isn't life. What future will my daughter have? Will you have? Dancing. Falling in love. Marriage.

Children. Grandchildren. Germany will not stop draining the life from France and her people until either they are pushed out or there is nothing left of us."

Rosalie wished she could look away, could gather her things and hurry home, but Monsieur Dumont's gaze held her in place.

"Maybe one person alone can do nothing. That is why we must come together, organize, and plan." He held the box with the radio a little higher. "That is why this is so important. It connects us with England and other Resistance cells. Together, and only together, can we reclaim freedom."

Hope sparked inside Rosalie. He spoke with such passion, such belief that there would be a victory for them at the end. But hope was dangerous, and they were further from freedom than ever before. The spark faded, leaving her soul darker than before. "It's too late."

"You don't think we're too far north from the crash site?" Karl asked, walking alongside Franz through the French countryside, Brenner following along as usual.

"Depends how injured the pilot is." The small plane had been shot down just east of Sainte-Mère-Église. The aircraft, a British Lysander, had been found crash-landed, the pilot unaccounted for. Blood stained the seat in the cockpit, and it was possible the man was already dead somewhere, whether moved under his own power or hauled away by one of the locals. "Either way, this is the region we've been assigned." The countryside crawled with a search for the pilot. Every house, every barn—they were to search everywhere.

"And when it's too dark?" Brenner asked.

Franz looked to the west and the lowering sun. At most they had an hour, maybe two, before they lost their light. "Hopefully, we'll find something before then." But even as he said the words, he didn't feel them. He didn't want to find the pilot, didn't want one more life on his conscience.

Franz watched as his men spread out, disappearing into orchards and behind rows of hedges and stone paths. He started away from them, separating himself, seeking a moment or two of solitude. Though why, he wasn't sure. When alone, he was left with the voices in his head, the nagging guilt, the numbing compliance.

The low rays of sun shot beams of light through the leaves overhead. Small birds sang out their final farewell to the day. A cricket or two joined in with the melody. Franz kept walking, wishing the sense of peace that surrounded him could penetrate deeper.

A twig snapped behind him, and his hand jerked to his sidearm. Nothing. He continued, needing to escape further. Just a moment of solace. He craved it as much as breath. Needed it. He walked for a while longer, gradually becoming aware that he was no longer alone. Someone trailed him, slowly growing closer. Either one of his men had followed him. . .or he was being hunted.

Franz came to a stone fence and followed it west, into the horizontal rays of the sun. No more sounds of pursuit. Perhaps he had imagined it. Too long at the eastern front had made him jumpy.

The ache in his hip grew, and he slowed. He should turn back, but he could not manage it, with the torment in his soul so acute.

He stepped past the edge of the stone fence, and a young Frenchman stepped in front of him. The barrel of a gun pressed against his chest. Recognition sparked, along with the realization he was about to meet his God. . .and he would find no peace there.

⋛ CHAPTER 9 ⋛

Pistol pressed over his heart, Franz met the boy's eyes—and saw his own fears and torments mirrored. Time suspended upon a breath while he waited for death. A moment passed. A trickle of sweat down the boy's brow. Hesitation.

Franz grabbed the boy's hand, shoving the weapon aside while throwing himself forward. They fell in a tussle of arms and legs. The gun dislodged from the boy's hand. They rolled, and Franz met the stone wall with his back, knocking the air from his lungs. A fist caught his chin. He returned the strike, and then brought his forehead into his opponent's face. The boy fell back, and Franz drew his own revolver. He found his feet.

"Shoot now," the boy huffed, hate and terror perfectly mingled in his dark brown eyes, so different than his sister's. "Kill me." A plea—to not be taken, to not be interrogated about the local underground, to not see his family hurt for his crime.

"Get up." Franz tested his jaw. A bruise might be inevitable, but the skin was intact.

The boy stood, but his chin jutted in deeper defiance.

"Get out of here."

He looked confused, then his eyes widened.

"Go home."

The youth backed away several steps before darting past the wall and out of sight. Franz dropped his hand and leaned into the wall. He'd had enough encounters with death over the past four years; it was strange to be so affected by this one. Men died every day, and yet somehow, he survived. Why? Why would God allow him to live—unless it was punishment for his betrayal?

"I'm glad I can fight at your side."

Heinrich had given his life, had sacrificed himself for their cause, and yet here Franz stood, his heart still beating in his chest, blood still pulsating. Life. But for what purpose?

Franz gazed heavenward at the overcast sky growing dimmer each minute. "Why am I here?"

His whispered question fell back on him with no strength to penetrate the clouds above, never mind reach God's distant throne. He pushed away from the cold stone and kept walking, avoiding roads and farms. The sun lowered behind the treed horizon. Still, he felt no desire to turn back. He hardly cared that his men would start to question his absence. Would they look for him or return to the barracks when night fell? He pictured them stumbling upon his dead body, shot through the chest. There would be inquiries, searches for the assailant, French civilians—whether guilty or not—punished for the death of a German officer, a note sent to his mother informing her of his death. And then nothing. The war would go on. The Nazis would continue to tighten their hold on the world. Nothing would change.

But you aren't dead.

The thought came to his mind, but it had not been born there. He looked up again as the first cool sprinkles fell on his face—more of a mist than a rain.

"Still changes nothing," he said quietly. He would do as ordered, just as he had done for the past four years. He would survive. And nothing would change.

He walked a few more paces, until his feet refused to take him farther. They rooted him in place, a weight pressing down on his shoulders.

You aren't dead.

It felt as though someone were trying to tell him something, but. . . "I don't understand."

A low groan touched his ears, so soft he questioned if it were real. He searched the thickly treed area he had wandered into, but with the sun almost gone, little remained visible.

The moan grew with the murmur of words he didn't fully understand.

Franz followed the voice to a fallen tree still heavy with new foliage, probably a victim of the last storm. He drew his gun and stooped to peer underneath. Boots, scuffed and dark, attached to the long legs of a man. Black marred the man's face. Nein. . . Blood coated his face from a gash on his head. Crimson stained the British pilot's uniform as well, but the shadows made it hard to tell the extent of his injuries. Either way, the man seemed in no condition to put up a fight.

Holstering his gun, Franz crawled farther under the branch and felt for any weapons. He unhooked the extra revolver from the man's belt and removed the knife from his boot. The left pant leg was mangled near the knee, but the damage was hard to assess. He gripped the pilot's belt and good leg then dragged him out. The man cried out in pain but offered no resistance.

Once free from the brush, Franz dug into his pouch for his single dose of morphine.

The man murmured something in English, and Franz shook his head. He knew very little of that language.

"Bitte, my leg," the man said, his German not much better than Franz's English.

Franz nodded.

"Broke."

Franz cringed. Between the leg, head wound, and who knew what internal injuries he'd sustained in the crash, the likelihood of the pilot surviving was not great. Especially as a prisoner of war. After any information could be extracted from him, there would be little need to keep him alive.

You aren't dead.

The words came again to him along with another thought.

You can change.

A chill settled through Franz. After so long of doing what he was ordered and keeping his head down, dare he choose a different path? Dare he risk everything?

The deep blue eyes of a certain French girl appeared in his mind, followed by the darker blue of his childhood friend.

"I'm glad I can fight at your side."

Franz looked at the British pilot who struggled to maintain consciousness—a man who'd risked his life for a higher purpose. It had been so long since Franz had fought for his convictions, he hardly knew them—or himself—anymore.

He swallowed against the constriction in his throat. Was it too late to go back?

———— ≈ ————

Rosalie caught sight of Marcel darting across the yard to the cottage.

Leaving Maman to finish in the greenhouse, she slipped through the steady drizzle and followed her brother up the stairs to his room. Hair plastered to his face and jacket dripping water, Marcel threw a bag on his unmade bed and began grabbing clothes from his armoire.

"What are you doing?" Her voice betrayed the tremble that moved through her. Something must have happened. Something was wrong.

He didn't even glance at her but grabbed his belongings and pushed past her. A pair of pants still hung out of the bag, unnoticed as Marcel hurried to the kitchen and rummaged until he found the half loaf left from supper.

Rosalie grabbed his arm, forcing him to confront her. "It's already dusk. You can't go out after curfew."

He jerked away.

"At least tell me where you're going."

"Away from here." His voice pitched with panic as he started for the door. "If the underground can't help me out of France, I'll join the Maquis farther east."

She staggered after him, her head spinning with the desperation she saw. "What's happened?"

He swore. "I hesitated." He paused, breathing hard. "He was right there in front of me. All I had to do was squeeze the trigger."

"Who? A German?"

Rosalie flinched as another curse spewed from his lips. "That new officer who keeps coming back here. I was going to take care of it so we wouldn't need to worry anymore."

Rosalie slumped against the wall, the meaning of his words carrying an enormous weight. She'd lost Papa, and now she'd lose Marcel too.

"Maybe you and Maman should come with me. It won't be safe. He knows who I am. He'll take revenge."

"How can we?" Everything they had was here. Their home. The gardens. Food. A chance at life. But if what Marcel said was true, could they risk staying? "We must talk to Maman, see what she thinks best."

Marcel snorted. "You think she's capable? She's broken, Rosa. I know you see it too. Ever since Papa was killed, she's been burying herself deeper and deeper in that garden."

Tears stung Rosalie's eyes. She did know it, but she wanted to believe she had a whole parent, one who could guide them through things like this, to take charge so she didn't have to. "I can't do this."

"What choice do we have?"

"What choice?" Her pulse quickened and heat rose through her. "You could have stayed away from the Resistance. You could have stayed away from that German. We had plenty of choices, but you took them away from us."

"I only did what I had to."

"No, Marcel, you didn't have to! No more than Lucas did. Nothing you do makes a difference!" Her voice cracked, and tears tumbled free. "You could have kept your head down. We could have waited this out together."

His lip curled, and he snorted a laugh. "There is no waiting this out, Rosa. This war will only end if we fight back. We will never regain our freedom if we don't take it." He shoved the bread into his pack and stomped to the door. "I can't stay. I'll try to come back for you and Maman. Be ready." He reached for the handle.

A knock echoed through the room.

They froze.

"The cellar," Rosalie squeaked, rushing to pull up the rug.

Marcel lunged to open the trapdoor, but a gust of night air announced their failure. They twisted to see a German officer force his way into the room. . .another soldier draped over his shoulders. The uniform was different, though—blue, not gray—and with a dark sheepskin jacket. A British pilot?

"I need help." Dripping rain onto the floor, the German kicked the door closed behind him.

"Who is he? What do you want?" Rosalie stammered. Was this some kind of perverse trap? Why would he need such theatrics if he already knew enough to have them stand before a firing squad?

The German officer dropped to his knees and rolled the man from his shoulders onto the floor. Rosalie grimaced at the bloodied mess of the pilot's face and uniform. He appeared unconscious—if he wasn't already dead.

"Je suis désolé," the German apologised. "I didn't know where else to take him. He needs medical attention and to hide."

Marcel inched behind her but remained silent. She cleared her throat. "I don't understand."

The German looked up at her, his own confusion apparent in the lines creasing his brow.

"Are you trying to help him?"

His eyes closed momentarily, and he nodded. When he looked at her again, more than rain glistened in his pale blue gaze. "I will do my best to protect your family if you will help me."

She glanced at Marcel, whose mouth pressed tightly as his eyes pinned on the man he had tried to kill. She had so many questions, but there was no time, not with their ally bleeding on the floor. The danger in hiding him here was real, especially with a German officer involved. Could he really protect them?

She reclaimed her voice. "What does he need?"

The German's chest deflated, and his shoulders relaxed a little. "First, to be hidden. There are other soldiers searching for him. It's only a matter of time before they come here."

Rosalie nodded and turned to finish uncovering the cellar. Her hands trembled with the motion. They would come here. What if he was discovered?

She fetched blankets and made up a bed on the dirt floor of the cellar. Her light was blotted as Marcel appeared above her with the Englishman's legs. The German followed down the stairs, hands clasped under the man's arms and across his chest.

"What is this?" Maman sputtered from behind them.

"Maman, the door!" Rosalie had to wait until all the men were past her before scurrying up the stairs and past her mother who remained in the doorway, a downpour steady behind her.

"That soldier. Why is he in our house?"

Oh, how to answer that? Rosalie pulled her inside and shoved the door closed. "He's a British pilot, Maman. He was shot down and needs our help."

Maman said nothing but glowered downward at the German uniform.

Rosalie was too weary to try to explain something she didn't understand. She bolted the door and made sure the curtains were properly drawn, then hurried with the kettle. Hot water, fabric that could be used as bandages, soap—her head spun as she gathered what they might need before returning to the cellar.

The small area and empty shelves lining three of the walls provided little room to maneuver past the German officer. Marcel moved out of the way but stood by while she knelt and began to clean the blood from the pilot's head. Seemed practical to start there and work down.

The German officer seemed to think differently. He tore away the bloodied pant leg and grabbed a rag. She had just prepared a needle and thread for stitching the huge gash across the hairline when the German braced himself at the man's foot. "I need you both to hold him down. I must set the bone."

Rosalie held an arm and shoulder, but she could not watch. The British pilot flinched and cried out, and she tightened her hold.

"I need something for splints."

Marcel scampered up the stairs, and Rosalie glanced at the German. "How bad is it?"

"The break is below the knee, and only one of the bones, so it should mend well enough. His knee took damage as well, but it appears mostly on the surface. If we can keep infection at bay and he has no internal injuries, then he might live."

The dance between life and death seemed so delicate. She picked up her needle and hovered over the bleeding scalp. *Don't think about it. Just like stitching cloth.* How hard could it be?

Her stomach lurched, and she fought to keep its contents where they belonged.

A warm hand braced her shoulder. "I'll do it," the German officer said. "Hold this." He handed her a rag and motioned her to apply pressure to the tear in the man's leg.

Managing a nod, Rosalie traded places with him and did as directed, very aware of his touch as he brushed behind her. She glanced at his profile as he crouched and began the meticulous stitching, his jaw set in concentration. He'd lost his hat, and blond hair fell across his brow, which glistened with either sweat or the rain. The gray of his uniform and the insignia on his chest and shoulder seemed at odds with everything he did.

What sort of man was this?

They spent the next hour washing, stitching, and bandaging until the pilot was tucked under a blanket. They piled his soiled uniform and boots in the corner to be dealt with later.

Rosalie finally climbed the steep stairs and went directly to the sink to wash her hands. Maman stood near the stove and soon placed a cup of steaming tea on the table. "Drink."

Rosalie nodded her gratitude and sank onto a chair. Moments later, heavy boots plodded from the cellar, and they looked over as the German officer appeared, his shirtsleeves rolled to his elbows, his jacket now draped over one arm. Maman turned away.

His mouth tightened. "I'll go." He pulled on his jacket. Its sleeves still wore crimson.

A strange feeling of concern swelled within Rosalie. "How will you explain the blood?" He looked down and muttered something in German.

Rosalie pushed herself back to her feet, trying to ignore the ache rising from her soles and the wave of uncertainty at the thought of helping this man who should be, perhaps still was, her enemy. She took the cup of tea with an unsteady hand and motioned to his sleeve. "I'll wash it." As soon as he had removed the jacket, she handed him the cup. "Sit."

His eyes widened with surprise, and his mouth softened. "*Merci.*" He lowered onto the nearest chair.

Maman stalked from the room.

"I'm sorry I brought him here," the German said softly. "I fear I am putting you in danger."

Rosalie poured cold water into the sink and tried not to ponder on Maman's disapproval or the danger, instead focusing her thoughts on scrubbing the sleeve of his gray coat, the uniform she hated.

CHAPTER 10

Rosalie held the jacket toward the single light bulb hanging in the kitchen, examining it for any discoloration. Finally clean. She sighed and turned to its owner. "Here."

The German had slumped forward in his chair, his head resting on his arms, eyes closed. She let out a breath, and a degree of the tension she'd been holding since he'd stepped into their home dissipated. How strange to look at him now, his blond hair mussed, his shirt wrinkled and rolled to his elbows. He almost appeared like any other man.

He's still the enemy.

Wasn't he?

How could she be sure one way or another? Could this be some elaborate ploy to infiltrate or ferret out more information about the Resistance and its local leaders? He could easily use the British pilot. . . and her.

But the concern in his eyes had seemed genuine, not only for the wounded man but for her and her family.

Perhaps he was a talented actor.

She draped the wet uniform over the back of a chair and sat across from him, her gaze glued to his face. "Who are you really?" she whispered.

The German stirred, and his head rose from his arm. He stifled a yawn behind a fist. "I apologize. I must have fallen asleep."

"Oui, but not for long."

He looked from her to the coat and pushed to his feet, wincing at the motion. "I must thank you again. You have been. . .truly kind."

"I didn't do it for your sake," she quipped before thinking better of it.

He nodded and slipped on his coat, not seeming to mind that it was still wet. "The tea was very good and appreciated."

She followed him to the door, the limp she had noticed in the past more pronounced now, and she wondered whether it caused him much pain. Just as quickly she pushed the concern aside. Marcel seemed to have disappeared again, and Maman was probably in her bedroom, leaving Rosalie alone to escort the German from their home.

"Watch for fever. Barring that, he might survive." He paused and turned back. "I will try to bring the supplies you will need for him when I can."

The promise surprised her. "Pourquoi? Why do this?"

"You don't trust me." Resignation hung in his voice.

"The only thing I really know about you is that uniform."

He glanced down at his coat. Then at his hands. "My name is Franz." A long pause. "I wasn't always one of them. But I'm not sure how to go back. I can't change the past four years, though I might wish for it." He looked up, but not at her. He peered past, unfocused. "Maybe it would have been better," he said softly. "I should've stayed."

"Stayed where?"

He glanced at her as though awakened from his thoughts. "It doesn't matter anymore. We can't change the past. I must go."

She closed the door behind him and slid the bolt into place. *Franz.* She was more confused about him now than before.

"He's gone?" Marcel asked from the stairs to their bedroom, though he looked no more ready to retire than she.

"You heard." Rosalie started to the kitchen. The teacup perched on the edge of the table, and rags tinged with pink crowded the counter. She drained the water from the sink and buried the rags in the trash. With a clean cloth, she wiped down every surface. "Leave no sign."

"What?" Marcel leaned against the doorframe, his arms folded across his chest.

"We must make sure there is no sign of the British pilot." Even speaking those words out loud sent chills through her. "Let's not even speak of him, not like that."

"And you trust the German?"

"Oui. Non. I don't know, but what choice do we have?"

"What if this is a way to uncover our relationship with the Resistance?"

"*Your* relationship," Rosalie snapped. "And yes, I have considered that. I've considered everything." She strode into the parlor to mop the floor where the man had first been laid, and Marcel followed. Her hands trembled as she gripped the rag. "I'm scared."

"You think I'm not?"

Rosalie glanced at her brother. For a moment she'd almost forgotten how young he was. Still just a boy at sixteen. And already so deeply entrenched in a movement that would get him killed. How close had he come today—attempting to assassinate a German officer? Her fear for him far outweighed what she felt for herself.

"What do we do?"

Now he asked? She released a breath and threw her frustration into scrubbing. A trace of blood had engrained itself in the floorboard, once beautifully polished but now worn raw. "We take care of the man, nurse him back to health as best we can. I will sit up with him tonight, try to get him to drink some broth if he wakes. You will visit Monsieur Dumont and see if there is a place where we can move him, somewhere safer."

"Safer? There is nowhere safe in France. And how do you suppose we move him when a radio was so dangerous to transport?"

Giving up on the floor, Rosalie hurried back to the kitchen to rinse her cloth. "You can still speak with Monsieur Dumont."

"No. We might be watched. We must wait."

She spun back. "For how long?"

"I don't know," Marcel snapped, panic coloring his tone. "Until we know it's safe."

"You just said nowhere is safe." She gritted her teeth. "I assume time will not change that." How long could they keep the man here? Sooner or later, someone would come looking. And if they found him. . .

A sharp knock cracked like rifle's fire.

Rosalie froze, staring at her brother. No one they knew would come this late and risk breaking curfew.

"Quick," Marcel said, flipping the rug back over the cellar.

"Quick?" And do what? What was left? The teacup still sat on the table where the German officer had sat. The cloth was still in her hands. She grabbed the cup as Marcel opened the door and heavy boots pounded into their home. The teacup fell from her trembling fingers and shattered. She grabbed for the pieces as a uniform appeared above her. The blood-stained cloth in one hand and the broken glass in another. She gripped the fine porcelain and felt it bite the skin of her palm. She dropped the fragment of cup and shoved the rag against her wound as she came to her feet.

"What is this?" Franz towered over her, eyes narrowed, soldiers flanking him. "We are searching for a British pilot who crashed near here. Have you seen anything?" His accent rang with severity, and a tremble moved through her.

Of course we have—you are the one who brought him here!

"Non," she replied evenly.

The man beside him said something in German, and Franz nodded. "What is that blood?"

"I—I was clumsy and cut myself." She held open her palm and winced at seeing the seeping gash.

Something flickered in his eyes, but otherwise his expression remained unchanged. "You must take greater care, mademoiselle." He stepped back and motioned to his men. "*Suche uberall.*"

Rosalie glanced to Marcel who stood silently by the door, to Maman appearing in her nightgown and robe while a soldier shoved past into her bedroom. Franz had stepped aside but made no move from his position on the rug, directly over the cellar door.

≣ CHAPTER II ≣

The next morning Rosalie jerked awake to the flickering flame of a dying lamp, a throbbing hand, and a man's groan. She blinked back sleep. Her eyes, gritty and sore, begged to remain closed. Instead, she stretched her neck, painfully kinked from a night leaning against the stairwell. The pillow she'd brought into the cellar had made the night tolerable, but barely. She shrugged off the blanket and leaned forward to examine her patient.

His chest rose and fell in steady rhythm, and his skin felt warmer than she liked but not feverish. He groaned again, his head tossing.

"Shh." She placed her good hand on the side of his swollen face.

His eyes flickered open, and he jerked from her touch. "Where am I?" he said in English.

Thanks to her father's insistence, Rosalie was much more familiar with English than German. And living so close to the Channel, it had come in handy on several occasions.

"Somewhere safe." The words came stilted with lack of use and were accompanied by images from last night. The German soldiers searching their home. Franz standing over the hidden room until he finally ordered them out.

"My plane?" The man blinked rapidly as though searching his mind.

"Crashed."

"Yes. I took fire. Over Normandy." He spoke slowly. His eyes closed, and after a moment Rosalie wondered if he had fallen asleep again. Then he murmured, "I remember a German."

"He came. . . He brought you here."

The pilot squinted up at her, then searched the room with his gaze. "Where is here?"

"Our home—in *le cellier*." She was not sure what the English word was. "We hide you from the soldiers."

"But you said. . ."

"He is *ami*. A friend."

"I don't understand." He groaned and touched the bandage wrapping his head.

Neither do I, but she would keep her doubts to herself for now. "It must hurt badly. Stay awake a little longer, and I will make you tea."

"As much as I crave a fine cup of tea, I would settle for water to quench this thirst." He shifted and grunted, wincing in pain. "Either that or something stronger than tea."

She pushed to her bare feet. "Water. I will get. And then tea." She hurried up the stairs to the kitchen and fetched a glass of water, taking an extra minute to put the kettle on the stove. Dawn glowed in the windows, the hour early, with no sign of Marcel or Maman. Not surprising after the night they'd had.

Back in the cellar, the man appeared asleep until she stepped close. He blinked and then settled on a squint.

"You are still tired?"

"Immensely, but mostly my head has a frightful pain in it. I don't remember what I struck it on." He gently prodded the bandage. "Is it bad?"

She nodded. "I wish I had something more to help with the pain."

He held his hand toward the glass she held. "Water will help, at least with the ache in my throat." He coughed and took the glass with unsteady hands. She placed hers over his.

"I will help." Rosalie left one hand on his to guide the glass while the other stole under his head to ease it upward until he could take a sip. She ignored the spike of pain in her injured palm. He forced the glass farther and downed several gulps until a cough forced him to pull away. "There is more when you are ready. My name is Rosalie, if you need anything."

"Rosalie." His gaze focused on her face, and his mouth softened into a smile, though pain still pinched his eyes. "I'm Robert Wyndham." His brow furled as though remembering something. "Captain Robert Wyndham."

The kettle's whistle grew shrill, so Rosalie slipped away and hurried to fix two cups of tea with fresh peppermint leaves. Hopefully, the herb would help wake her from the sleep that still tugged at her limbs. Maman appeared, still in her nightdress, and sat at the end of the table. Black rings hung around her eyes, and her braid was more messed than usual.

"Would you like some tea as well, Maman?" Rosalie combed her fingers through her own hair, hoping she didn't look as rough after such a long night.

"*S'il te plait.*" Maman massaged her temples. "The British pilot is still here?"

"I'm afraid he probably will be for some time. He is in no condition to be moved, and it would not be safe with the Germans still searching the area."

"I don't like this, any of this."

"None of us do." Her only consolation was they had already been here and would probably not return soon. One small blessing of last night's raid. Rosalie set a teacup in front of her mother, feeling more like the parent than the child. The weight of it laid over her—the life of a man, the protection of her family—and yet she had so little control over anything.

She set the cups of tea and slices of two-day-old bread on a tray and returned to the cellar.

"*Des tisanes*. . .tea is hot." She stumbled over her English, her fluency diminished with lack of use. "You would like food?"

"Please."

She sat on an upside-down pail beside him and held out the thin slice of bread. How she wished to have some preserves or even just a little butter to improve its flavor.

He took the offering with no complaint. "You speak very good English."

She groaned. "Not good at all."

"Better than my French, despite having spent time in Paris as a youth."

She leaned forward, resting her elbows on her knees. "What brought you to Paris?"

"My mother is in love with that city—of all things French, actually. And she very much enjoys travel."

"And you accompanied her."

"A few times." He closed his eyes again while he nibbled the bread. More of the color had drained from his face.

"Don't speak so much, Captain."

"Please, call me Robert." His small smile turned into a wince of pain. "But I think that is wise."

"I saw your leg, watched as it was stitched. Must be very painful."

"Understatement." He spoke between gritted teeth. "But better than when I first came to after crashing." Again, his eyes slipped closed, but he continued. "I took fire just after I crossed the Channel. Never felt a plane lurch like that. I couldn't regain control enough, not for a safe landing. But I was too low to bail. No other choice but to take her down."

The stairs squeaked, and Rosalie glanced to see Marcel perched on one of the top steps.

When Robert said nothing more, Rosalie stirred in the dribble of honey she'd added to his tea and helped him sit up enough to sip. "A miracle you survived."

"Yes." He took another a long sip and lay back down. "And a miracle to be found by your. . .*friend*."

The word and the terseness of his tone sat heavy in Rosalie's empty stomach. She wanted to refute that a Nazi officer could ever be a friend, though she had implied he was. To hear it from the injured pilot put her on edge. Though perhaps the German's role was the greater miracle.

Her gaze drifted to the charred Bible she had set on an empty shelf the night before. She considered the book good luck, but maybe there was such a thing as miracles, not just as a turn of phrase.

A knock sounded from above, and Rosalie looked to Marcel. He jolted from his seat, and the cellar door slammed, followed by the soft thud of the rug over top. How dark this pit suddenly felt.

"What's happening?" the man beside her whispered.

Not daring to speak, Rosalie shook her head and lifted a finger to her lips. Voices rumbled through the floorboards but not loud enough to hear who spoke or what was said. The door closed, and footsteps padded across the floor above them.

A longer pause. She held her breath.

Please be a friend or neighbor or someone who wanted plants for their garden.

The floor creaked directly overhead, and a beam of light broke through as the trapdoor opened. Marcel tromped down the stairs, a scowl on his face and someone on his heels. Honey-blond hair under a cap. Blue eyes that held so much. But no uniform.

"Franz?"

———— ≈ ————

Rosalie's voice brought Franz to a halt on the stairs. The surprise in her voice did not surpass his own at hearing his name on her lips. When everyone looked at him, he forced his feet back into action. "I brought supplies," he said in French. "What I could find."

Marcel stood out of the way, arms folded over his chest. The pilot's eyes narrowed in suspicion. Rosalie looked Franz up and down, brows raised. "You aren't in uniform?"

"I'm off duty and thought it best to keep a lower profile. Besides," he said, tossing a glance toward Marcel, "I had a near brush with death last time I was out." Though he kept his voice light, how safe was he with his would-be assailant mere inches away? Marcel probably wouldn't hesitate a second time if he felt his family was threatened.

Rosalie glanced at her brother, a crease between her eyes.

Franz pulled the satchel from his neck and opened the flap. "I brought another dose of morphine and clean bandages, but that's all I was able to gather in so little time. I wasn't able to return to my quarters until late."

She took the bundle he handed her. "Your men continue their search?"

"Yes, but with less enthusiasm. I am sorry for returning here with them so suddenly. I met them shortly after leaving and delayed them as long as I could but felt it best to be present for their search."

She nodded but still looked concerned.

"I also brought meat." He hurried to pull the wrapped beef roast from his satchel. "And cheese. I thought they might be useful for you."

"Very." She motioned to her brother. "Marcel, will you take them to the kitchen and boil more water."

Marcel reached for the food but didn't leave. It seemed he had decided to play guard as long as Franz remained. His welcome was spent. . . but at least he hadn't been stabbed in the back. Yet. "I want to check his leg before I leave."

"Very well." Her tone flat, Rosalie seemed more resigned to his presence than grateful for it. Rightly so, but the understanding left his chest with an odd hollowed-out sensation.

"I will wash my hands first." He slipped past Marcel and up the stairs. Marcel followed. No one spoke while he took off his tweed jacket and rolled up his sleeves. Marcel and his mother watched—or glowered at him—while he washed.

"More light would be useful." He tried to smile to lighten the mood, but it seemed to have the opposite effect. He turned to the cellar.

"Here."

Marcel took an oil lamp from a shelf above the sink and lit the wick. The kitchen light flickered above their heads but thankfully stayed on. With how frequent power outages had become in the area, no wonder they kept a lamp close at hand.

"Merci." Franz returned to the cellar and tried to focus on the tasks at hand and not the woman beside him smelling of her garden with hints of lavender and mint. Or the narrowed gaze of his patient. At least the man's wakefulness was a good sign he'd recover. Franz administered the dose of morphine first with hopes of easing the mounting tension in the tiny space.

"Thanks," the man grumbled in English, one of the few words Franz recognized. He nodded his reply and then motioned to the bandaged leg. The man seemed to relax a little while Franz checked the wound, which appeared to be healing despite the weariness and haste in repairing it last night. A little redness and warmth surrounded the gash, but not enough to signal an infection had set in. He applied salve to a clean bandage and wrapped it firmly under the heavy stares of Rosalie and the Englishman.

He rose and gave a tight smile. "I'll be on my way."

No one said a word as he gathered his things and mounted the stairs. Marcel met him in the kitchen and followed him as he donned his coat and crossed the parlor to the door. Franz turned and straightened his collar. "Should I be worried?"

The young man's jaw tightened. "I was trying to protect my family— my sister, my mother."

"Then I wasn't a random attack. You searched me out."

The boy's eyes spoke the truth though his mouth remained a tight line.

"You might have gotten them both killed." Surely Marcel knew the possible rebuttal if he'd been discovered. Franz frowned. "Do you think I still present a risk?"

"Don't you?"

Franz lowered his hands to his sides, his heart constricting. Yes, he did. He had gotten Heinrich killed and now he risked this family—he risked *her*—while he walked away, just as he had done before. "I'm sorry. I will do everything I can to keep your family safe."

"I wish I could believe that." Marcel turned back into the house and the door closed.

Franz stood for a moment longer, his past and present colliding. Would the future be as bleak? He trudged toward Sainte-Mère-Église.

The rain had stopped in the night, leaving the roads soggy under his boots. The sun was still low and struggled to show itself through the thick foliage. Not quite penetrating. Not quite reaching him. Leaving him alone.

He'd only made it a short distance before footsteps slowed him. Sergeant Bayerlein stepped out from behind a hedge. "What is this? Commander?" He motioned up and down at Franz's clothes. "I did not recognize you, Leutnant Kafka. With no uniform?"

"I no longer answer to you, Unteroffizier." Franz started past.

"Nein, nein, of course not. You answer to Hauptmann Meyer. And he has nothing against his officers finding some pleasure. The fräulein is beautiful."

"What are you talking about?"

Bayerlein smirked. "Nothing, obviously. It is just interesting what can be seen when you keep a watchful eye." He saluted and strode past Franz, heading toward the village. "*Guten Morgen,* Leutnant," he called over his shoulder.

⟁ CHAPTER 12 ⟁

"Your German has not returned?"

He is not mine. Rosalie settled on the overturned pail beside Robert. He reclined, propped up with several pillows. Almost a week of healing had brought color to his face and eased pain to his head and leg. "No, he hasn't. Probably for the best." Food and supplies were running low, but they would make do.

"What is your plan with me, then? Or will he come as soon as I am mended?"

Rosalie raised her brow as she laid a short length of board across his lap. The spoon clanked against the flowered porcelain as she set the warm bowl of soup on the makeshift tray. "You expect me to know his plans? I am hoping that he will leave us all be, that his actions have been as kind and straightforward as they seem. But as you noted, he is German."

Robert steadied the bowl with his hand but made no move to eat. "I've upset you."

"You call him *my* German, like I have any involvement with him."

"Don't you?" He watched her closely as though analyzing her reaction.

"Non. I don't. I am sure I like the Germans less than you do."

"Really? And yet one just happens into your home, handing over a British officer with little more than a by-your-leave. I assume he took my gun and my knife. Or have you hidden them somewhere?"

"You had no weapons when you arrived here."

"No, of course not." His eyes narrowed. "Are you working with the Germans, or just him in particular?"

Rosalie's jaw slackened. "You have been here for six days, and that is the conclusion you've come to?" She pushed to her feet. "And here I thought you were a German spy."

"Sent to find out what, exactly?"

"Fine, not a spy, but possibly useful all the same." She crossed her arms. "Don't you think it a clever plan? Leave a British officer with persons possibly with the Resistance, and then watch them closely to see how they get him out of France?"

His head tipped, his sandy hair falling over one eye. "Out of France and into a POW camp in Germany?"

Rosalie glared at him, losing patience with his accusations. A week of saying almost nothing, and now she wished she could shut him up.

"I am trying to understand how the German is involved."

"Other than saving your life?" She threw her hands in the air. It was the truth, though, no matter what his intentions. "If he had not found you, you would have either died out there or been captured by the Germans. They have searched everywhere since locating your plane."

"But not here?"

"Here as well." And again, Franz had stepped in to keep them safe. "We kept you hidden. And non, I do not know how to get you out of France. We haven't dared contact our friends for fear we are watched."

His amber eyes bore into her. "So, you are with the Resistance?"

"Not me. My brother." Rosalie lowered back to the tin pail. "I do not know what is going on any better than you. For now, we help you heal, while we wait and see."

"And the German?"

She sighed and shook her head. "I want to believe he is trying to help. But I'm afraid."

He finally leaned back and ate a spoonful of soup. The last of the broth from the beef Franz had brought them. "At least you aren't too naive."

The suggestion stung, but she made a show of rolling her eyes. "I have lived through enough of this occupation to lose all naivety."

He smiled tightly and continued eating. Rosalie had enough of interrogations. She would collect his dishes later.

"Wait? You're leaving?"

"I have things to do."

"Maybe, but it is awful dull down here day after day."

She flashed a coy smile. "Then perhaps you should make better conversation." She started up the stairs.

"Must you go?"

"If you are bored, there is a Bible on that shelf," she said with a backhanded motion.

In the kitchen she finished washing the bowls her family had used for their meal and wiped the counters. She was in no hurry to return to her patient but didn't want to leave the house until she'd gathered his things and closed up the cellar in case any unwanted guests appeared. Again.

She jumped as the door opened and Marcel hurried to the kitchen. His brow wrinkled, and sweat pooled in the creases.

"Now what?" she questioned.

He held up a thin slip of paper. "Monsieur Dumont wants me to come. I missed a. . .job for him."

"You can't possibly. It's not safe. For him or you."

"But if it's important and they need me? And the—" He nodded to the cellar. "Dumont should know so plans can be made. There must be a safer place for him."

"Not until that leg is mended and he can be moved without drawing attention." As much as she didn't like the risk of having him in their home, she wouldn't risk his life either. Especially when he had been shot down trying to help France.

Marcel had taken up pacing the length of the kitchen, not a large space to work out his energy. "Maybe you are right, and I shouldn't go."

Good. Rosalie relaxed into a chair, suddenly quite weary, but at least Marcel wasn't taking unnecessary risks.

"You could go."

She jerked upright. "Non!" The memories from delivering the radio still brought chills.

He pulled a chair up across from her. "Women are less suspected than men—"

"Or *boys*."

He scowled. "You could pretend to be visiting Yvonne."

"I think it's you she'd rather see."

"What?"

She shook her head. He was probably oblivious to the girl's attraction to him. "Nothing. I just don't see how my making social calls helps anything."

"You can talk to Monsieur Dumont. Ask him what to do about the pilot and tell him about our problem with that German officer."

"The German officer who spared your life and saved a British pilot?"

She wasn't sure why the sudden need to speak on his behalf. Maybe it was because of the suspicion laid at her feet minutes ago for being associated with him. What little association they'd had. "Fine. I'll go." It would feel good to get away even for a couple of hours. And this time it would be safer. It wasn't like she needed to transport a radio or some other contraband.

She returned to the cellar to find Robert turning her Bible over in his hands. "Decided to give it a read, did you? Despite it being in French? I'm afraid I'll need it for a short time."

He glanced up, one brow rising. "I'm not sure how anyone can read it, French or not. It's in horrible condition. There are even pages missing."

"Yes, well, I have a different Bible for reading." Not that she'd spent much time with the large family one. "This is for. . .*comment le dis-tu. . .* good luck."

He held out the book. "And what do you need good luck with today?"

"Not attracting any more Germans." She smiled tightly. "While I risk my life to ask about getting you home, Captain."

His face sobered. "I'm sorry. I should show more gratitude and less suspicion. It's just that German who brought me here—I can't trust that, can't settle it in my head."

"You think I can?" She took the book, a memory flashing in her mind about the day she had found it and the German who had picked it from the rubble.

The June heat pounded down, allied with intense humidity that beaded moisture on Franz's skin. What he wouldn't give to shed the heavy coat of his uniform, but their orders were to keep up a strong presence on the streets to keep the citizens in line. Major Kaiser was not pleased that the British pilot had never been found, nor did he like the flourishing black market in the area. What did they expect, that the French people simply bow to their order and starve?

"I don't dare ask you what's on your mind," Karl said from beside him. "That is quite the scowl."

Franz tried to neutralize his expression—not an easy task with most of a week passed since he'd checked in on Rosalie. And the British pilot. The latter seemed to fade in consequence with thoughts of the first. Was she well? Did they need more supplies? Did she still hate him so fiercely?

"I think it's getting worse," Brenner observed with a laugh.

Franz glanced at the boys and forced at least the corner of his mouth to turn up. "Don't tell me you're enjoying this heat."

Karl made a coughing sound in the back of his throat but shrugged. "I prefer it to being cold." He gave a small smile. "Though I doubt that is the cause for your mood."

"Maybe not." He watched a group of three French laborers across the street huddled in conversation. Since the incident with Rosalie's brother, he'd grown more cautious. There seemed a restlessness in the air that increased with each week. Was it the French. . .or him?

"You worried about them?" Brenner asked.

"Those men? Nein. Most likely complaining to each other about one thing or another." Like the scarcity of food and younger men to do the labor required.

"Or complaining about us?"

"They do that behind closed doors," Franz said, Rosalie again pestering his thoughts. How much longer would her brother be allowed to remain with his family before someone decided he should slave away like so many Frenchmen in one of the factories feeding the Nazi war machine?

Karl shook his head. "It was hard to imagine what it would be like out here when sitting back at home, attending Hitler's youth, listening to everything happening in the war. But you get here and see the way people look at you."

Franz caught sight of Bayerlein interrogating a farmer parked with his truck at a check stop coming into town. He always seemed close at hand these days. Either that or Franz was becoming paranoid. "Some soldiers like the effect they have on the locals."

"I did for a while," Karl admitted. "It felt like respect—that we were mighty, and they cowered before us."

"Not anymore?" Franz watched the boy closely. He liked Karl and hoped he would find at least somewhat of an ally.

Karl shook his head. "It's not respect. It's fear and hate. Mostly hate."

"But to be hated for the sake of the Third Reich. Besides, these people are French and not like us. They are so corruptible and not wonderfully Aryan." Sarcasm edged Franz's words more than he should have let it, but he was pleased his young companions wore frowns. Franz clapped Karl firmly on the shoulder. "After a while, they seem an awful lot like a bunch of normal people, don't they? It's easy to forget why we are here, why we must cause so much. . .harm."

Brenner's brows pushed together with confusion, while Karl looked straight ahead, his face somber but resolute. "Because it is our duty. To the Fatherland." He filled his lungs, but his voice droned on with the same old rhetoric. "There are things we might not understand, but we must trust that our leaders know what is best."

"Ja. Our duty." The words tasted as bitter as when Franz had first said them to Ernst Rintelen with as much feeling as he put behind them now. Because he hadn't believed them then, and he still didn't. What duty he'd had was to his mother, and she was in the care of a leader of the mighty SS. Did what became of Franz Kafka make any difference anymore? Was it only *his* life at stake?

He pulled up short at the sight of Rosalie pedaling toward the temporary check stop. Karl paused beside him. "Are we waiting for something?"

"I want to observe from here. Just for a minute."

The boys settled at his side, and they watched as one of Bayerlein's men questioned Rosalie, their voices no more than a murmur on the breeze. Even from here, he could see the tightening of her shoulders, and he felt his own tense. He clenched his fists when Bayerlein confiscated her bag to be searched. Franz leaned into the balls of his feet as he strained to make out any of their words. Not until Bayerlein returned her bag and she mounted her bicycle again did Franz's breathing relax. She rode past the guards and was on her way.

"Ah, the girl from the rainy day at the market."

Franz looked at Karl while forcing his hands to relax. Maybe he needed to be warier of this boy.

"I have noticed her a few times since then." Karl's smile appeared. "Do you wish to follow her and see where she goes?"

"No. I have no interest in her." And the last thing he wanted was to draw anyone else's attention to Rosalie or her family. As much as he wanted to find a way to see her alone, to ask her if there was anything she needed and how the British pilot fared, he had no option but to keep his distance a while longer.

"Your interest is the Unteroffizier then?" Karl nodded toward the man in question, who glanced their way. Bayerlein tipped his head, his usual smirk rising to his lips.

"Just keeping a watchful eye," Franz said, mulling over how much of a threat Bayerlein posed. There was no love lost between them, but did the man dislike Franz enough to hurt Rosalie? What if her association with Franz put her in as much risk as the secrets they shared?

≣ CHAPTER 13 ≣

What had she gotten herself into now?

Rosalie tucked the small package under the Bible in her handbag and climbed onto her bicycle. *"Don't look inside,"* Monsieur Dumont had directed. *"Keep it well hidden and deliver it as instructed."*

It was past noon already. There was no time to ride home and tell anyone the change in plans and still make it to Valognes and back again before dark. Despite not knowing what the package contained, she dared not keep it with her longer than necessary. *"It's for the best you do not know,"* Dumont had assured her.

Not at all reassuring.

He probably figured she'd refuse to deliver it if she knew.

Why did I agree to this?

"For Marcel," she whispered—better her than him. And for Captain Robert Wyndham. If he had been willing to fight for France, shouldn't she be willing as well? She pedaled in slow rotation, not wanting to draw attention to herself. Just a pleasant ride through the countryside to visit a possible employer in Valognes. Monsieur Charles Petit owned a bakery, apparently.

She rode south out of Sainte-Mère-Église to avoid the check stop that had made her pause on her way into the village. The route would take her half an hour longer, but she should still be able to make it home well before curfew. As soon as she passed the last grouping of homes at the edge of Sainte-Mère-Église, she sped up, adrenaline powering her pace. The breeze was warm against her face and bare arms. If only she could forget the secreted package, she'd be able to revel in the rush of air through her loose hair and the flashing of shade from the trees along the road.

"The more you focus on pedaling, the easier keeping your balance will be."
Papa released the bicycle's seat with a push.

*"Walking might be easier." Even if it did take more time for her to make
deliveries. The bicycle wobbled from side to side. At least walking would be
less embarrassing. At fourteen, a young woman had her image to consider,
and riding astride a contraption determined to dump her in the dirt was not
something she wanted displayed in front of the whole community. Thankfully,
the country lane near their home allowed some privacy under the umbrella of
beech trees.*

"Focus on where you want to go, Rosa, not where you are."

*A small growl escaped her, but she managed to lift her gaze from her feet
to the bridge up ahead. She pressed one pedal then the other. Just until the
bridge. Then she would convince Papa to sell the bicycle or save it for Marcel.*

*But with her focus on her destination, the bicycle soared in a straight line
with increasing speed. A giggle escaped her, and she heard her father's call.*

"Now you know freedom, my Rosa."

*She tried to focus on the exhilaration of flying. . .and not question how
she would stop.*

But life was no longer carefree rides across the countryside. One
misstep would mean the end.

Rosalie checked off each landmark in her mind, calculating how far
she had come and the distance remaining. The first small community
she passed through was hardly inhabited and had no sign of Nazi soldiers. She cycled through Hemevez and Le Rauge with similar finding.
The German presence was much stronger in Valognes, similar in size
to Sainte-Mère-Église. Thankfully, with fewer important crossroads,
Valognes did not seem quite the wasp's nest.

Following the directions to the Petit Bakery, Rosalie worked her way
toward the crowds waiting outside. A long queue of people with ration cards
in hand. Several scowled as she tried to make her way to the front door.

One woman smacked Rosalie's shoulder when she tried to step past.
"What are you doing, girl? Back in line."

"I'm not here to buy anything."

"Back of the line."

Rosalie fell back a step as more began to grumble. She sent a glance to
the soldiers across the street. One looked their direction and took a step.

Rosalie hastily backed to the end of the queue and prayed no one
would hear the thundering in her chest. Too many people watched. Too
much attention. She stood restless as the sun sank ever lower in the

west. Another hour at least passed before she leaned her bicycle where she could see it through the window and was allowed to step inside. The small room bustled with activity and noise, the line continuing to the counter where a short man passed loaf after loaf across to waiting hands and bags.

"You have your ration card?" a woman demanded as she approached the counter.

"Oui, but that is not why I have come. I was sent to—" She cleared the tightness in her throat, feeling a surge of nerves. "I was sent to Monsieur Petit for employment. A mutual friend sent me."

"I know nothing of needing more help. Move along."

"You don't understand. I must speak with Monsieur Petit."

"We do not offer charity here. On your way." The woman waved her to the door while turning her attention to the next in line.

Instead of retreating, Rosalie slipped to the next counter. "Monsieur Petit?" When he nodded, she continued. "Monsieur Cartier told me I might be able to find employment here?"

His eyes widened though ever so slightly. "Ah, Cartier. I have missed my old friend. Is he well?"

"Oui." Though saying the name as Dumont had directed felt like an announcement of her true purpose in coming as a transporter of goods.

"Come, and we will see if we can help you." He stepped to the end of the counter and beckoned her to follow him into the back. "Make do without me for a moment, Danielle."

The woman at the other counter sputtered with protest as she attended the crowd on her own.

"Come quickly," he told Rosalie once the door closed. He led her through the large kitchen, down a hall, and into a room with thick curtains already drawn. He switched on a single lamp on a desk and held his hands out. "What word has he sent?"

"A package."

He took it eagerly and unwrapped the brown paper binding. Inside were folded documents, identification, and travel papers. "*Parfait,*" he murmured, setting them aside to unwrap the final contents bundled in a handkerchief. Rounds of ammunition. Her jaw tightened, and her breathing grew jagged. She had risked her life for this—death a certainty if she had been discovered, not just for her but her family.

"Merci, merci," the man said. "We will keep this safe."

She nodded numbly and headed out the door, retracing her steps, pushing through the crowds and back onto the street. Across the street, a gray-clad soldier looked up and caught her eye. *Act normal.* She diverted her gaze and mounted her bicycle. The sun was already hugging the horizon. This had taken too long, and she could not delay her return.

Rosalie took the more direct route toward home, sweating more from the angst of what she'd done than the vigor with which she pedaled. She kept up the pace until the outskirts of Montebourg—almost halfway home. She took a minute to rake her fingers through her hair and make herself presentable before riding slowly through the small village. The German presence was hardly noticeable, but her senses had never been so keen. Daylight faded quickly, draining with it the hope of arriving home before dark.

"*Halt.*" A soldier stepped onto the street from where he and another had been speaking and waved for her to stop.

Rosalie pulled her bicycle to the side of the street and dug in her purse for her papers, so grateful the delivery had already been made. Her fingers brushed the Bible. *Keep me safe, God.*

The soldier spoke to his companion in German while he looked over her document, and the other man chuckled. The first returned her papers but didn't step out of the way. "Where are you coming from?"

"Valognes."

"But your home is in Sainte-Mère-Église." His tone demanded a reason for her travel.

Rosalie wanted to say she was visiting friends and leave no connection to herself and the bakery, but she knew no one in Valognes in case someone tried to confirm her story—not unheard of. "I was told of the possibility of employment."

The German again made a comment to his companion, the leer on his face and the way he eyed her not making it sound flattering. It was frustrating and nerve-racking to not understand their words, but finally he waved her on her way, his conversation with his friend never pausing. She wondered if they would speak quite so freely if the surrounding people knew what they said.

The miles passed under her tires, fatigue growing as adrenaline ebbed. The sun dropped away, and the sky blackened until she was forced to slow. The wheels jostled over ruts in the road and stones she might have otherwise avoided, and the trees deepened the shadows. A light flashed up ahead, a vehicle—no, two—heading her direction. Not the first she had passed, but it was late now and possibly well after curfew.

Her bicycle dropped off sharper than she'd anticipated into the ditch. She jumped off and jogged into a stand of trees. The rumble of engines neared, coming around a bend in the road, and she ducked down. A stone dug into her knee, but she ignored it with a glance back to the road as the vehicles passed. Her heart's rapid thudding almost drowned out the crickets' songs and a distant owl.

Rosalie waited a few minutes before returning to the road. Relief poured through her when she finally reached the smaller lane leading home and the glow from the windows appeared through the black. She dropped her bicycle against the side of the cottage and jogged up the walk. The door refused to open, so she hammered her fist against it, needing to be inside, to feel safe.

Marcel opened the door a crack, and she pushed through.

"Where have you been?"

"I had an errand to run to Valognes."

Maman stepped from the kitchen. "Thank goodness you are home. You mustn't. . ." Her voice cracked. "Mustn't be out so late." She turned into her bedroom.

Rosalie leaned back against the closed door to catch her breath, not completely unaware of the strange surge of accomplishment rising through her. She'd done something to rebel against the Nazi occupation, as little as it had been.

≡ CHAPTER 14 ≡

The next morning, Rosalie took the Bible along with breakfast for the captain. He propped himself up with the pillows she'd provided and offered a tentative smile. "Good morning."

"Bonjour." She returned the book safely to an empty shelf.

"What is the story behind that Bible?" Robert asked from behind her. "That cover screams *intrigante*."

"Intrigante?" She smiled at his use of the French word. She lowered onto the stool and set the tray of "green" eggs, named for their color when heavily seasoned with herbs, and toasted baguette on his lap. "I suppose."

He looked at her, brows raised.

"What? You want me to tell you?"

"You suggested I make better conversation." He gave a quick smile. "I thought I would attempt it."

"A strange way to begin." A groan silently scored her soul at the thought of that day—the day Maman learned of Papa's death and began withdrawing, and Lucas had been killed. So much about that day she would rather not remember.

"Was it bad?"

"I found this Bible the day the Nazis marched into our village." She leaned into the shelves behind her, not caring how they dug into her back. "My brother injured. Maman has not been the same since. A good friend. . .a good friend killed."

Rosalie pictured the moment, sitting in the small shed, her brother bleeding, her heart racing, the German soldier picking the book from the trash, his face softening and so similar to. . .no. *Impossible*. It was only her imagination trying to see Franz as the soldier who had spared them. There were plenty of blond Germans with blue eyes.

Robert shook his head. "You're correct, I am a horrible conversationalist. Will you give me one more chance?"

She almost smiled at the flat tones of his vowels as he spoke. "Dare I?" Spending too much time with him would not be healthy. He could be quite charming when not accusing her of fraternizing and conspiring with the enemy. Though she would do better to ignore the sensation, her girlish heart quite yearned for the attention.

"Has your family always lived in Normandy?"

"Oui. My father inherited this cottage and land from his father." Another victim from another war. "My mother. . ." Rosalie stopped. Her mother wasn't from the immediate area, she remembered that much—more from what others said than her parents. Had it ever been mentioned?

"Is something wrong?"

"Non. . ." Rosalie gave a throaty laugh. "I just don't remember where my mother's family is from." *What family?* Three brothers dead in the last war. Grandparents. . . Maman hardly spoke of her parents. Only her mother in passing. And when Rosalie asked, the subject was always subtly changed.

"You've had a lot of stress and other things on your mind," he said gently.

She almost laughed at that as well. He had no idea about her mission last night, and she wouldn't speak of it. Time for another change of topic. "You know this area well, from flying over?"

He lifted one shoulder. "I have been studying quite a few maps. When you fly at night, you need to know which towns are where and the exact miles between them. You guide your plane by miles, speed, and the time it takes, not by sight."

"It must be frightening to fly at night. Not knowing where the enemy is. Where you are. And then to be fired at?" She shook her head. "And for what? You are not French. You risk your life for us?"

"You are not worth it?" His smile appeared again. "I am certain you are."

Heat crept up her neck to her cheeks. Hopefully, he didn't take too much notice. "I do not speak lightly. What do you gain by fighting for France?"

"Besides your company?"

She chuckled and shook her head.

"Very well," he said, eyes beaming. "First of all, we strengthen England's borders. With the Germans dug in right across the Channel, keeping them at bay has not been easy. But also, you are our allies. We haven't given up on you. It's only a matter of time before we strike back. I don't know where or when, but we'll be coming."

"Like at Dieppe?"

"No. Not like Dieppe," he said sharply. "That was a fiasco and not well planned."

She sighed and straightened, hands planted on her knees. "I wish I could believe that freedom is still possible. . .but I don't think I do."

"You just need a little bit more faith." His hand covered hers with warmth, and he squeezed. "Maybe you should read more of that Bible of yours and not just keep it for good luck."

"Maybe so." *Especially after yesterday.* Her heart sped every time she thought of the risk she'd taken—and her strange lack of regret. Instead, she felt emboldened and strong. She had finally done something to fight back.

His hand withdrew. "I can see that brain of yours is working."

"What?" She returned her focus to him.

"Something lit a spark in your eyes. I'm sorry if I've offended you."

"Oh, no, not that. I—you are right. I should read more. Papa and Maman took us to church sometimes. I. . .believe in God." A warmth touched her center.

He really does exist.

The warmth swelled.

"I should go back to work," she whispered, not wanting to chase away the feeling growing in her chest, but too aware of Robert's studious gaze. Besides, there were gardens to weed, plants to water, soup to cook. . . and a Bible to read. She would somehow find the time.

"I understand, but will miss your company," Robert said. "Thank you for the breakfast, and the conversation. I will endeavor to make mine even more enjoyable at the next opportunity."

She stood and picked up the Bible again from the shelf. "The improvement is noted and appreciated."

Rosalie closed the cellar door behind her and slipped into her room to leave the Bible on her bed. Before setting the book down, she cracked it open. Isaiah. She cringed, remembering Maman complaining about understanding anything in the book. Still, she read the first verse that her eyes found at the beginning of the fifty-seventh chapter.

" '*The righteous perisheth, and no man layeth it to heart: and merciful men are taken away, none considering that the righteous is taken away from the evil to come. He shall enter into peace: they shall rest in their beds, each one walking in his uprightness.'* "

"Papa," she whispered. Papa was as good a man as they came. Strong but kind. Merciful. Moisture gathered in her eyes, blurring the words. He was spared the pain and fear France had endured the past three years. He was at rest.

She slowly closed the Bible but held it a moment longer, savoring the strange peace that had come over her, that undefinable understanding that all was well with her father.

Voices at the front of the house compelled her to set the Bible aside and hurry downstairs and outside to investigate. She burst from the front door and stopped. "Yvonne? Why have you come?"

The younger woman stood with a blue kerchief around her head, speaking with Marcel, who leaned on the spade he'd been weeding the garden with. She appeared almost disappointed that they had been interrupted as she glanced between the siblings.

"Papa was worried and wanted me to make sure you arrived home safely."

Rosalie wanted to appreciate the sentiment but wondered if he were more concerned about the package and what she knew and could tell the Germans if interrogated. "As you see, I am well, but it is not safe for you to be seen here."

"Why not?" Her eyes carried innocence. She likely had no idea what her father had Rosalie do, the danger he had put her in. "We are friends." She sent a sideways glance at Marcel.

Interesting. They were friends now, were they? Rosalie forced a half smile. "Just be careful." She wasn't sure who she meant the words for. They all needed to be cautious as they proceeded. The Nazis had eyes and ears in the most unlikely places.

As she turned back to the house, a movement caught her eye, and she looked past the front beds to the road. A man stepped behind a hedge. He was fair with a cap pulled low and a tweed coat she recognized. What was Franz doing here?

Curiosity overwhelming her usual caution, Rosalie moved out of sight of her brother and Yvonne and then raced across the side gardens, jumped over a low stone fence, and followed a row of beech trees as the road curved before crossing over a small bridge. She reached the road before the man and remained out of sight until he stepped past.

"What are you—"

He jerked around and caught her in his arms, taking her down. Halfway. Franz froze with her suspended a foot or two above the ground, his blue eyes wide. He yanked her back up and set her on her feet but didn't let go.

"What are you doing here?" he questioned.

She struggled to catch her breath. "That's what I was about to ask you."

"I'm sorry. I didn't hurt you, did I?"

"No, no, I'm fine. Just startled me." She looked down at his hand, still bracing her arm. Warmth spilled through her.

He withdrew. Then glanced around and took her arm again to guide her off the road. "Better for us not to be seen together."

Obviously. "Then why are you here? What is the point of spying when you already know everything?"

He led her past the beech trees, following the stream. "I don't know how you're doing, if you have the supplies you need, how our *friend* is faring."

"Well enough. He seems to be healing." She watched Franz closely for a reaction. His expression relaxed. His hand again lingered at her elbow. She should pull away.

He finally came to a stop behind a large oak. "And you? Your family?"

"We're surviving."

"If you need anything, you have only to ask. I did not bring anything today. I was only planning to—"

"Spy on us?"

"Of course not." His lip twitched a hint of a. . .smile? "I was admiring your flowers."

She couldn't help but raise her brow at that. "Our flowers?"

He released her and pulled a book from his satchel. Rosalie tried not to miss his touch while she opened the cover to once blank pages now covered with charcoal renditions of poppies, clematis, and tamarisk. Another page showed an intricate sketch of rosebuds at the cusp of opening. Beautiful.

She glanced at their creator.

Color infused his face under her stare. "My mother. . ." He cleared his throat, and his voice deepened. "My mother is very fond of flowers."

"These are for her?"

"I will send some of them." He gave a lopsided smile that made her want to follow suit. How had she not considered what a handsome man he was—when not in uniform?

She shoved the book back in his hands and straightened. The pictures were too beautiful, too alive, to be sketched by a German officer. Despite his accent, it was becoming difficult to see him entirely in that light anymore.

"Are you upset that I sketched these pictures for my mother?"

How did he read her so well? "No, it's the fact you have a mother."

"I couldn't help that. Every living thing has one of those. Kind of necessary," he teased.

"Yes, but that's the problem. I don't want to see you like that." She wasn't making any sense and she knew it, but more and more he left her disarmed. He was the enemy, wasn't he? "You confuse me."

"Because I have a mother and enjoy sketching?" He got a strange look on his face. "Does it make me too human?"

She nodded.

He looked down at the book in his hands. "If it helps, my mother recently married an officer in the SS. And I haven't sketched in years, not since I joined the army. For the past five years I have been every bit a heartless machine as you wish to think of me."

"What changed?" Because that wasn't what she saw in the man before her. Maybe only because he was out of uniform, but she wanted to believe he was changed. Their lives depended on it.

≣ CHAPTER 15 ≣

Franz met her gaze, his mind churning through everything that had brought him here. His mother's marriage. The past he could no longer ignore. A charred Bible. A good look at death. *And her.* "I don't know that I can explain it. But I'm not the man I was even a month ago. I'm tired."

"Of the war?"

"Yes. And of what it has made me." Shame filled him, standing before her, reliving his sins since he had walked away from Heinrich that night in Berlin. Fear had driven him for too long. "Is it so hard to believe that many of us would prefer to be home with our families? Have you considered that some of us have no more choice than you?"

"Non. I don't want to consider that. I want to hate you—I *need* to hate you."

Her words detonated within him like mortar fire, scoring his soul instead of his flesh. He nodded, weariness dragging him lower. She was right, she needed to keep her hate. How else would she continue her fight against them? How else would she recover her freedom?

Silence settled between them, drowned out by birdsong. A breeze carried a hint of the ocean, though miles away, and rain—frequent in this area. What would it have been like to meet at another time—not that they ever would have crossed paths without the help of the war. But the question still emerged from the depths of his thoughts.

Something about her captivated him, especially now with the determined tilt of her chin and purse of her lips. Dark hair hung loose just past her shoulders, the perfect frame for her face. Her eyes crowned them all and froze him in place. Large and dark like a storm over the Channel and still holding too much fear. But something else glinted within them now—a fire he'd not seen there before.

"I don't mean you personally," she said softly, almost a whisper. "I don't hate you. Not anymore." She turned and started toward her home. He watched her until the very last, before returning to the road. The walk back passed far too quickly, and he was not ready for Karl to meet him on the outskirts of the village.

The young man raised a brow. "Interesting choice of clothes, Leutnant."

"The uniform gets restrictive after a while." He tugged on his collar and kept walking.

Karl kept pace. "And I suppose it helps you blend in better with the locals."

Franz paused. "Are you spying for Unteroffizier Bayerlein now?"

"No. Should I be?"

He narrowed his eyes at the youth, wondering how quickly Karl would betray him should the occasion arise. The boy might be inexperienced as far as war went, but he'd participated in Hitler's Youth and grown up in the Nazis' Germany. Betrayal was a common language.

"You should not mind Unteroffizier Bayerlein as much as you do." Karl chuckled. "He's jealous that you were promoted over him, but I'm discovering his hiss is worse than his bite."

For now. Franz had known too many men like Bayerlein to let his guard down. But neither could he stay away from Rosalie. He needed to help her more, to not remain forever on the sidelines. But how could he do so without causing harm?

"I was trying to find you."

Franz brought his head up. "Why?"

"The major sent someone for you. Best get back into uniform." Karl followed him to the barracks, but nothing more was said. The morning was still early, but he had lingered too long in the countryside, and the village was wide awake now. Several soldiers gave him strange looks while others smirked, probably thinking he had snuck out to pursue pleasure of another sort. There were too many French women and girls willing to entertain an officer or soldier for an extra ration of food, chocolate, or wine, and who could blame them. Fear and hunger often brought out the worst in people, just as it had in him. Not Rosalie, though. She'd almost refused his help already to avoid indebtedness. While even the appearance of such an arrangement would keep them safe from suspicion and allow him to come and go with more freedom, she would never agree to it. The shunning she might receive from her own community would never be worth it.

Back in uniform, collar tight around his throat, Franz walked to the major's office only to find he had already left. An Unteroffizier directed Franz to the parkade where a group of officers climbed into cars and a transport truck. The major frowned when he saw Franz but waved him over.

"I sent someone to find you over an hour ago, Leutnant Kafka." An accusation more than a statement.

"My apologies, Major. I just received your message and came directly."

He grunted his acknowledgment. Or his doubt? "Where were you? Someone reported seeing you leaving town in civilian clothes."

No use denying it. "Yes, Major."

"And why is that, Leutnant?" The major climbed into the front seat of his car but left the door open.

"You tasked me with uncovering local Resistance movements. How am I to discover anything if they can see my uniform from a mile away?" He had learned quickly not to stall with answers lest he gather suspicion, but he now wished he had left the Resistance out of his excuse. Not if his movements were traced to Rosalie and her family. "I also am quite fond of a brisk walk through the countryside in the mornings."

The major motioned to the back seat. "You will ride with us." Then slammed his door.

Franz climbed into the car as directed and waited for the interrogation to continue. An officer sat behind the wheel, while another sat in the rear across from Franz. He reported to Hauptmann Meyer, but the other man he'd only met briefly in the past.

As soon as they reached the main road heading east, the major resumed. "Leutnant Kafka is about to explain his efforts in uprooting the underground here in Sainte-Mère-Église. I would hope you take every precaution, Leutnant, after your predecessor's unfortunate murder."

The image of Marcel's revolver against his chest flashed through his mind. "One of the reasons I feel more comfortable out of uniform when out by myself."

Hauptmann Meyer, sitting across from him, laughed. "You are quite a bold man, Kafka."

"Probably from his time at the front." The major chuckled. "Life here must seem rather dull to you."

Franz forced a smile and a chuckle of his own. *Play along.* "Of course, but my leg appreciates the rest."

"Ja," Hauptmann Meyer replied with an understanding nod. "Were you quite seriously wounded?"

"It felt like it at the time," he said, keeping his tone light. "It required six months of recovery and returning to Berlin."

"Was Berlin your home before the war?"

Franz answered in the affirmative, and the conversation continued, the major again bringing up his relation to an honored member of the SS.

As they drove in convoy toward the coast, Hauptmann Meyer addressed him. "Back to the underground, Leutnant. We have seen no further signs of the pilot from the British Lysander bomber. Do you believe they found him before we did, and if so, would he still be in the area?"

Franz took a contemplative breath, his mind racing through every logical course, and which would lead to the best outcome. "Very possible, Major. There are quite a few more French in the area than us. Knowing we were searching, if he was not badly injured, I doubt they would have left him here any longer than necessary. Unfortunately, he may very well be halfway back to England by now."

"Yes, you are probably correct." The conversation moved to the other officers and the men they commanded. Franz didn't ask the purpose of their journey and was quite surprised when they stopped on the bluff overlooking a sandy beach and miles of the English Channel. The cool breeze rising off the water struck his face, and he breathed in the salty air. Followed the others while they walked to the edge of the grass. The major disappeared into the nearby bunker.

Franz stared across the water, the only thing separating them from England. As soon as the British pilot was healed, they would have to find a way to return him home. Looking at it now—the rolls of barbed wire, signs warning of land mines planted in the sand, huge beams of iron strapped together in X's to keep vehicles from being driven up the beach—the task seemed impossible.

"There is no way they will consider landing here," Hauptmann Meyer told the man next to him. "We are too far from England."

"Yes, but where will they come? It's only a matter of time before the British and Americans make another attempt."

Franz drifted away from the group and the conversation, his mind on the Englishman hidden away and the possibility of an Allied invasion. One thing seemed certain—no one was getting off this beach alive, in either direction.

⧈ CHAPTER 16 ⧈

A week after her conversation with Franz, Rosalie's thoughts were still in a tussle. Even now, kneeling in the dirt pulling weeds from rows of spinach, memories of his sketches refused to leave her, the texture and life he had created in tones of gray. Along with the open apology in his cornflower-blue eyes. If not for his accent and truly Germanic appearance, it might be easy to...

Rosalie forced her train of thought to derail, not daring explore where it might go. Her knees were sore, so she wiped her hands clean and picked a handful of tender spinach leaves to add to lunch. Salads were a welcome addition to their usual meager fare. They had already begun to sell and trade their produce to others in the village, which added greatly to their dwindling funds and supplies. More and more such trade was done out of sight of the Nazis, who tried to oversee all movement of goods and food.

Dark clouds crowded out the sun's rays. The wind carried a taste of rain as it teased the branches above. Hopefully, the change in weather would not impede Marcel's work on one of the local farms. And Maman? Rosalie looked toward the greenhouse and the blurred form of her mother repotting herbs. Not much had changed despite the British pilot living in their cellar. There was a new nervousness in Maman's eyes, but she said little of their guest or the dangers he brought.

On her way to the house, Rosalie paused near the door of the greenhouse, wishing she knew how to broach the subject of where her mother had grown up and what had become of her family. It shouldn't be that difficult to ask such a simple question from one's own parent, but she stood in place, feeling more distant from her mother with each moment that passed, and more lonesome for her father.

"Patience has many rewards," Papa had told her.

He nodded toward Maman, who walked toward the greenhouse with the empty pots from what they had just planted, her stomach swollen with a sibling for Rosalie. "There is the most beautiful of all the flowers of these gardens." Papa lifted Rosalie high on his shoulders. Even at eight, she was a small thing and loved seeing the world from this vantage point. "And you look just like her. A miracle for her sake." The last she barely heard though her head rested on his.

"Does that make me beautiful too?"

He chuckled. "It does. God made you, my Rosa."

Rosalie paused at the door and breathed deep. She'd never thought much on her father's words about God, but with her recent study of the Bible, they soothed her soul.

God made me.

She pushed into the house and skidded to a stop. Robert reclined in the rocking chair, his leg propped up on a stool, eyes closed. The door slammed harder than she'd intended. "What are you doing up here?"

His eyes batted open. "Breathing air that doesn't reek of moldy onions."

"But if anyone comes—"

"They would have come by now." He shrugged, but it was accompanied by a wince. "Besides, don't I look French?" He tugged at the pale green collar of the shirt they had given him. Papa had been just a little shorter, so the pants hung high around Robert's ankles and bare feet, but otherwise the clothes fit well enough. At first it was hard to see him in Papa's clothes, but he would have approved of their use.

Rosalie set a hand on her hip but gave a thoughtful pause. "You might pass well enough unless you open your mouth. Then you are obviously English."

"I'll just leave all the speaking to you. You speak French well enough."

"I do, don't I?" She rolled her eyes at him.

"With how well your English has improved the past couple of weeks, you might soon speak that better than me as well."

Rosalie shook her head and stepped into the kitchen to rinse the spinach and wash her hands. A minute later Robert hopped to the table, using the wall and anything in his way to help his balance while keeping all weight off his broken leg. He really shouldn't be up here trying to get around with his leg still healing, but she couldn't argue with his need for a breath of fresh air and to stretch his back.

"Do you know any other languages?" he asked, dropping into a chair.

She laid the spinach out to dry. "Like what, German? If only."

His eyes narrowed. "Why is that?"

Rosalie ignored his question, pulling a pan from its hook and collecting the handful of petite potatoes she'd brought in this morning.

"Why German?" he asked again.

"You still worry I might work for them?" Rosalie glanced over her shoulder. She didn't like how pale he'd become since moving.

"No, simply curious. Why German? And why now, after three years of occupation?"

She sighed. "I am tired of standing at a checkpoint with them making remarks to each other and not knowing what they say. What if they said something important that might help the Allies? I stand right there and know nothing."

"So, what you really want is to spy on them."

"Oui." Exactly what she wanted. A way to fight back. "Do you not think I would make a good spy?" Her teasing mellowed as she reached for a knife and a cutting board. "Perhaps not a good one. I am terrified of all this. Of what would happen if they found you here—not just for us, but for you. And the other things I have done. One mistake, one German who looks too close, and everything is over."

Robert grunted as he lifted his bad leg onto a nearby chair. "Like the one who was here, who found me?"

"I think—and pray—we can trust him."

The conversation paused briefly and then moved on to more pleasant topics. Robert spoke of his home in Sussex and his worried mother. His father was an officer who contributed to the war effort from England, and a brother served with the infantry. Two married sisters and three nieces and a nephew brought endless smiles. Just hearing him speak of them tugged at Rosalie, filling her with yearnings for family. She loved Marcel and Maman, but a distance more pronounced than miles pulled them apart. And what of children? If not her own, then Marcel's. Was that something to hope for, or would it only bring more pain if she lost him as well?

She didn't sense the same despair when Robert spoke. Despite being wounded and stranded in Nazi-occupied France, his voice portrayed hope of return, of seeing his family again.

"And a wife?" She didn't know why she'd asked such a forward question. Or did it just feel forward because *she* was asking. Might he think she wanted to know because of an interest in him? *Did* she have an interest in him?

His gaze zeroed in on hers, and heat crept to her cheeks. Oh, heavens, he did suspect! But he smiled. "No wife. I did have a fiancée, but she was not interested in being the wife of an RAF officer." He grimaced, but there was a lot of sorrow there too. "A lot of us don't make it home."

"But you will," she said, forcing confidence into her tone. "We will find a way to get you home."

Robert watched her for a moment, then pushed to his good foot and maneuvered toward her. He leaned heavily against the counter while brushing his fingers down her bare arm. A tingling sensation skittered through her. "Thank you. But at the moment, I can't admit to being in a hurry." He leaned forward and pressed warm lips to the corner of her mouth. The touch was brief, but the sensation of it lingered even after he withdrew.

Rosalie stood in place, not sure how to proceed. Did he have feelings for her, or were his kisses just kisses? She wished she were more experienced, but there had been no one since losing Lucas.

When she didn't say anything, Robert simply smiled. "I think you are right, though. I should probably lie back down for a while." He turned toward the cellar when a tapping came at the door. He looked at her, and she grabbed his arm. No time to climb below—not with his leg in the shape it was. She motioned for him to sit.

"Stay here." Rosalie closed the cellar and pulled the rug over the trapdoor. "Who's there?" she called out as she hurried to the door, praying they wouldn't have to test how well Robert passed as a Frenchman.

"Yvonne." A voice sang through the heavy wood.

Rosalie sagged against the door. "Thank you, God," she whispered in gratitude. Though there was a strange feeling of regret as well that Franz had not returned. But of course not. She greeted Yvonne with a smile and stepped outside. The fewer people who knew of Robert's presence in their home, the safer for all involved. "What brings you out this morning?"

"Papa sent me with a message." She leaned one hand against the wall and removed her shoe, then handed Rosalie the tiny paper tucked in her sole.

Important pickup from Caen. Go to Librairie *Monette and ask for a book about growing ivy. Ask about sending your friend home. Wear extra makeup.*

"I can't. Caen is too far. It will take most of the day just to get there."

"He said to make sure either you or Marcel agreed," Yvonne said quietly.

Marcel. The makeup wouldn't do him any good, so obviously Dumont thought her the best one for the task. Not to mention, the thought of her brother making such a journey sat like a stone in her gut. And he would go too. Eagerly. "Fine. Tell him I'll leave first thing tomorrow morning." If there were no delays, she might make it home in one day.

Yvonne nodded and hurried down the walk. Rosalie read the paper one more time, committing it to memory before returning to the kitchen and putting a match to it. The paper curled and fell to ash. Rosalie dropped the last corner into the sink.

"I couldn't help but overhear," Robert said from his chair at the table, his leg again propped up. "Will it be dangerous—what they have asked you to do?"

"Everything is dangerous. Having you here. Clandestine meetings. Deliveries. Curfews." She lifted a shoulder. "But this is war. When the Germans first arrived, I thought that if we did as we were told and kept our heads down, we could get along. We could survive." She shook her head. "They killed my father and so many others. And now they try to starve or work to death the rest of us."

He stood and touched her shoulder. She leaned in, craving the comfort, and he wrapped her in an embrace. "I'm still so frightened, but how can I pretend it doesn't affect me any longer?"

"Want to know a secret?" he mumbled against her hair.

She sniffled. "What?"

He pulled back enough to look into her eyes. "We're all frightened. Every time I receive a new mission. Every time I fly. Every time. And now, wondering how in the world I'll get out of France. Terrified. But that can't stop us. We can't let it."

Rosalie nodded and straightened, steeling herself. Fear was the Nazis' strongest weapon, the reason they controlled the radios and newspapers. The reason executions of Resistance members were usually public and broadcasted. She'd no longer give them that power over her. "I won't."

≡ CHAPTER 17 ≡

A burst of laughter from the two other soldiers standing at the side of the road did nothing to lighten Franz's mood. The sun shone hot and only a few clouds adorned the sky—an almost perfect summer day despite the humidity making his shirt cling to his skin.

The soldiers manning the check stop halted their antics as a truck pulled up to be inspected. Sweat beaded the driver's forehead—whether from the heat or the nervousness of having his load inspected. Despite the dwindling possibility of an enemy pilot in the area, their searches retained their vigor—though Franz suspected it was more from boredom than expecting to discover anything.

Franz crossed his arms and leaned into the small building constructed on the side of the road to provide limited shelter and house a small radio unit. He listened to the young soldier drill the driver about his home, his destination, his purposes in traveling, while the other looked over his paperwork. When they were content everything was in order, they lifted the barricade and allowed him on his way.

The road was relatively busy, the afternoon spent, and anyone who traveled for work anxious to be home. At least these people still had that much. A home. He wasn't sure he did. He couldn't imagine returning to Berlin now that his mother had remarried. He would never be comfortable living in the large estate Ernst Rintelen had moved her into recently. If rumors were to be believed, it had been confiscated from a wealthy Jewish businessman. Franz didn't want to contemplate what had become of the man or his family. He wished he could escape any knowledge of concentration or death camps—to forget the stories he'd heard.

Nein. There would be no going home, even if he survived this war.

"Well, well," Soldat Fischer crooned, stepping out to intercept a woman on a blue bicycle. Franz's jaw loosened. Rosalie had painted her lips a bright red, and her eyes appeared even larger and more vibrant than usual. Though he recognized the uncertainty in her gaze, she hid it well behind a coy smile which made her lips appear even fuller.

"*Guten Abend*," Karl said, meeting her. He cast a glance over his shoulder at Franz before returning his attention to Rosalie. "Reason for travel?" His well-rehearsed French phrase.

She stepped off her bicycle and walked the last several feet. "I had business in Caen and am on my way home."

"Business?"

Her smile remained in place. "Books. There were books I needed. On plants I grow."

"*Bücher?*" Fischer snorted. "I'd like to see a book worth riding all that way for," he muttered in German.

Karl nodded toward the basket fastened to the back of her bicycle.

"S'il te plait." Rosalie leaned the handlebars toward Karl to hold while she pulled out a volume on ivies and another on the cultivation of herbs. A third about roses. Under them in the basket lay the charred Bible Franz remembered so well.

"I find it hard to believe she went all that way for books," Fischer repeated. "What else is she hiding?"

Franz watched Rosalie as she returned the books to their place, her gaze dancing between the two soldiers as they spoke back and forth in German, anxiety growing in her expression.

"We must search you." Fischer gripped her arm.

"*Halt!*" Franz lunged to intercede, while forcing his face to not reveal the panic pinging every nerve. "I will take care of this. Continue with the others in line." He gripped Rosalie's elbow and pulled her and her bicycle off the road. He propped the latter against the building and led Rosalie inside before switching to French. "What are you doing here?"

The small booth allowed for no more than a foot or so between them, but Rosalie pulled back as far as she could. "Now for the real interrogation?" she asked. "It is just as I explained to them."

"Yes, I heard." He forced his voice lower. "But books? Do you not have enough at home?"

She folded her arms. "My father said a person should never stop learning. He loved books. Especially on plants and flowers."

Franz swallowed the apology that threatened to choke him at the mention of her father. "Now is not the time to be taking chances," he said instead. He looked out the small window to where Karl had moved to better see what they were doing while Fischer motioned another vehicle through the checkpoint. Franz doubted Karl had heard much of the conversation, but he should have paid more attention. How would he explain his actions and why he'd taken a personal interest in this woman?

"You are the one who—"

He wasn't sure what she was about to say, but something probably better left unrecorded. He pulled her against him and pressed his mouth to hers. The action was for the benefit of the man watching, but he quickly faded from Franz's mind. Rosalie tasted of sweet peppermint and smelled like the flowers she loved. What he had planned to be a quick kiss lengthened, and he brought his arms around her. Hers moved slower but followed a similar course up his back. Her lips moved against his with a gentle reply.

A hammering on the door pulled them apart. Karl motioned from the other side of the window at an approaching car, one wearing Nazi insignia and swastika.

"You best be on your way." He led her back outside to her bicycle. He held it for her while she mounted and watched as she rode away. A few more miles and she'd be home. *She'll be fine.*

Would he? The taste of her mouth lingered on his and made him hunger for more.

Karl raised a brow and shoved a handkerchief into Franz's hands. "Might want to clean off that lipstick before anyone sees." He strode away to man the barricade.

Franz turned away and wiped the cloth across his mouth, removing the smudge of red. The rumble of the car drew close.

"Leutnant," Fischer called.

Franz tucked the handkerchief into his pocket and turned to see Hauptmann Meyer motion for Franz to join him beside his car. "Leutnant Kafka. Just who I wanted to speak with. Have you had much traffic through here this afternoon?"

"Only what one would expect." He squared his shoulders and prayed he'd removed every trace of red.

Meyer hummed. "The Gestapo in Caen suggest there has been more communication between an underground cell there and smaller towns in the area. Sainte-Mère-Église was at the top of his list." He looked up the road to where Rosalie had just disappeared. "What about the woman on the bicycle? She fits the basic description of someone seen at the Monette bookstore."

"A bookstore?" Franz glanced and was relieved to see his men manning the barricade and out of earshot.

"Yes, a station of the underground, it seems. But we will continue to watch a while longer. Who can say what we might find." He nodded back toward the road. "What was that woman's business?"

Franz swallowed against the sudden fear spiking through him, one he was too familiar with. This time it centered wholly on Rosalie and her safety. "The woman is a personal. . .acquaintance of mine."

Hauptmann Meyer raised a brow. "Ah, I see." His mouth curved upward. "I see no harm in 'personal acquaintances' so long as they don't interfere with your duties."

"Of course."

"Good. See that I have a detailed report of all travelers from Caen today." He nodded at Franz then looked to the men at the barricade.

Franz gave the order to remove it. Gravel ground under his superior's tires as the car pulled forward.

A heavy breath seeped from his lungs as the barricade lowered back into place. He had no choice but to chance another meeting with Rosalie. Anticipation battled his dread.

———— ≈ ————

Perspiration trickled down her spine by the time Rosalie pulled her bicycle along the side of the house and removed the contents of the basket. With the books bundled against her chest, she hurried inside and pressed the door closed. Marcel rushed in right behind her, probably having seen her return.

"Are you alright? I don't like you taking chances like this."

"So it's fine when you do it, but I shouldn't? I'm older than you." And probably much more cautious. She was glad she had gone instead of him, especially with the checkpoints. Franz wouldn't have been able to intercede nearly as easily with Marcel. She tasted her lips but tried not to dwell on how Franz's kiss had affected her. Better to push that right out of her mind. Not think about his hands bracing her against him. The rise and fall of his chest.

"I want you to be careful."

Oh, blessed distraction. Rosalie nudged her brother. "Now you know how I feel." She took the pile of books to the cellar, Marcel clearing the way as they went. Robert sat up as they climbed down the steep stairs.

"You're home. Hallelujah. Everything went well?"

She cracked a smile, the adrenaline still bleeding away. "Yes. I met my contact and have both a message"—she held up the book on ivies where certain passages were marked for someone who had the right code—"and a part to replace the one I guess was broken in the radio." The latter remained wrapped for safekeeping in the hollowed-out book on herbs. Her heart had almost stopped when the soldier had examined the books. Thankfully Franz had intervened...though she questioned his methods and the lingering feelings his kiss had given life to.

"Marvelous," Robert said.

"Yes." She set the books on a shelf. "I will deliver them to our local contact tomorrow. "But I also have something for you, Monsieur Matisse Desrosiers."

"What?"

She chuckled at his expression and pulled a full set of forged documents from the pages of the Bible. "Everything you need to travel, including ration cards. They are incredibly detailed."

"Matisse, eh?" Robert smiled up at her as he took the papers.

"I think it fits."

"You are amazing."

Rosalie shook her head, but there was a thrill that came with out-maneuvering the Germans, by being defiant. A thrill she could get used to. She quickly told them about her journey to Caen, leaving out names and exact locations as she'd been directed. The fewer who knew specifics, the safer for everyone.

"When you are ready to leave, we will contact them again. They will plan your route back to England."

"I wondered if it would be possible." His eyes grew earnest as they focused on her. "Thank you."

She nodded her acceptance and stood. Leaving everything but the Bible in the cellar for safekeeping, she returned above. She was famished and probably not the only one. The sunset glowed with ribbons of pinks and blues through the western window in the parlor. Switching on the lights, Rosalie caught a glimpse of herself in the hall mirror. She'd worn some makeup before the occupation, but little since. She barely recognized the woman looking back at her, nor the fire in her eyes.

The door rattled against its lock, followed by a rapid tapping. Maman appeared from her bedroom, hesitancy in her expression.

"One moment," Rosalie whispered, closing the cellar door with Marcel and Robert still below. She nodded to her mother to open the door.

As soon as the door latch clicked, Franz pushed past Maman. He shoved the door shut behind him and jerked the curtains closed on the nearby window.

"Why are you here?" Venom edged Maman's tone.

Franz didn't look at her, his gaze steady on Rosalie. "We need to speak. In private." He finally cast an apologetic glance at her mother, who glared for a moment longer before lowering onto the small sofa, her spine rigid.

"Maman, please," Rosalie said. She didn't know what Franz wanted to say to her, but if it had anything to do with their kiss, she did not want her mother overhearing. When her mother refused to move, Rosalie strode past and motioned Franz to follow out the back door and behind the greenhouse, which blocked them from view of the road. As soon as they were out of sight and earshot, she looked to the German officer, still in uniform.

"Why *are* you here?"

He glanced around. "You mustn't return to the bookstore in Caen."

"What?"

"The Gestapo know someone there is working with the Resistance. They are watching it."

A chill moved through her despite the lingering heat of the evening. Madame Monette had been everything warm and kind. "They must be warned."

"They will be. I'll find a way, but it cannot involve you going anywhere near there again. It's too great a risk."

"A risk to everyone. They could say something to the—" She glanced at his uniform. Exactly what she feared. A pulsing ache grew behind her temples.

"Yes, if interrogated, they could betray far too much information. Do they know who you are, your name, where you live?"

"My name, no. I was told never to give my name. But they know what I look like, and that I live near Sainte-Mère-Église." Not to mention the contact they had with Dumont. "And they also know of Robert."

"Robert?"

"The fact we are hiding a British pilot."

Franz's frown deepened.

"How will we warn them?"

"Not *we*. I will think of something else." He paced the area, hat in hand, his feet trampling the grass. His blond hair flopped forward, giving him a youthful look despite worry deepening the creases at the corners of his eyes.

"What about you? What will happen if you are discovered helping us?"

He paused, a breath escaping between his lips. "As an officer, I will probably be afforded at least the appearance of a trial before the firing squad."

The image flashed in her mind and then struck her heart like an electric current. "Then why do it? Why risk yourself?"

His mouth tightened as he looked away. "Because it doesn't matter if I'm found out." Franz adjusted the grip on his hat. "I shouldn't be alive anyway. I should have been executed five years ago at the side of my best friend."

He lifted his gaze to hers, and she glimpsed the torment of his soul. "Instead, I betrayed him for the sake of my own skin."

⚡ CHAPTER 18 ⚡

Franz watched Rosalie's brow scrunch with question in the dimming light. He owed her more of an explanation—especially if she was to trust her life to him. But he wasn't sure he was ready to return to Berlin, to *Kristallnacht*, to watching friends and acquaintances dragged into the streets while their homes and businesses were looted and burned. Or to the many nights afterward, hidden away in Heinrich's attic, the tapping of the typewriter and the scratch of his pencil bringing the truth of what was happening to light.

He attempted to clear his throat but still felt as though he were being strangled. "We wrote leaflets, dozens and dozens. We had no choice but to attend Hitler's Youth, but we couldn't understand how the others could believe the government's lies. We listened to the BBC, my friend translating what was really happening. That is what we wrote." He pictured Heinrich, hunched over the radio, his brow furrowed with disbelief as he reported Germany's doings from Britain's point of view. Franz's task had been to type out what was said. He'd had a way with words back then—but now they wedged in his throat, choking him.

"What happened?" Rosalie prompted, though he could tell she hesitated to ask. Just as he hesitated to tell.

"We handed the leaflets out to everyone we knew, but in secret. Already the Nazis tried to regulate what was said, going after those who were spreading 'false information' and 'propaganda.' We didn't dare reveal ourselves. Instead we slipped our papers into coat pockets at church, taverns, and schools. Even posted them around the city with sketches I drew. We wanted to wake people up to what was really happening."

"You were against Hitler and the Nazis?"

"With everything I had."

"But now you wear their uniform, an officer no less. I don't understand."

Franz sighed and dug deeper into his memories. Heinrich met him there with his quick smile, his brown eyes glistening with mischief when they were boys, before they knew or cared anything about politics. It had been Franz's idea to fight against the Nazi propaganda. Heinrich had followed along willingly.

"I'm glad I can fight at your side."

"We were together one night working on our leaflets. It was late, past curfew, before we finished. He told me to stay for the night, to not risk being caught on the streets."

"You worry like an old lady."

"I insisted I couldn't stay. My mother would be frantic if I didn't return. I couldn't do that to her." He lifted his shoulder. "Besides, I was invincible. Or so I believed, until that night. I was caught and beaten by some Brown Shirts, local government thugs. Spent the night bleeding in a cell, fearing the worst. The next morning, an acquaintance of my mother arranged my release."

"And your friend?"

"A few days later, Ernst Rintelen, the *Schutzstaffel* officer who had helped me, came to our apartment and informed me that my friend had been discovered with our leaflets and charged with conspiring against the government. He told me Heinrich would be sent to prison or a work camp, or worse. But my involvement could be covered up. I had a choice. I could join my friend. . .or the Wehrmacht."

She straightened away from him. "You turned your back on your friend and joined your enemy?"

Her words gave voice to the guilt that had gnawed at him for so long. Bile rose from his stomach, stinging his throat. "Ja," he whispered, his voice barely audible to his own ears.

She folded her arms across her stomach, withdrawing further.

"I was a kid and I was scared. I'd heard enough rumors about what they did to people, the executions of political enemies. I'd already been bloodied by them. I didn't want to die."

Shame lowered his gaze. He couldn't bear the disappointment and questioning in her eyes. Regret pierced deeper than she could ever know. Years of following orders, becoming everything he hated and had fought against, crashed against him with accusation. His sins against God and innocent civilians. . .

"And now?"

"And now. . ." Could he change his course, give his life for his convictions? "I don't know."

She sighed, her shoulders dropping. "I want to believe you, to trust that you are earnestly trying to help and not lay some bizarre snare for us. I—I think I do trust you. But then I see that uniform, and my doubt, my fears, return. When I hear your accent, I hear the taunts, the orders, the threats from other soldiers."

"And you hate them." He forced the corner of his mouth up in a rueful smile that hopefully didn't betray the pain swelling in his chest. "And have every right to hate me too. I hate myself. I thought if I played along, if I didn't draw attention to myself, I'd be able to get through this war. But there is no middle ground. I've become someone I didn't want to be. I've done—" Images flashed across his mind, tormenting. "I've done horrible things."

She glanced down at his uniform. "Why change now?"

The stone fence pressed into the back of his thigh as he sought some support. "I stepped away from it all for long enough to clear my brain. I was badly wounded and sent home for a few months to recuperate before coming here."

"Your limp?"

He nodded and held out his right hand so she could see the scarring in the low light. "The most pain I've ever endured was in those first weeks. The field doctors questioned if I'd survive, never mind keep either of my limbs. I wanted to die, even prayed for it. But now, I'm almost grateful. Then seeing that Bible of yours again—"

"Again?" Her head snapped up. "It was you."

"I remembered you and your brother, and the feeling of doing the right thing. And then watching you, seeing your courage. You reminded me of who I used to be, who I want to be."

She relaxed her arms. "I'm not so very brave."

He could almost laugh at that, but she seemed to believe it. "I disagree. You are one of the bravest people I've ever met." But how to help her understand the effect she'd already had on him. His mind detoured to their moments alone at the checkpoint. "I need to apologize."

Her brows rose.

"Earlier, when I kissed you."

Her cheeks reddened. "Let's not speak of that. Better to forget it happened."

"Of course." Though she asked the impossible.

Rosalie walked to the front of the greenhouse and peered around to the front of the property. "I wish I knew how this would all play out," she whispered. Then turned back to him. "You will find a way to warn those at the bookstore?"

He nodded, though he had no idea how to go about it yet.

"I need one more thing from you." Her jaw jutted with determination.

Uncertainty battled with the need to prove himself to her, whatever she might ask. "What is it?"

"I want you to teach me German."

"German?" The last thing he expected her to want.

She squared her shoulders. "Know your enemy."

———————≈———————

"Where is he?" Rosalie asked out loud. They'd agreed to meet where they had talked once before under the large oak next to the stream where no one would see them—something neither of them could risk. To be seen fraternizing with a German soldier would soil Rosalie's reputation beyond repair. She was not one of those women who sold their dignity for food or a taste of wine and chocolate. Even if she had enjoyed Franz's kiss too much.

Rosalie blew out her breath and tried to focus on the Bible in her hands, the worn leather wrapped in a cloth cover she'd made. She needed to put Franz's kiss out of her mind completely.

A minute later she gave up on her reading and gazed out over the stream. A mist still hung over the water in the earliness of the day. Every morning for the past week she'd waited here, and he'd come twice. Their meetings had been brief, a few words and phrases given in German for her to practice before he had to hurry back to the village and his duty.

"Know your enemy," she said out loud. The language was coming slow, mostly focused on things she might hear at a check stop or during a search, with appropriate replies. But what if she was coming to know her enemy too well?

She set the Bible down and walked to the edge of the stream. "*He's not your enemy.*" Not anymore. But she would keep her distance. He had a purpose, but once he'd served it, she would gladly see the last of him.

She tossed a stone into the rippling water and fought against the rising irritation over his absence this morning. Again. Three mornings and no sign of him. Had he changed his mind about teaching her?

Giving up, Rosalie tucked the Bible under her arm and started home. Maman looked up from where she sautéed some vegetables for breakfast with what little butter remained. Now that the garden was producing, they were able to trade for most things they needed, all under the noses of the Germans.

"Where were you?"

"Just out for a walk." Rosalie made a show of setting the Bible on the edge of the table so her mother would not suspect any other purpose for her early outings.

Maman turned her attention back to the pan, but her body still showed an unspoken tension. The cellar was open, and Rosalie fixed a plate for Robert's breakfast before heading down. He sat up and stretched his arms. "I heard you leaving again."

"You heard me?"

He pointed to the open ceiling above. "Every morning. Your brother is heavier on his feet. Was he there?"

"Marcel never—"

"I don't mean Marcel."

Rosalie glanced up the stairs and cringed that her mother might overhear. She raised a finger to her lips and shook her head. "Non."

"Good." He said it under his breath as though not intended for her.

She sat on the upside-down pail and handed him his breakfast. "Why do you say that? He can help me."

"I don't trust him alone with you."

"I think we have no option but to trust him."

He mumbled something more under his breath that she didn't catch, but evidently, Robert didn't like her meetings with Franz. "Is it so wrong I want to understand what they say with their smug looks, thinking we don't understand?"

Robert folded his arms across his chest. "Do you think they would speak differently even if you knew? They're pigs."

"You're probably right, but if they think I don't know what they are saying, they may say something that will help the fight against them. I can't sit on the sidelines anymore."

The corner of his mouth turned up. "You are hardly on the sidelines." He motioned to himself. "In fact, you are right in the middle of it, hiding British officers, working with the Resistance."

She shifted on the pail. A wave of helplessness overwhelmed her despite his words. "For the little effect it will have on the turn of the war."

His warm hand stole over hers and squeezed. "No one soldier will win this war. But each is needed for victory."

She glanced at their hands, not sure how she felt about the gesture.

"But please, even if you trust this German, even if he is ready to aid us, he is still a warm-blooded man."

Rosalie met the studious gaze of the man beside her.

"And you are an attractive woman."

"Attractive?" She raised a brow in an attempt to lighten the heaviness settling over the small room.

He smiled. "You're beautiful."

Warmth spread through her.

"Rosalie!" Maman called from the top of the stairs.

"I need to go." She hurried away, breathless by the time she reached the kitchen. "Oui, Maman?"

Her mother didn't look at her, but Rosalie could feel the tension mount between them. "Take some vegetables to the Fourniers after you've eaten."

"Of course." Rosalie paused at the edge of the counter to wait for her heart rate to return to normal. If that was possible. The sincerity of Robert's flattery stirred something within her—a desire to be looked at the way he looked at her, to be seen. . .to be loved.

≡ CHAPTER 19 ≡

The sky wore gray to match the uniforms so prevalent throughout Sainte-Mère-Église. The heavy humidity suggested rain would start soon, so Rosalie pedaled quickly toward the Fournier home. As always, the sight of the brick cottage with its white shutters and creamy curtains brought pangs of regret and loneliness, memories of Lucas tugging at her heartstrings. Today guilt accompanied her. But surely it was not wrong to allow her affections to turn to someone else. Lucas would not fault her for that—especially if that someone fought for the very thing Lucas gave his life for.

Claude Fournier answered her knock and waved her in, staggering out of the way. She followed cautiously toward the kitchen, aware of the fermented odor drifting from the man.

"We have a guest," Claude announced, then dropped onto a chair at the table. "She brings vegetables." His words slurred.

Aline hustled across the room, pulled her husband back to his feet, and shoved him toward the door. "Off with you until you are presentable."

Rosalie stood back until Lucas's father had stumbled out the door and his mother waved her to sit at the table. "Forgive him. He's struggled since his return. Being held in those horrible prisoner-of-war camps. And then learning about Lucas. It's not been easy for him." She swatted a hand in the air as though to clear away the emotions running so high.

"You don't have to explain." Rosalie only wondered where he'd found the alcohol, not a common commodity anymore. She unloaded her basket onto the table. Small carrots, beetroot leaves, onions, lettuce, and spinach along with a few herbs.

"Oh, bless you, child. I don't know how we'd manage without you and your angel mother."

Rosalie lingered and helped clean the vegetables. "About Maman. . ." Perhaps the story was not only her mother's to tell. "Do you remember when she came to the area?"

Aline looked up in surprise. Then nodded. "Of course I do." Her gaze drifted. "Seems only a few short years since then, though I was so busy with Lucas, he a new baby. The war had ended, and your father arrived home in uniform, new wife at his side. They met while he was away to war and had married at the end." She swished the assortment of green leaves through the water. "Your mother was expecting you by the time they arrived here, I believe, just starting to show."

"Do you remember where she was from?"

The older woman gave her a curious look. "Your mother hasn't told you?"

"Not that I remember. I've asked, but she seems reluctant to speak of it."

Aline seemed to consider that for a moment. "I suppose I can understand why. She was a quiet one when she arrived, but your father explained it to us, trying to soften the way for her in the community. The girl had lost her family while her village endured a horrific battle. Verdun-sur-Meuse. That was the name. She fled toward Paris with her mother and a sister. Yes, that's right."

"Maman never mentioned a sister. Just her brothers that were killed in battle."

"Her sister died if I remember correctly. Her mother too, but near the end of the war when food was scarce and the Germans were withdrawing. I don't know all the details, and your mother never spoke of it. Perhaps it's still too painful."

"Perhaps." Rosalie set the small bunch of washed carrots on a cloth and collected her basket. "Thank you for telling me."

She mulled over what she'd learned as she pedaled toward home. Halfway there the heavens opened with a downpour, but she let it wash over her. Poor Maman had lost her entire family in the last war, and now Papa.

"Verdun-sur-Meuse."

Something about the name seemed familiar. Maman had met Papa during the war and had come home with him as his wife. With her family dead, nothing would have held her to the home she'd known before the war. "Dear Maman." What pain did she keep bottled within her, allowing no one to share her grief? Would Rosalie react the same if she lost Marcel and Maman?

As she pedaled, her thoughts shifted to others who risked themselves and their families. Worry scratched at her insides. Why hadn't Franz returned? Had he been able to warn Madame Monette, or would they be arrested and questioned? She'd heard torture was used against Resistance members. Was there enough information to lead back to Sainte-Mère-Église?

"Don't borrow trouble, my Rosa." She heard her father's voice, a memory from years ago, as a thunderstorm had brewed above them. *He wrapped an arm around her and squeezed. "If we have no control over what will come, then leave it to the only One who does."*

"Who does?" she questioned as the dark clouds billowed and lightning lit the darkened sky.

"When you figure that out and know it for yourself, you will no longer fear storms. Instead, He will speak to your heart: 'peace be still.' "

———— ≈ ————

Dawn glowed on the horizon, but the sun had not quite showed itself as Franz hurried toward the stream. An entire week had passed since he'd last met Rosalie there. The deep grasses washed his boots with the heavy dew. He jogged the last few yards, a strange nervousness mingling with the anticipation of seeing her again. If she was there. With his long absence, duty and discretion keeping him away, he would be surprised if she hadn't given up on him and remained home to enjoy her morning away from mosquitoes and the cool, moist air.

As he neared the oak, resignation and disappointment settled into his chest.

She might still come, he reminded himself.

A form moved, rising from a large rock behind the tree. She turned, and the corners of her mouth lifted. "You're here."

"I'm sorry it's been so long. It's not always possible to get away."

She closed the Bible and hugged it to her chest. "You told me as much when you agreed to meet."

He stopped near her and tucked his hands into the pockets of his tweed coat to keep them from reaching out to her. "What would you like to learn today?"

She held up a finger to hush him. "First, I must know if you were able to warn Madame Monette."

He nodded. "A note that she and anyone else involved with the bookstore were no longer safe. No one remained when the Gestapo raided the building two days ago."

Rosalie glanced heavenward and murmured a prayer of thanks. The smile she rewarded him with, though slight, made the risks he'd taken all the more worthwhile. "*Danke schön.*"

It was his turn to smile. "*Sehr gut.* You have practiced?"

"A little," she replied in turn, then leaned against the tree. She switched to French. "There is so much left to learn, things I might hear when they stop me to look at my papers."

"*Ihre Dokumente?*"

"Ja. But also, what they say to each other."

He knew exactly what they might say, as it was often enough on his mind. "*Was für eine schöne Fräulein.*"

She raised her brows, waiting for his translation, and warmth crept up his neck. Perhaps he should have started elsewhere.

"What a beautiful woman." It was impossible to say it without some of the sincerity he felt.

She cleared her throat. "I suppose that is a good phrase to know."

"I imagine similar is said often of you."

Her cheeks flushed, and she glanced at the babbling stream. "I wish they wouldn't."

"It's impossible not to notice." Though thankfully they would most likely never see her as she was now—the morning light glowing in her hair, her eyes bright but softened by the mist, and her lips pursed in thought. He ached to pull out his book and sketch her as he had the flowers near her home.

His thoughts must have been evident in his movements as she looked to his satchel with questioning in her eyes. "What did you bring?"

"Only my sketchbook and pencils."

"Show me."

He pulled the book from its place and surrendered it to her. She glanced over the flowers she had seen before, then past the buildings in the village that had caught his eye. She paused longer at a hurried sketch he had done of Karl and Brenner laughing together. Her brow furrowed, and he wondered if she was able to look past the uniforms they wore and see the innocence of youth he had tried to capture. She turned the page and froze on the images of the beaches just miles to the east, the shore marred with fortifications.

"Is this what it looks like now?"

He nodded.

"We used to swim and play on those beaches in the heat of the summer. And now. . ."

Now a person would be shot for stepping foot on the sand.

She closed the book and handed it back to him. "I must admit to preferring your sketches of flowers."

He gave a rueful smile. "And I prefer sketching your flowers, but my pencil draws what is on my mind." Thankfully she had not turned to the back of the book, where he had started images of her, none doing her justice. He returned the book to his satchel, but when he looked up again, her gaze was on his hands. Her fingers smoothed over the scarring on the back of his right hand, sending a cascade of sensations through him.

"My father's were scarred like that," she said softly. "From the last war. Sometimes they hurt him."

"Sometimes it does." He had kept every finger, so it was easier to look past the discomfort.

"Do you know what happened in Verdun-sur-Meuse, during the last war?"

The turn of topics caught Franz by surprise. "Verdun?" He took a minute to remember what he'd been told and what he'd read. "It was the longest fought battle—almost ten months if I remember correctly."

"I wonder if that was when they died."

"Who?"

She shook her head. "Never mind." She pulled her hand away. "I just don't understand why we must have wars. Why fight? Does anyone actually win?"

"No. No one does." He already missed her touch.

"We should focus on why we came here."

"*Sicherlich.*" He straightened away from her despite the aching need to pull her close. Distance was safer. "Of course."

≣CHAPTER 20≣

August 1943

The business of survival was not an easy one. Summer days slipped away, bringing thoughts and fears of enduring another long winter under Nazi control. Allotted rations were again cut, leaving little expectation of food for the colder months once the gardens ceased producing and the bulk of their harvest was turned over to the nearby depot. Most of it would probably be shipped to Germany or sent to feed their army. "Sicily may soon be free," she whispered to herself. That was what Franz had told her this morning. Maybe France would follow.

Rosalie set the tray of oregano in the sun to dry beside the mint she cut that morning. In her mind, she rehearsed the German words she had learned over the past weeks. Franz constantly praised her for her quick mind in learning his language, but she had less patience with herself.

"*Bitte haben Sie Geduld*," he would remind her. "Have patience."

She returned to the house to find Robert pacing the floor with the cane Marcel had furnished for him. He seemed to share her impatience, though his was focused on getting back to England so he could continue the fight. Unfortunately, with Madame Monette and her contacts fled and Monsieur Dumont silent on the matter, "just across the Channel" never seemed so distant.

"How is the leg? You mustn't push yourself so hard."

"The leg is fine." He hobbled to the nearest chair and dropped onto it. Sweat beaded on his brow. "Well enough, at least."

"Haben Sie Geduld," she murmured.

"What was that?" Robert leaned forward on his elbows, eyes narrowing.

Rosalie crossed into the kitchen and washed away the green staining her hands. She already knew very well how he felt about her meeting with Franz.

"Is that from your latest lesson with *him*?"

"You say it like it's a crime."

"Fraternizing with the enemy isn't?"

She turned a glare on him, and he held up his hands in apology.

"I just want you to be careful." He pushed to his feet and came behind her.

"I am always careful." But the longer Robert remained here, the more his frustration grew, as well as the dangers. "And he is not our enemy. He brought news of the Allies. They have landed in Sicily."

"How?"

"Mostly by sea, but he said they had. . .*parachutiste*?"

Robert thought for a moment. "Paratroopers."

"Ah, oui. Paratroopers were also used."

He leaned into the counter beside him. "I think they will have to do the same here. There is only one way to get enough men onto French soil quick enough, and that is from the shore. Paratroopers would be extremely useful for taking control of bridges and other strategical points."

The thought of freedom and an end to this war sent a thrill through her. "And we, what can we do?"

"Depends on if you can be contacted and given instructions before the operation. By radio or something."

Rosalie nodded. What had become of the radio Marcel had helped Monsieur Couture assemble? Monsieur Dumont might know.

Robert gently tapped his finger to the side of her head. "What is going on in that beautiful head of yours?"

"Nothing." She managed a weak smile. "I only hope they have success in Sicily." Because if they couldn't take that small country, what chance would France have?

"They will," he declared. "We're ready for this fight. We've been learning from our mistakes, growing wiser and stronger."

"You wish you were there, non?"

He sighed and kissed her head. "I do. I'm not ready to sit out the rest of the war. I want a front seat as we drive the Nazis back into Germany for good."

Rosalie allowed herself to lean into him for a moment but didn't feel the same. She just wanted her family to be safe, to not relive her mother's past. That would be enough for her.

Marcel burst into the cottage, out of breath and grinning. He pushed the door closed and bolted it.

Rosalie left Robert and stepped into the main room. "What's happened?"

He held up a finger for her to wait while he slipped off his left shoe and pulled an envelope from the sole. "From Monsieur Dumont."

She snatched the missive from him before he had a chance to object and hurried back into the kitchen. She sat to rip the note free. Two train tickets fell to the table. From Caen to Pont-l'Évêque for the 19th of August—the day after tomorrow. She emptied the envelope of its final contents. Travel documents for *Matisse Desrosiers*—Robert—and herself.

"You're going home," she breathed, not quite believing it was finally happening. Not quite sure how to feel about it. She read the note through one last time before passing it to Robert, who had pulled his chair beside her.

Marcel leaned over Robert's shoulder to see, shoe still in hand. "About time."

Robert gave a tight chuckle. "After all my complaints about taking so long, I'm suddenly hesitant to leave." He read through the instructions then passed the paper back to Rosalie. "We should probably destroy this."

She tossed the note into the fireplace and set a match to it. She watched until the paper flaked to ash before turning back to the table where Marcel and Robert waited. "We have one day," Rosalie said, her voice lacking strength. So much to do, to plan for.

"Back to England. Hardly seems possible. I only wish you could come all the way with me. It's not much safer for you to stay, not with what you're doing."

"I should go," Marcel said, leaning forward. "It will be easier to fight from the outside, to join Monsieur De Gaulle's men."

"Non." Rosalie sat across from him. "The journey is too dangerous. And you are needed here." She needed him—to know he was safe and not storming the beaches of France into the onslaught of German fire. "Best for both of us to stay and continue our fight from within."

His mouth turned up. "*Our* fight?"

She nodded and glanced at Robert. "We'll be ready when the Allies come." Just as he'd promised.

"If I make it out of here alive, I'll be with them. And someday, I plan to come back, Rosalie. I'm not ready to leave and forget about you."

The intensity behind those last words burned into her chest along with thoughts of brief kisses and lingering in his arms. Was there really hope of a future with him? "I will watch for you."

Marcel cleared his throat with an exaggerated sound.

Rosalie slapped his arm. She took the tickets and slid them into her handbag. Robert knew France well enough from the sky, but not from the streets. That would be her role. "We will prepare everything tomorrow and leave early the next morning." Which meant she could meet once more with Franz at the stream. *If he comes.* Would it be better to inform him of their plans and ask for assistance. . .or to stay silent and not risk anything being leaked back to the Nazis?

No. The less he knew, the better.

Rosalie bid the men good night and slipped up the stairs to her room. Anxious energy sparked through her, making it impossible to settle. She packed a small bag and attempted to read until her eyes burned and she turned out the light. She lay in the dark for hours, playing their journey through her head, trying not to consider what would happen if she or Robert were discovered.

Her eyes batted open at the earliest rays of breaking dawn in her window.

Franz. Maybe she needed to confide in him. Oh, how she wanted to seek his help!

The rooster crowed and the light spread across her floor while minutes ticked by on the clock near her bed. She pulled the covers to her chin, forcing herself to stay. Too many people were already involved in this plan.

She worked in the garden until the sun's heat beat down on her, driving her back inside. The afternoon was spent gathering what they would need for their journey, including her Bible. As she worked, Rosalie rehearsed the instructions Dumont had sent. When she joined Marcel and Robert in the kitchen, her brother held a revolver and ammunition.

Robert took the weapon and turned it over in his hands. "Not sure where is best to hide it."

"Let me." Rosalie could barely keep the tremble from her hand as she reached for the gun. But she knew the checkpoints and had seen how much more thoroughly they searched men. A woman with a quick smile created a different distraction. She would have Marcel load the pistol and it would go into her handbag, wrapped in a scarf under her Bible until they reached their next contact. "This will be best." So long as she could keep her nerves controlled when they passed through the checkpoints.

The rattle of the door jarred them from their preparations. The knocking grew more intense as they scurried to hide what they had gathered. Rosalie gave Marcel a nod, and he stepped to answer. The door flew open with the same motion that brought Yvonne into the room. Her arms flew around Marcel.

"They've arrested him."

"What?" they said in unison while Rosalie rushed past to slam the door closed.

"Papa. The soldiers came and searched the house." She hiccuped a sob. "Then dragged him away."

Marcel extracted himself from her arms. He hurried to the window and peered out. "You are sure no one followed you?"

"I don't think they did. I don't know!" Her voice pitched with panic.

"What do we do?" Marcel glanced to Rosalie as though expecting she had any answers. Her own fear rose. How was she supposed to know what to do? She was a follower, not a leader. Robert watched them with a concerned but confused expression, and Rosalie quickly summed up in English what had happened, one thing becoming clearer to her with each moment—they couldn't stay here. No doubt Dumont would do everything he could to keep their identities secret, but what if he had no choice? Or maybe the Germans already knew of their involvement with the Resistance, from the same source that had betrayed Dumont?

Franz?

No. She couldn't believe he'd betray them. The Germans would already be at their door if he had.

Either way, she refused to sit here waiting for soldiers to descend upon them and drag them to their deaths.

"We need to leave. Now." She hurried outside and around the side of the house to where Maman hung bundles of lavender to dry in the greenhouse.

Maman glanced at Rosalie and fumbled the bundle in her hands, and it tumbled to the ground. "What has happened?"

"Monsieur Dumont has been arrested by the Germans." Her voice sounded surprisingly calm to her own ears. "Yvonne is here, but it might not be safe for any of us."

Maman blinked but otherwise remained frozen in place. "Where will we go? There is nowhere safe in France."

Maman was right, and there was no way to escape France. Even the tickets to Pont-l'Évêque might be compromised. "For tonight, go and

137

stay with the Fourniers. You've had no involvement with any of this. Stay there and out of sight until we send word."

Her eyes widened, and Rosalie recognized fear. "What of you and Marcel? Will you not come with me?"

Rosalie shook her head. "Our names may be known. And Yvonne will need to hide. And Robert." So many lives at stake, and far too much responsibility pressing on her. She stiffened under the load. "But go quickly before curfew and stay from the main streets. I will pray you pass safely." She kissed her mother's cheek. "I love you, Maman."

"Be safe," Maman whispered. Rosalie barely heard the words, but they were enough.

Minutes later they locked the doors and parted ways, Maman into town, and they to the north. Rosalie led the group through the trees and around hedges as the evening darkened the sky. With every step she worried for Maman. Had she been right in sending her to the village? Would the Germans be angry when they couldn't find them and seek her instead? Would Maman be made to pay for their crimes? Rosalie glanced over her shoulder again, tempted to go after her and bring her as well.

She'll be fine, Rosalie repeated to herself. The Germans wouldn't have her name or know where to find her. If they came looking, it would be for Rosalie, Marcel, and their British friend.

Through the trees, she could make out a low light from the Guillaume home. She led the group to the left where a woodshed stood dark. With the summer weather, the building stood almost empty but for a few remaining logs smelling of moss and decay. "Close the door."

She turned on the small torch she had brought and inspected the floor littered with old leaves and twigs. An unseen rodent scampered into the corner. As much as she wished to believe it was nothing more than a mouse, judging from the size of droppings across the floor, it was probably a rat. For all she knew a whole family of rats lived behind the small stack of logs.

"We can't stay here," Yvonne whimpered.

"We have little choice," Marcel said, tossing down the bundle of blankets Rosalie had shoved at him back at the house.

With one laid out near the door, she sat down and motioned Yvonne to join her. "There is nothing else to do right now but wait." And pray they weren't discovered.

Rosalie pulled her handbag from around her neck and reached past the Bible. She extended the pistol to Robert, who would have the most experience with a gun, then settled back against the wall. "We should try to sleep while we can." And in the morning. . .only God knew what tomorrow would bring. She bowed her head and addressed her pleas to Him. She prayed for the life of Monsieur Dumont, that he would be spared and released. She prayed for Robert, that they would find him a safe way back to England. For Yvonne and Marcel and Maman, that they would be protected. For herself, that she would know what to do.

Rosalie closed her eyes and pictured the beaches only a few more miles to the northeast. If only they could sneak past the Germans with a boat or somehow swim to England and safety. If only they weren't trapped.

≣ CHAPTER 21 ≣

Franz woke the next morning to a buzz of talk. An older Frenchman, Antoine Dumont, had been arrested the night before. A leader in the Resistance who was linked to the Monette bookstore. An order for Franz to meet with other officers arrived within the hour, and he quickly readied himself, his mind in a spin. If this man was in the Resistance, did he know of Rosalie or her brother and did this put them in danger?

"The man tells us nothing," Hauptmann Meyer grumbled as he reported to Major Kaiser and the others. Franz stood near the door, wishing he could forgo the meeting and check on Rosalie but knowing that any information he gleaned on her behalf was vital.

"And the daughter is nowhere to be found," Meyer continued.

"I have no patience for this," the major said from where he stood behind his desk. "Make the man an example for any others who think to fight against us."

"A public execution?"

"Whatever you see fit, but I want it done today." The major waved them out and turned back to the large map of Europe nailed to the wall that seemed more interesting to him than Meyer's report.

Franz fell in step behind the others. Hauptmann Meyer seemed disgruntled with the brevity of the meeting and turned to the man beside him. "What has the major so distracted?"

"You haven't heard? We lost Sicily yesterday."

A low string of curses tumbled from Meyer's mouth, while Franz fought back a sudden urge to smile. A fleeting urge as he remembered the man about to be executed for trying to help his people. Too many had already been sacrificed. Would there be an end? Would he be able to keep Rosalie safe?

Franz broke away from the others and made his way to the edge of town on the most secluded roads. Though he was already late for their usual meeting at the stream, maybe she'd waited for him. He would go to her home if necessary. She needed to know to keep a watchful eye and avoid any further connection to Dumont.

The stream rushed over rocks and logs with bubbling current, and the birds sang as though there were no worries in the world. Tall grass along the side of the bank had been trodden, but otherwise there was no sign of Rosalie. He blew out his breath but found he couldn't turn away yet. He craved the simple peace the small meadow portrayed.

"Franz?"

Rosalie came from behind him, as though she'd been watching for him from out of sight. She approached cautiously, and as she neared, he could see the dark hue under her eyes and the pinches of concern at the corners.

"You heard about Dumont. You were working with him, weren't you?"

A single nod. "Now what?"

Franz lifted his palms. "He's to be executed."

She shook her head, but he continued.

"He has said nothing about your or your brother. And his daughter is missing."

"I know."

"She came to you?"

Another nod.

Franz groaned. First the British pilot and now this? He didn't like the risks she took.

"We were supposed to be on our way to Caen this morning."

"We?"

She lifted her brows, questioning how he didn't know who she spoke of.

"The pilot? How was Dumont involved?"

"He arranged the tickets to Pont-l'Évêque, where we were to meet another contact."

"You can't use them."

She threw her hands up. "I know that! But what are we supposed to do? The Germans"—she motioned to his uniform—"are closing in on us, and I now have two refugees to get out of France. Or at least to Pont-l'Évêque. But how do we know that contact is safe? How do I know they don't have my name and aren't on their way here right now?"

"They aren't," Franz assured her.

She huffed. "They sent you alone?"

Franz felt the sting of her words, of the underlying suspicion. "I've had nothing to do with this."

"Then find a way to free Monsieur Dumont. His daughter is frantic with worry. There has to be a way you can save him."

"It's out of my hands."

Her jaw tensed, and she shook her head. "You're an officer among them. You could order the guards to release him to you."

"You think that would go unnoticed? With no explanation for my actions, I'd join him in front of the firing squad."

Rosalie flinched but recovered quickly, her eyes glinting. "You haven't really changed. You let them take your friend. And you still won't risk your own life for someone else. You'll let them shoot a good man because you're still afraid."

Franz took a moment to find his tongue. He forced himself to hold her gaze despite the guilt drilling into his gut. "Yes, I am. I'm terrified. But not of dying, like you think." The realization of his true fears stopped him short.

"Then what?" she demanded.

He dipped his head. "I'm not ready to meet God." *To be judged.*

She stared. "No. You're not."

Franz watched her go, his feet numb. He noted her path and then turned back toward town. She was right to be angry with him, but what solution was there? Trying to free Dumont wouldn't solve anything. There was no way to get him out of the area. Or himself. Franz wasn't ready to give up his life in a vain attempt.

I'm not ready to meet God.

The truth of it settled, heavy in Franz's chest. It really wasn't death he feared. Truthfully, death might even be a release from the misery of this world. But to stand and be judged by God? His hands were too stained for that.

He walked back, taking his time to mull over every possibility. Order the guards to release Dumont, steal a car, and try to get away? They would radio the first check stop and he'd be shot without questioning. Try to make it cross-country? There was nowhere to go or hide.

"Where have you been?" Bayerlein raised a thick brow, his eyes narrowing.

"I don't believe that is any of your business, Unteroffizier."

"Of course not. Though you may be interested to know I was tasked with organizing men for the firing squad." His stance broadened. Did Bayerlein really think this a great honor? "Dumont is quite a prominent citizen here, and a close friend of their mayor, Renaud. Though I suppose not everyone likes him, seeing as one of his own denounced him. Either way, his death will cause a stir."

"No doubt." Franz's stomach turned. Dumont had been betrayed by a neighbor? Would the same person have any knowledge of Marcel or Rosalie's involvement? "Who do we have to thank?"

"Major Kaiser has kept the man's name to himself. Apparently, some information is even above you, Leutnant." Bayerlein threw up a salute and walked away.

Franz went through the motions of his tasks, his gaze frequently going to his watch, counting down the hours until eighteen hundred hours—six p.m. The minutes dragged painfully by, while the hours passed too quickly. By three in the afternoon, he felt half mad from the tension building in him. He made his way to where they held Dumont and asked to speak with him. No one seemed to question Franz's request, and he was quickly allowed into the small room containing only a table and two chairs, one which was broken into several pieces. Dumont slumped against the far wall, the high afternoon sun angling down on him through the barred window. Fresh blood mingled with crusted crimson on the side of his head and his nose, swollen along with both eyes.

Franz waved the guard back into the hall. "I'll only be minute. I doubt the prisoner will give me any trouble."

The door closed behind him.

"Confidence cometh before the fall," Dumont's voice rasped in French.

"Then I will be quite safe," Franz replied. He stepped nearer as to not be overheard. "If I had any confidence, you might not be facing your death today."

The man squinted up at him. "I don't understand what you imply."

Franz held the man's gaze. "I am not your enemy."

Dumont choked out a broken laugh.

"Your daughter is safe for now with your friends, though one was upset that she couldn't move forward with the plans to return a certain captain home. Mostly though, they are worried for and praying for you."

The man's jaw sagged, and his eyes wept. "You are the one who. . ."

Franz nodded.

"I couldn't believe it was possible when I heard what you'd done.

I warned them it might be a way to trap us. I still don't know if I can believe you."

"I know. But I am not this uniform. And I would—" His voice cracked. "If you had any plan for escape, I would do everything in my power to save you."

The older man shook his head, though he winced at the motion. "No, save the others. Help my daughter get away. Watch over our friends."

"That would be easier if I knew who your enemies are, someone who would hate you enough to denounce you."

He shook his head. "Impossible to know. Food. The promise of protection. There are too many incentives. Not just hate."

Franz was halfway through his nod when the door creaked open behind him. His heart stalled as he jolted to his feet and glanced at the guard. At the same time Dumont flinched away as though he'd been struck again.

"I can tell you nothing," he murmured, raising an arm over his head. "I've told them I know nothing."

Franz caught his breath and forced any compassion from his face and voice. "Then there is nothing I can do for you, old man." And the truth of it soured in his soul. "Goodbye." He strode past the guards and forced himself to not look back.

———— ≈ ————

They sat in the shed most of the day, Rosalie venturing out only twice—to meet with Franz and collect some foodstuffs and more blankets from the house, and then again to sneak into Sainte-Mère-Église to check on her mother. Claude Fournier met her at the door, a scowl on his face but his eyes clear. "What has your mother upset? She won't say a word to us, just that she can't go home."

Rosalie pushed past him and forced the door closed. "It is better I don't say anything either, but thank you for letting her stay."

He leaned close until his stale breath washed over her. "Are you putting us in danger?"

"I don't believe so."

"Rosalie!" Aline bustled past her husband and pulled Rosalie into the parlor where Maman sat in the rocking chair, eyes steadfast on the wall. She glanced over at the commotion and slowed her rock. Expectancy and dread widened her eyes.

"Marcel?"

"Marcel is well." Rosalie moved to her mother, who appeared to not have rested since they'd parted ways. "He is safe."

"Is that what this is about?" Aline asked from behind her. "Monsieur Dumont is to be shot this evening."

Rosalie's chest crushed against her ribs. "This evening?" Not so soon. Somehow, she had harbored hopes that Franz would find a way to save him or she would have time to convince him. Now there was no time.

Aline's face lost all color. "You and Marcel have worked for him. Have the Germans come after you too?" She crossed herself and offered a quick prayer heavenward.

Rosalie struggled to find her voice and any rational thoughts. "Non, we had heard of his arrest and wanted to take precautions. It's better Maman stay here a little while longer if you will have her."

"Of course. She will be safe here for the time being, though we will keep her presence hushed. I'm sick over what will be done to Monsieur Dumont. And his daughter, what will become of her?"

"I wish I knew," Rosalie replied. The fewer people who knew Yvonne's whereabouts or their continued involvement with the Dumonts, the safer for everyone. "I should go." She turned but stopped at the door and hurried to her mother's side. "Au revoir, Maman."

Her mother was unresponsive to her farewell kiss, and Rosalie bit down on her lip to keep her emotions in check until she was free of the house and away from the village. The tears rolled down her cheeks as she crossed the fields. Did Maman not realize the danger her children were in and that she might never see them again? Of course Marcel she worried over, cared for. But would she be sad if Rosalie met the same fate as Monsieur Dumont?

Pity for herself fell away, washed from her with a surge of utter helplessness on Dumont's behalf. He was hours, maybe minutes, away from death. The day already grew so late. As she approached the stream and the old oak, she silently prayed Franz would be waiting for her with a plan for freeing Dumont.

The breeze teased the tall grasses and rustled the leaves above. No Franz. No plan. Rosalie hugged herself, mind churning. *There has to be something that can be done. Something.*

A rifle's report pierced the sky.

Non. Then a heart-shattering symphony of rifles discharging in perfect unison.

Her throat swelled, and her eyes ran over. She could see him, speaking with her father about the gardens while she unloaded plants from the truck, or laughing with the mayor at a community gathering. She saw his warm brown eyes as he pleaded with her to join the fight. Saw him standing stalwart as rifles cut him down. He was dead. Rosalie knew it with every fiber of her heart, as much as she wished for some doubt, some hope.

A sob tore from her chest.

Why had they attempted to resist? They should have stayed quiet, stayed safe.

It's too late.

A cry rose from the other side of the stream, and Rosalie raced across, not caring that the water soaked to her knees. Yvonne appeared through the trees, coming from the shed, her eyes set in the direction of Sainte-Mère-Église. "Non! Please no, no, no."

Rosalie met her as she collapsed to her knees in sobs. They clung to each other while Yvonne wept. Rosalie pressed her eyes closed but couldn't dam the flow of her own grief. The helplessness gnawed her. All Dumont wanted was a normal, happy life for his daughter.

Now he knew how impossible that was.

This was *normal* now.

"*This isn't life,*" she heard him say.

No, this was death, and misery, and broken hearts. Rosalie knew Yvonne's pain too well—the loss of a beloved father. For a moment she saw her mother as a young woman. She would have been about Yvonne's age when she'd lost her father and brothers. How acute must her pain have been? And who would be next? Rosalie glanced to Marcel. Robert stood a few yards back, leaning on his cane.

"*Germany will not stop draining the life from France and her people until either they are pushed out or there is nothing left of us.*"

Did it even matter whether they fought or stayed to their shadows and hoped not to be noticed? In the end only death and pain awaited. Would it not be better to fight, then? There had to be a way to get Robert out of France and Yvonne away from here. It was too late to use the tickets to Pont-l'Évêque, but she knew the contact's name and might be able to find him. New plans had to be made.

Yvonne trembled, and Rosalie rubbed her shoulder, offering what very little comfort was available. Antoine Dumont might be dead, but how could Rosalie let his death be in vain, or the death of her own father? They had both fought for the same thing.

"What future will my daughter have? Will you have?"

≣CHAPTER 22≣

With word from Franz that the Germans had learned nothing about Rosalie and her brother from Antoine Dumont, they returned to their home, but even two weeks later Maman remained in the village with the Fourniers. Rosalie did not encourage her return. The busyness of spring was far past, and summer drew short. They continued to work the gardens for all the produce they could preserve or sell for funds during the winter months—after the Germans took their half. Robert paced the floor with growing restlessness, and Yvonne remained for the most part cloistered in Rosalie's bedroom, burying herself in her grief.

In work, in studying her Bible, and while trying to sleep, Rosalie rolled around in her mind every possible escape route from France. With each day the dilemma increased. She had no radio for communication and few connections to other members of the Resistance. All she had was the name of the contact in Pont-l'Évêque but no way for the three of them to travel there except by foot. Multiple checkpoints barred their path.

She considered returning to the bakery in Valognes, and perhaps that was her only option. But she would travel alone first and discuss their needs with Monsieur Petit, though how would she get the needed travel documents, and what if he had also been compromised? Would she be drawing unneeded attention by contacting him? Again, fears and desperation collided with no sure solution.

Rosalie pushed into the cottage with a handful of carrots for lunch to find Yvonne bent over the table, face on her elbow, crying. Robert stood out of the way, looking uncertain how to proceed.

Rosalie set the carrots aside and pulled a chair close. She rubbed her hand across the girl's back, wishing she had words to accompany what she hoped was a soothing motion. Obviously, everything would not be all right. Instead, all Rosalie could offer was a "You go on and cry. It's normal to hurt like this. . ." *To feel as though you've been ripped in two.* She wished someone could have offered the same understanding a few short months ago when she'd learned the truth of her papa's death. Instead, she'd been expected to keep going as though nothing had changed.

Had it been the same for Maman as a girl? She'd at least had her mother and sister according to Aline. Had she cried on their shoulders, or had they looked to her for strength? And when they'd been taken from her, had she no one to turn to, or had Papa found her by then?

Marcel burst into the cottage, out of breath though she had seen him outside just minutes ago. He carried a sack and dropped it onto the table in front of her. "He says you have ten minutes."

"Ten minutes for what?" Robert questioned. He spoke in English, but at least his understanding of French had come a long way since his arrival.

Rosalie shook the bag out on the table. A German uniform, everything including polished boots.

"Your officer friend drove by in a fancy car. Said you have ten minutes for all of you to be ready." Marcel gave Rosalie a pointed look. "You too."

"Me?"

"*Apparemment,*" Robert grumbled, holding up a pair of silk stockings.

Her jaw slackened. "What is that man thinking?" she questioned in English.

"The more important question is how well do you trust him?"

"Well enough." She took the stockings, so smooth between her fingers. A second pair stared up at her from the table. "But even if I didn't trust him, do we have a choice anymore?"

"I guess not." Robert took up the uniform and hurried to the closest bedroom to change.

"Come, Yvonne." Rosalie pulled her friend to her feet and led her up the stairs to quickly freshen up. Judging from the gifts, his plan required a little more class than a dirt-stained skirt. She changed into a dark blue dress that still fit well despite years of being left on a hanger. A summery yellow one suited Yvonne's fairer complexion, and they both ran the brush through their hair a handful of times. While Yvonne pulled the stockings on without apparent hesitation, Rosalie hemmed and hawed as the minutes ticked away.

"Hurry," the girl urged as she headed from the room.

Rosalie sighed and yanked the luxurious silk past her knees, not allowing further thought before hastening back downstairs where she was met by the startling appearance of Robert in an enemy uniform.

Their time had all but passed when they jogged down the walkway to the waiting car, a beautiful machine glistening with polished black paint. Franz jumped from the driver's seat to open the passenger door for Rosalie while directing the other two into the back seat with their bags.

Despite the urge to demand what his plan was, Rosalie settled into the leather seat and waited. As difficult as it was to sit still, she would demonstrate her trust in him. She owed Franz that much.

The car rolled forward and sped down the dirt road before he supplied answers. "Major Kaiser has been offered a new car, a supposedly nicer one, but the trade is to be made in Paris."

"You are taking us to Paris? How does that help?"

He rested his free arm over the back of the seat and glanced at the others. "I thought a detour through Pont-l'Évêque would be warranted." Franz cracked a smile.

Rosalie was learning to like that smile. She almost had the urge to kiss it with the sudden gratitude she felt. The thought brought back a memory better forgotten. She pushed past it, needing one more question answered. "And the silk stockings?"

"When I volunteered for the errand, Hauptmann—Captain—Meyer questioned my motives, guessing from our last meeting that I might be wanting to get away with a particular someone."

"He saw us?" Her face reddened, and she hoped Robert didn't follow their conversation too closely. She could only imagine what Yvonne might think.

"He saw enough and. . ." Franz's face flushed. "I may have suggested I had a personal interest in you."

"You what?"

He planted both hands on the steering wheel. "He saw you and thought you fit the description of someone they were looking for— yourself, in fact. I told them that was unlikely because I knew you. . . personally."

Well then! "Hence the silk stockings?"

He tapped his finger to a thin box between them on the seat. "And chocolates. A gift from Meyer with hopes that my short leave might be more enjoyable."

A feminine chortle broke from the back seat.

Rosalie gaped at Yvonne. "This is highly inappropriate." As amazing as the silk felt on her legs...and as nice as it was to hear something besides sobs from the girl. "Though we really shouldn't allow good chocolate to go to waste." She opened the box and held it out. Yvonne popped one in her mouth and then settled back, closing her eyes to savor the treat.

Rosalie offered the box to Robert, but he frowned and shifted in the uniform that fit him all too well. With the cap perched over his furled brow, her confidence grew that he would pass a general inspection at any checkpoint. So long as he wasn't required to speak.

Taking a chocolate for herself, Rosalie returned the box to the seat and looked back to the road. She tallied the time it would take them to reach Pont-l'Évêque. Not more than three hours unless they were held up at a checkpoint, but usually the Germans drove past the lines of waiting civilians. They would reach their destination by six in the evening, leaving a few hours to find her contact. And if she couldn't...They would worry about that later. For now, she allowed a pool of dark chocolate to form on her tongue and set her hand over her purse and the Bible within.

Guide our path, Lord.

"I see at least the chocolate meets with your approval." The corner of Franz's mouth curved up a little.

Rosalie sighed, unable to deny how much she enjoyed the creamy flavor. "I don't remember the last time I ate chocolate."

"Far too long ago," he supplied.

"Papa used to order a chocolate cake every Sunday," Yvonne said softly from the back seat. "Even after the occupation, he bartered for several canisters of cocoa and hid them away. Every Sunday we would make something, even just hot cocoa. But he never ate it anymore. It was for me, he said. He wanted me to remember happier times, and hold on to the hope that they would come again." Her eyes glistened, but her lips formed a slight smile at the memory.

Rosalie took another chocolate and handed one to the younger girl. She held hers up as though a glass. "To happier times and their return."

Yvonne nodded, and a tear tumbled. "And to Papa."

"And to your papa, one of the best men I've known." She met Robert's gaze and then stole a glance at Franz. Two more good men, so different and yet they fought toward the same goal, though not for their own gain—for France, for her.

⋛CHAPTER 23⋛

As they neared the first checkpoint, moisture gathered on Franz's palms. He eased his grip on the steering wheel and rolled down his window, greeting the soldier with a nod. He handed over his orders from Major Kaiser and tapped his fingers against the wheel. "*Macht schnell.* We wish to be on our way."

The soldier looked past him at the women, his gaze barely pausing on the Englishman seated not three feet away impersonating a German officer. Rosalie was brilliant and flashed a smile at the soldier, stealing his attention completely, a wonderful strategy despite the surge of jealousy prickling his chest. Though not a frequent occurrence, he preferred when her smiles were directed his way.

"Can we go now?" Franz questioned, the impatience in his voice requiring no extra effort.

"Oh, of course. One moment." He disappeared for a moment to stamp the papers and then returned them to Franz. A second soldier approached from behind and looked over the passengers. He grinned at the ladies and then centered his focus on Robert. "Where are you stationed? I don't remember seeing you before."

Franz glanced back to see Robert's mouth open...with a laugh.

Franz did the same and yanked his documents from the first soldier. "Do you know everyone so well? Leutnant Becker is not here long, but I am surprised you even ask." He started rolling forward while they scrambled to lift the blockade from his path. He rested his arm on the window and took a breath. "Laughter. A surprisingly effective response to put off questioning."

Rosalie flashed him a smile. "I'm glad you approve."

"That was your idea?"

"I suggested it in case he was questioned." She shrugged. "A smile, a laugh, to pretend you don't despise them—whatever is required to keep them from seeing the fear."

He looked at her. He'd seen her fear, but most of the time she seemed confident, cheeky even. Was it all a front?

The Englishman said something Franz didn't understand, and he suddenly wished he'd spent as much effort learning English as Rosalie had learning German. He settled into driving while Rosalie twisted to speak with the man in the back seat. Franz couldn't make out more than a handful of words, just enough to guess they were discussing what would happen once they reached their destination.

He watched Rosalie from the corner of his eye, admiring the gentle wave of her hair as it fell past her shoulders, the fullness of her lips, and the determined glint in her eyes. She was far too attractive in the blue dress, but it was only part of what drew him to her.

"Will we have much time in Pont-l'Évêque?" Rosalie asked him.

Franz quickly redirected his thoughts. "I can stay as long as tomorrow morning. If needed, I can leave you in Pont-l'Évêque and pick you up in a day." Though he would rather not. He'd rather not let her out of his sight until she was safely home. Though, if he were being honest, not even then.

He focused back on the road as the French countryside rolled past them. It would be too dangerous to allow any feelings to develop between him and Rosalie. First, because she would never return any affection. Second, they were in the middle of a war, and they could not afford to let their guard down or lose focus. That was how people got killed.

She would be worth dying for.

Even his conscious thought could not argue that away. Whether he wanted to admit it or not, he loved her.

He stole another glance at her, and the realization cemented. He tensed his jaw.

"Is something wrong?" Rosalie asked, peering at him.

"No, nothing. Trying to make out what I can of your conversation." Not the full truth, but she was better off remaining ignorant of his feelings. For both their sakes.

"I'm sorry. We have three languages between the four of us, and no one has them all."

"Except you."

She groaned. "My German is horrible, and my English barely passable."

"I can't judge your English, but you have been very quick at learning

154

German. You should be proud."

"I'll be proud when I can put it to good use." The edge of her tone spoke to her meaning. He wished he could hear her laugh again. "It is your French I am impressed by," she continued. "Where did you learn it so well?"

"School. At least for the younger years." He maneuvered around a cluster of potholes. The road, like most in France, was in great need of maintenance. "I enjoyed it, so I kept it up. Perhaps not as useful as English might be when listening to the BBC, but the French broadcasting has been helpful."

Her lip curved up a little. "Do you really enjoy it? Why not learn English instead?"

He shook his head. What he didn't want to mention was how much better his French was since the occupation. If they had landed on England's shores, maybe he would be fluent in that as well.

Robert mumbled something while tugging at his collar.

Rosalie shifted in her seat and replied in English.

"What's wrong?" Franz questioned.

"I don't like this," Robert said in passible French. It seemed he had been practicing as well. His agitation needed no translation.

"What, exactly?" Franz asked.

"This uniform."

It was better when they couldn't communicate. "I don't much like it either."

"But if I am caught, I will be shot as a spy."

"If you are caught, we all will be shot."

Dumont's daughter shook her head, her face losing all color. "Please, let's not talk of this."

Rosalie reached over the back of the seat and took her hand. "All will be well. You'll see." Again, the confidence she was able to portray astounded him.

"You can't promise that." The girl pulled away, crossing her arms and looking out the window.

Rosalie sighed. "No, I can't," she whispered. She shifted to face forward again, her hands going to her purse and withdrawing the old Bible with its tattered cover. She held it on her lap, eyes closed, perhaps with a prayer.

Not much more was said the next two hours as they drove through Caen and continued east. Two more checkpoints passed without incident, and they arrived at Pont-l'Évêque by dusk. "Where do you want me to drop you off?" he asked Rosalie. It had already been decided she would hunt out the contact while the others came with him to a hotel where Robert could change back into civilian attire.

"Église Saint-Michel. Stop a block or two from the church and I'll walk."

The car purred through the village, which was perhaps even smaller than Sainte-Mère-Église, and few people were out in the twilight. The tall stone bell tower and triangular windows appeared above the smaller homes, and Franz slowed.

"S'il te plait, drive past."

He did as directed and continued on for another two blocks before pausing so Rosalie could jump out. She flashed him a nervous glance before walking quickly back the way they had come. He knew her thoughts easily enough. What if she couldn't locate her contact or they were unable to help? He had no answers.

Franz drove away, wishing she didn't have to go alone. Instead of seeking out a hotel, he cruised around the immediate neighborhood and then extended his parameter. Generally, the streets were quiet, and he probably had nothing to worry about. They passed a few soldiers, but they seemed content to mind their own business for now.

He finally accepted that all was fine and headed in the direction of the main road where he'd seen a hotel. A familiar car caught his eye, but it was probably nothing, as they were common enough. The German officer climbing out of the driver's seat was not, however. Hauptmann Meyer. What was he doing here? Franz was aware he'd left several hours before them to tour some of the coastal villages, but why Pont-l'Évêque, and why now?

Franz spun the wheel, curving onto the closest street, just shy of where his superior was parked. With luck they had not been seen. He circled back to the old church and its grand windows and ornate stone works.

"Why are we going back?" Yvonne Dumont asked, sitting up.

"Where?" Robert questioned in French.

Swallowing a curse, Franz glanced out the back window to make sure they were not followed. "We're not safe here."

———— ≈ ————

Rosalie walked past the solemn graveyard with its stone markers, trying not to consider how many of her people—fathers, brothers, and even mothers and sisters—had been added to churchyards and common graveyards across the country in the past few years. She didn't know where her father was buried. Did he have his own spot in an open field, or had he been dumped in a hole with strangers in a mass grave?

She let the ache in her chest swell until it enveloped her, her movements forced as she continued to the front of the church. Her father was with God now. That is what she chose to believe. She stepped through the great arched doors into the church, and her breath caught. Silence enshrouded rows of pews and arched ceilings highlighted with hues of gold as the evening light glowed in the high windows.

"Can I help you?"

She started at the voice and turned to the man in overalls, hat perched over his brow. "Oui, I was sent to find Monsieur Gaillard."

He looked her over. "What business do you have with him?"

From Monsieur Dumont's description, this was probably the man she sought. "I am looking for a man buried here." Even whispered, the words seemed to echo through the empty chamber.

His brows shot up. "I would think you too young to know anyone here."

"Perhaps, but a friend sent me. I was supposed to come almost two weeks ago, but there were. . .complications."

"I heard rumors our friend was discovered."

"He was shot." A fate any of them could easily meet.

"I am sorry."

"But I still need help." She stepped nearer and lowered her voice. "I have Yvonne Dumont, his daughter with me. She will not be safe in Sainte-Mère-Église. And a British pilot who needs to get out of France."

He nodded slowly. "Where are they now?"

"Waiting. I wanted to make sure we were safe here before I brought them."

He gave a sad smile. "Nowhere is safe, mademoiselle." He motioned for her to follow him when the door of the church cracked open, and a gray uniform slipped in. Franz sprinted toward them.

Gaillard flinched like he wanted to run, and Rosalie seized his arm. "Please wait."

"Have you betrayed us?"

"He's a friend." She spun to Franz, while keeping her grip on Monsieur Gaillard's sleeve. Thankfully, he didn't pull away. "What are you doing?"

"We have to go. Now."

"But what about Robert and Yvonne? Where are they?"

Her question was answered by the opening of the door again. Robert trudged to them, suitcase in hand, Yvonne on his heels. "Does someone else want to explain what is going on?" he demanded in hushed English.

Rosalie looked to Franz for an explanation.

"Meyer, who I told you of. He's here, in Pont-l'Évêque."

"The officer with the chocolates?"

Franz nodded. "He knows I am on my way to Paris with you, but the others will be hard to explain."

She focused back on Gaillard. "Are you able to help?"

"What will happen to us if we can't get away from France?" Yvonne whimpered at Rosalie's side.

Rosalie squeezed her hand but looked to Franz. "How long do we have?"

"It's a small village. The longer we stay, the greater the risk."

Monsieur Gaillard spoke next. "You swear, on all that's holy in this church, that you are in earnest and these people are who you claim them to be?"

She met his piercing gaze. "I do. Can you help my friends?"

He hesitated, then made the sign of the cross. ". . .*mais délivre-nous du mal. Amen.*" He gritted his teeth. "Your friends may stay, and we will do what we can for them."

Rosalie's breath left her as a burden lifted from her shoulders. "Merci!"

Franz clapped Robert on the shoulder. "Change quickly."

Monsieur Gaillard motioned Robert through a side door. As soon as they left, Yvonne threw her arms around Rosalie. "I wish you could come with us. I've never been so scared."

"I know, but I'm needed here." She wasn't sure that was true anymore, but she couldn't leave Marcel and Maman. "Robert will take care of you. You will be safer away from here."

The girl hugged her tightly. "Thank you for helping me."

Rosalie nodded, too many emotions choking back her words. *If only I could have done something for your father.*

She felt a steadying hand on her arm and glanced into Franz's understanding gaze. Was it possible he read her thoughts, maybe even shared them?

Gaillard returned, and moments later Robert followed, dressed again as a French civilian. He handed the bundled uniform back to Franz and gave a nod which Franz returned. Robert stepped to Rosalie and braced her arms. "Be safe."

"I was going to say the same thing to you. I will pray for your safe return to England."

"Thank you for. . ." He seemed uncertain how to continue, then pulled her into his arms. His mouth captured hers with a kiss, firm and fervent. She allowed herself to relax into his embrace, swept away by the passion in his touch. But as they drew apart and the moment faded, she became all too aware of Franz watching on.

"If I make it out of this alive, I swear, I will be back," Robert whispered.

She nodded, not sure what to say, not sure what he expected.

Franz took her arm and directed her into the warm evening air and to the car. The car trembled as the door slammed closed. Rosalie glanced back at the church with her friends hidden inside. She'd done all she could for them, but it was hard to leave them in another's care. Her lips still tingled from Robert's kiss, but now wasn't the time to explore what she felt. What was the point? Despite his promise, she might never see him again.

ECHAPTER 24E

The purr of the engine his only company, Franz glanced at Rosalie as she dozed, her head leaning against the car door, pillowed by her arm. They hadn't spoken since leaving Pont-l'Évêque. Probably a good thing, as his thoughts and feelings were in a muddle after watching Robert kiss her.

Jealousy wrestled with the knowledge that he needed to accept what could never be between them. Robert was her ally, while he... He wasn't sure what he was, really. Some misfit stuck between two existences. A German soldier who wanted the war to be over and the Nazis to lose. If only his people wouldn't have to pay the price, but they had been already paying it for the past six years with the blood of their men and tears of their women. And for what? There was no real purpose to the war but the gain and power given a few men.

He sighed with another glance at Rosalie. She should be home tending her flower gardens, safe with her father and mother or married to some local boy who wanted nothing more than to make her happy. Not here, risking her life for others, disparaging her reputation if seen with him. She should not know this much pain.

It was dark by the time they reached Paris, and Franz reached over to rouse her. "We are almost there."

She jerked upright with a gasp and looked about. "Where are we?"

"We just reached Paris. We'll be at the hotel in a few minutes and then you can go back to sleep."

She shook her head, blinking the sleep from her eyes. "I shouldn't be sleeping." She covered a yawn.

"I disagree. We both need rest before our return trip tomorrow."

This time she nodded. "Do you think Robert and Yvonne will be alright? I'm so worried."

"I'm sure they are in good hands. You have done everything you could for both of them."

She moved her hand to the Bible she had read until the evening light had faded. "They are in God's hands."

"Ja," he whispered. Their fates were all in God's hands.

Franz followed the directions Hauptmann Meyer had given him to the hotel. A room had already been booked. *A* room. One single room between them both. He hoped Rosalie wouldn't object, and he really should have mentioned the arrangements before now.

He opened his mouth, but she spoke first.

"I came to Paris every summer with my father. We sold plants and flowers, but already the city was full of life and brilliance. And music. Especially in the evenings. Maybe it's just the dark and the curfew, but the city seems almost dead now—or in mourning, draped in black."

Franz had been through Paris on his way to Sainte-Mère-Église, but he didn't want to confirm that even during the waking hours, the life had been drained from this city, just as it had from most of Europe.

He pulled the car along the curb in front of the hotel and turned off the engine. "Rosalie."

She looked at him, and he realized this was the first time he'd spoken her given name aloud.

"I need you to trust me."

Her eyes narrowed. "Trust you? More than coming all this way and revealing secrets of the Resistance?"

"Oui."

"What's going to happen?"

Already someone approached the car. Franz hurried with his explanation. "Captain Meyer was the one who had the room booked."

"Room. As in one?" Her jaw tightened. "He has taken a lot of interest in your enjoyment of this trip, hasn't he?"

Before he had the opportunity to answer her, the porter opened her door. Franz shoved a breath from his lungs and hurried to her side of the car. "Allow me." He handed their bags to the porter and took her arm. He let the man lead the way and leaned close to her ear. "He is a strong believer in the morale of his fellow officers."

"We wouldn't want anything to damage your morale," she muttered.

With the reservation already made, they were quickly shown to a suite, which allowed them to avoid the leering gazes of the other German officers in the lobby and halls. It appeared officers of the Wehrmacht and *Luftwaffe* were the main patrons the hotel served.

As soon as the door closed, Rosalie faced him, arms across her chest. "What exactly do you propose?"

He lifted his hands in surrender. "A night's rest without being murdered in my sleep."

"I make no promises."

He crossed the sitting room and flicked the light on in the bedroom. "Well then, since I will be sleeping with an eye open, you take the bed, and I'll set up out here on the floor."

Her eyes softened. "I'm sure that is best. For the sake of your morale."

He smiled at that. "Go on and get some sleep."

She walked past him then turned. "I'm actually more hungry than tired. Do we have anything to eat?"

"Let's see." He walked to the small table where a basket sat with a couple of apples and a handful of small but deep purple plums. "We also have the last half of a baguette in the car. I can run down and grab it if you want."

"Fruit is fine."

He picked up both options and held them for her to inspect. "Which would you like?"

"Both." She cracked a smile.

He tossed the plum and then the apple. She caught them both with ease and proceeded to juggle them in one hand.

"Impressive."

She fumbled the fruit but caught them before they struck the ground. "It's been so long."

"Since you gave up preforming?" He winked.

"Since I've practiced." She tossed the plum up in the air and caught it. "My father taught us. Marcel and I used to compete with each other."

"So how many can you juggle?" He held out another plum.

She made a face. "Fine. But only for the sake of your morale."

He groaned. "Can we please forget that?"

She shook her head. "I think not. But take this." She threw him the apple. "Toss me another plum whenever I say *now*."

He waited while she moved to the center of the room where she would have more space. "Now."

He tossed her a second plum, and she began to juggle the two. "Now."

He tossed a third and she mixed it in with the others, alternating as they left her hands and flew through the air.

"Now."

A fourth joined the mix.

"Now."

She made the transition to five, but one of the plums tumbled from her hands, followed by a second and a third. She managed to catch the last two, then scrambled to grab the others from off the floor. "They are ruined. I shouldn't have tried."

"Nonsense. That was amazing. And the plums are fine. It just means you need to eat them all tonight, so they don't spoil."

Another hint of that smile. "Don't tempt me."

"Come on, when was the last time you let yourself relax and did what you wanted to?" He pulled off his cap and his uniform jacket and tossed them onto a chair. He could ask himself the same. But what did he want? The answer came without effort. The woman across the room—to make her happy. "One evening."

A fine brow rose. "What?"

"Let's pretend for one evening that there are no food shortages, no occupation." Franz loosened the top button of his shirt. "No uniforms."

"I'm not sure I can."

"Try." He bent and picked up one of the fallen plums. "For one night, can we pretend we're free?"

———≈———

Rosalie watched Franz sink into a chair. He leaned forward and raked his fingers through his shaggy blond hair.

"Pretend?"

He nodded. "Pretend I am just a regular man, and you. . .are you."

"What?" She picked up the other two runaway plums and dropped onto the sofa. "You get to pretend to be someone else, and I have to stay me?"

"I was going to try to be me." Franz shrugged. "Besides, someone else might not be able to juggle so well."

A laugh bubbled from inside her. It felt good. Maybe there was merit to his request. "Where do we begin?"

"Well, first with eating all these plums before they spoil."

She laughed again and tossed one at him. "You can help."

He caught the plum and cleaned it on his shirt. "Can, as in I may help myself as well, or I better or else?"

"Oh, there will be consequences if I have to eat these all myself, but you will probably be safe from them."

He chuckled, and warmth washed over her. She'd never seen him more relaxed, and it changed his countenance. He was rather handsome for a German. She chastised herself. Tonight, they were pretending. No sides. No enemies. Just a man and a woman.

Franz took a bite of the plum. "So, tell me about yourself, Rosalie. What do you enjoy about summer?"

She settled into the sofa, kicking off her shoes and tucking her feet up beside her. "Flowers." She took a bite and savored the sweet juice as it teased her tongue. "And fruit."

"Why does that not surprise me? About the flowers, that is."

"So, you are surprised I like fruit?" She smiled at him.

"Ha ha. No, I recognize that anyone named for a rose must like flowers." His teasing tone made her chuckle. "The extensive beds at the front of your house may have also made me wonder."

"Not at all. Those are my mother's beds, and my father chose my name, so your arguments make no sense."

"So, you don't like flowers? I will have to make note of that. No flowers for Rosalie."

She nibbled at her plum, thinking of what it would feel like to have a handsome young man show up on her doorstep with a bouquet of roses or lilies. It was easy to imagine him with blue eyes and sun-bleached hair. "No, I adore flowers. We used to raise fields of flowers, not just vegetables. Oh, we had a garden alongside the house for food and herbs, but flowers were our business, and our passion."

"I can picture that—you as a little girl, braids flying, skipping through fields bursting with color."

"Not a care in the world," she whispered, closing her eyes. Papa was there with her. She ran to him, and he swept her into the air—and suddenly the war was back, sitting between them with dark, ugly fingers reaching out to clasp her heart and remind her of everything she missed and longed for. As wonderful as pretending had been, it didn't bring her father back. She opened her eyes.

Franz frowned. He probably read her expression well enough. "What happened?"

Her eyes watered at the compassion on his face. "My Papa. . . I miss him so much. He'll never come home. I'll never see him again."

He leaned forward and clasped her hand. "I'm sorry, Rosalie."

"I hate this war—this helplessness I constantly feel. I despise it with everything I am."

"Me too."

She felt the gentle squeeze of his fingers and wondered if she should pull away. But she wasn't ready. She sniffled. If anything, she wanted to understand this man more. "What about your father?"

"I never knew him. He died before I was born."

"And your mother?"

"Last I heard, she was well, though I don't receive much news from her since she remarried this spring."

"Have you met your stepfather?"

Franz dropped his hands from hers, and suddenly she regretted the question. "I've known him my whole life," he said. "And I detest him the more I know him. He's one of the men who has made this war what it is, who's profited while everyone else suffers."

She followed her urge and took his hand again. "So very different from you."

"Is he?"

"You can't blame anything that happened on yourself. You couldn't have saved your friend. And. . ." She took a moment to find the right words. "*Tut mir Leid.*"

Franz looked at her in surprise.

"I'm sorry," Rosalie repeated. "I was wrong to blame you too. It's not your fault that Monsieur Dumont was killed. I shouldn't have said any of the things I did." She offered a sad smile. "It isn't as though I was any better. I didn't rush the prison and rescue him. Why should I expect you to?"

"Because I'm one of them."

She shook her head. "No, you aren't. Even you can't believe that anymore."

Silence nestled between them while both looked at their intertwined fingers. Franz slid a little closer, and his gaze rose to her face. . .to her mouth. His own opened as though he would say something, but not a word escaped his lips as he leaned in, pausing only inches from her. His breath brushed across her cheek with the scent of sweet plum. She had only to tip toward him, and their lips would touch. Would it be so wrong to go back to pretending? No war. Nothing to keep them apart.

Rosalie leaned away. She'd already lost too much. She couldn't risk her heart with no hope of a tomorrow.

"I'm sorry," she said again.

Franz withdrew, hurt in his eyes though his voice remained calm. "For having more wisdom than I?"

"For not being better at pretending."

of him,
t his abs

✺CHAPTER 25✺

November 1943

Limbo once again. September and October puttered by with uncertainty dragging out each day. Rosalie was supposed to take a handful of potatoes to the kitchen for dinner, but instead she sat on the upside-down tin pail that remained from when Robert had occupied the cellar. Two months and she'd heard nothing from him, Yvonne, or those who'd helped them. Had they reached England safely? Would she ever know?

"If I make it out if this alive, I swear, I will be back."

But as much as she wanted to see him again, she didn't want him to come back. Not until it was safe, not until this war was over—and she couldn't imagine that anymore. Another winter was on their doorstep, and the excitement of the summer had fled. No more secret deliveries or messages. Only silence. With Monsieur Dumont dead, they no longer had any contact with the Resistance. Most evenings Maman retired early, leaving Marcel to pace restlessly while Rosalie pored over the weathered pages of the Bible. She didn't know whether the book had brought her luck or whether God had taken an interest in her, but she longed to know for sure.

How else would someone like Franz end up in your life?

She almost smiled at the thought and pushed to her feet, three potatoes in hand. Franz was definitely an anomaly. She missed him too, though it felt strange to admit. The past two months had gone by without seeing much of him. Distance was safer—though she wasn't sure how she felt about his absence. Which meant it was probably for the best.

Back on the main floor, Rosalie had washed the potatoes and was reaching for a knife when Marcel burst into the cottage. Their gazes met, and he gave a tight smile, one without any pleasure. She set the knife aside and followed him upstairs as far as his bedroom door. "What's going on?"

He didn't look at her as he gathered black clothes. "Today is the eleventh."

"What has that to do with anything?"

He paused to give her a look of exasperation. "November eleventh."

The end of the last world war and the celebration of France's freedom. "I understand what the day is, but why does it require you to dress in black?" Already she had a suspicion that didn't bode well.

He shooed her from his bedroom. "We can't let the Nazis think they've broken us." His door closed.

But they had, hadn't they? Rosalie sighed. "What about curfew?"

"This only works after dark, trust me."

She trusted him fine, except where his safety was concerned. "Can you tell me what you're doing?"

"Non." A moment later he opened the door while shoving his arm into the sleeve of his black sweater. "You'll have to see for yourself."

"Not if you aren't telling me why we're risking our lives."

"Then I'll see you in the morning." He flung a salute her direction and jogged down the stairs.

One less potato she'd be making for dinner. Though she was tempted to cook his and eat it just to spite him. What a feast that would make. The Germans had already come and taken a large portion of everyone's crops. Some, of course, had been hidden away for her family's use and to be sold and traded with neighbors, but would it be enough when rations allowed by the Germans were constantly trimmed? If the war lasted much longer, would there be anything but bones left for the Germans to rule over?

The door squeaked closed below and footsteps padded across the parlor. She stared down the stairs. "Maman? It appears it will only be us again this evening."

"Dare I ask what your brother is up to tonight?" Not her mother's voice.

Rosalie hastened around the turn in the stairs, anticipation bubbling. "Franz?" She restrained herself from throwing her arms around his neck.

He removed his hat and gave a brief smile. "Sorry for not announcing the intrusion. I didn't wish my visit to draw unwanted attention. I saw your brother heading across the field. I hope Marcel will be careful.

The major was not pleased with their antics last night."

"They? What was he involved in?"

"It's assumed more than one person was responsible. The letter *V* was painted on signs, buildings, even sidewalks."

She felt a smile. "V for victory. In the last war."

"We gathered that. And spent the whole day washing off and painting over every one of them."

She feigned a grimace.

"I can see your regret for our suffering."

"Enough regret to wonder how to prolong it. Perhaps that is in the plans for this evening." She cast a glance out the window. How dangerous was tonight's mission?

"Try not to worry too much. No one expects anything to happen so soon. It's seen as a flash of mischief because of the day."

She sighed. "I still worry. I can't help it."

"Marcel is fortunate to have a sister so concerned." Longing pulled at his voice.

Rosalie tipped her head to study him. "You've never mentioned siblings."

"I don't have any, as much as I've wished for it. My parents hadn't been married long before my father left for war. He returned on leave a couple times, enough to. . ." He cleared his throat and glanced away. "He was killed before I was born."

Understanding created more of a bond than the rift she might have expected learning that his father had also fought against France. "Your mother never remarried?"

"Not until this spring." His smile looked more like a wince.

She remembered what he'd told her of the man. "I'm sorry."

He looked down at the hat in his hands. "I want her to be happy, and I hope she is. That this is what she wanted, but. . ." Franz motioned to the insignia on his sleeve. "He was the reason for this promotion."

"I see." But that was hardly on her mind right now as she stood in place across the room from him, neither of them moving. "Is that why you came? For Marcel, I mean?"

"No. Well, partly." He held her gaze as though looking for something there. "I overheard a broadcast from the BBC."

"You have my attention, and I'm thoroughly jealous."

"A report of the return of a pilot lost for several months and presumed dead."

Her heart skipped. "Really?"

"A Captain Robert Wyndham."

She couldn't withhold a squeal. "They made it. They're alive."

"Yes." He fidgeted with his hat. "I thought you would like to know since you and he were...close."

"We became good friends." She knew exactly where his mind went, and hers followed to that goodbye kiss in the church.

Franz nodded and started to turn. "I should go."

Something panged within her chest. Disappointment? She should feel nothing but elation that Robert was safe. But she wasn't ready to watch Franz leave so soon. "No German lessons today?" She switched to German, the language no longer as distasteful as it had been to her. "I've practiced a little."

He glanced back, and his mouth turned up at the corner. "Sehr gut. But I do not think it would be wise."

"Wise? To learn German...or for you to stay? Might someone have seen you?"

"Nein, not that. I took precautions."

"Then...?" Rosalie paused, realizing she'd been stepping toward him and only a few feet now separated them. "Have you been avoiding me?"

"Ja." He closed the distance with one step. "I do not trust myself." He touched her cheek, then pulled away. "Your Captain Wyndham will be back."

"I care for him, and I am so happy he is safe, but I have no claim on him." A few kisses, a sweeping infatuation. Since the night in Paris, any romantic feelings for him had been replaced by something else, something she couldn't put a name to, but centered on the man only inches from her.

"He loves you, I think."

"And do you?" Rosalie bit her tongue. She shouldn't have asked such a question! Heat rushed to her cheeks at her boldness and Franz's studious gaze which lowered to her lips. His breath cascaded across her skin, a pleasant sensation that made her insides tremble. Warmth brushed her mouth, and she closed her eyes in anticipation. It was his brief kiss at the checkpoint she'd been longing to repeat.

"I do love you," he whispered against her lips. "And I've never been more afraid."

She tipped against him and deepened their kiss. He loved her. She felt that love wrap around her as his arms pulled her against him. She was tired of fear and letting it dictate her life.

———————— ≈ ————————

Logic and emotion battled within Franz as he held Rosalie in his arms and spilled his heart into his kiss. This wasn't supposed to be. Keep his distance, keep her safe. That was his mantra the past two months. But how could he retreat now? She caressed his soul with healing and desire. And humanity. He'd felt life seep back into him since meeting her, and he was no longer the mindless machine they had created of him. His heart beat with a rhythm of its own, and his mind searched possibilities.

She drew away enough to search his gaze, and he managed somewhat of a smile, his thoughts still spinning. How could someone so beautiful and pure be in the middle of so much trouble? And how was it possible for her to be standing so close, her fingers intertwined in his hair, her lips full and pink from the kisses she'd offered so freely?

Rosalie wet her lips, and Franz leaned in for another brief taste. At some point he recognized they would need to step apart and discuss what this meant and how to proceed, but he didn't want to think about that now.

The door thudded behind him, and Rosalie jerked away from his touch. Horror showed in her eyes as she backed away another step.

"What have you done?" Her mother's voice held such venom, Franz instinctively stepped to shield Rosalie. "You have disgraced this family."

"Non, Maman." Rosalie pushed past him, at the same time distancing herself. Her hands clasped together as she faced her mother. "You know he is not like them."

Her mother's head wagged while her hand waved at his uniform. "He is not welcome here. He only pretends."

"Non, Maman."

The pain in Rosalie's voice spurred Franz into action. He glanced at her, wishing he could stay and fight for her, but knowing his presence was the problem. "I'll go."

Madame Barrieau circled out of the way as though he were diseased. She murmured a curse under her breath and slammed the door behind him. As much as he wanted to linger and know what would be said within the small house, he hurried to the road and put miles between him and the storm brewing in the Barrieau home. He should have delivered his message and kept his distance, but it was hard to regret the past ten minutes.

⫚CHAPTER 26⫚

Two days later, Rosalie stared at the black ink marks in the Bible, each a part of a word, a sentence, a book. Each in its place. Each needed. Unlike her. She heard the mumble of voices below and knew Marcel was home. She was surprised when he tapped on her bedroom door a few minutes later.

"Are you coming down to dinner?"

"I'm not really hungry. You and Maman go ahead without me."

Instead of leaving, he leaned into the doorframe and folded his arms. "What happened between you two?"

Not something she wanted to talk about. "Nothing."

He narrowed his eyes, looking so much like Papa it made her throat ache with emotion. "That's what you said yesterday, and she still doesn't look at you or acknowledge you live in this house."

Rosalie set the Bible on her pillow and flopped backward across her bed. "She hates me."

"I don't believe that for a moment, and neither should you."

"Maybe, but she'll never forgive me."

He sat beside her on the edge of the bed. "For what?"

Rosalie felt her face flame and covered it with her hands. Would she estrange her brother too with the truth of her actions?

"This has something to do with your German officer, doesn't it? Something happened when he brought news of Robert?"

She nodded. "But it doesn't matter anymore." She pushed to her feet and straightened her skirt. "We made a mistake, and it won't happen again, so why talk of it? I'm done waiting. Done hiding. I want this war over, and I don't care anymore what I have to do."

He raised a brow. "Feel like cleaning up a few things tonight?"

"What do you mean?"

"You know the Vs we painted?"

She nodded. After the Germans had painted over or washed off the first group, the locals had returned with five times as many. Everywhere. On every building and even a few vehicles. She had seen the Nazi retaliation in the village today. They had turned the Vs into crude swastikas, the sight sickening her.

"We're going back tonight." He reached into his pocket and handed her a small paper. She unfolded it and felt a smile pull at the corners of her mouth. Someone had cleverly taken the image of the V with the Swastika and transformed it into a V with a two-barred cross of the Cross of Lorraine, a symbol of French patriotism. "The first war we need to win is the minds of the people."

"I'm coming." And she would continue with the Resistance until no one, especially Maman, could question her loyalties.

She followed Marcel downstairs and forced herself to eat a few bites, ignoring Maman's snubs, before searching her room for a dark skirt and blouse. She found a black cardigan and handkerchief in her mother's wardrobe. Shortly after midnight, she met Marcel behind the greenhouse.

"Maman's asleep," he reported, gathering up a satchel of supplies. Once at the edge of the village, he handed her a small can of paint and a brush. "Best if we split up. I'll start a few blocks over, and others are covering the south."

Rosalie nodded her understanding, her pulse racing.

"Be careful."

"You too." She watched him go, then tipped her head with a prayer for her brother and the others out tonight. She ended her pleas with a quick cross and then shook her can of paint and cracked the lid. Working her way through the alley, she searched the walls for the paint markings. The broad swipes of black paint forming the Swastika clenched her stomach as she stepped to the first symbol and applied her own, transforming the image. Then moved to the next. Her ears attuned to every murmur of wind through the branches above, every scratch of cat, every creak of hinge on garden gates. One after another she worked her way down the street, adrenaline chasing away any thought of tiredness.

She'd completed close to a dozen when the solid thud of boots farther up the street froze her. They proceeded in her direction, and she ducked into a basement entry, behind a stack of firewood. Pressed into the gritty wall, Rosalie forced her breath to slow, though she felt she might suffocate.

"More here," someone grumbled in German from almost directly above her. They were looking at her artwork and didn't seem pleased.

Good.

More footsteps in her direction.

She slammed her eyes closed. *Please make me invisible.* She tipped her head forward so the scarf would hide her face. *God, make me invisible.*

"Still wet. They couldn't have gone far." Footsteps shuffled to the top of the stairs. She could feel the strength of the soldier's gaze brush over her.

Please, make me invisible.

Another set of footsteps moved past, searching the alley, but the first remained. Had he discovered her? Was he waiting for her to move and reveal herself?

Make me invisible.

Endless moments passed before the second footsteps returned. "Did you see anyone?"

"*Nein*," he muttered. "No one."

They moved away, and Rosalie dared to breathe again. *Thank you, God!*

Still, she remained in place, not daring to move from her hiding place for a long while, until there was no doubt they were gone. She gathered her brush and can and thought to head home, but caught sight of yet another swastika marring their victory. Indignation surged and she quickly fixed it with her paint and moved on to the next. For the next hour or so she worked silently, a shadow moving from building to building, until she caught sight of Marcel farther down the street speaking with someone.

Marcel motioned to her, and she hurried to his side. The man led them both into the nearest alley and around behind the church. Rosalie leaned against the cool stone wall to catch her breath. She couldn't recognize the man under the thick layer of black he wore on his face. Until he spoke.

"Like I said, we need someone to transport them," Monsieur Couture said.

She straightened. "Transport what?"

"Newspapers," Marcel whispered. "There is a Resistance cell just outside of Paris that has a press. They've been printing news of the war and the Allied advances—truth that our people need to know."

"Because the first war we need to win is their minds," Rosalie whispered, remembering what her brother had told her.

"Those were Monsieur Couture's words," Marcel replied.

"They need hope," the older man continued, "or they will not fight, and we will not be ready for the Allies when they come."

Rosalie's heart thudded. "Are they coming?"

"Soon. I know it will be soon. They have Sicily and now most of Italy. They will come, and we must be ready."

"Then I'll do it," Marcel said.

"Non." Rosalie set a hand on her brother's arm. "I will. I stand a better chance of making it through."

"Your sister is right. Young men have been the most active in our movement and attract the most attention from the Germans. A pretty woman is more likely to deceive them."

Marcel looked at her. "It will be dangerous, Rosa, more so than sneaking around at night."

"I've made deliveries for Monsieur Dumont. I know what is required."

"Yes, but this will be regular and consistent," Monsieur Couture said. "You will only have to go as far as Caen, but it will be the same route every week. You will need travel papers and reasons for your trips, as well as your pretty smile."

"But there isn't anyone else, is there?"

"Not in as good a position as you."

Rosalie nodded, the weight of her decision heavy over her. But Papa had already given his life for their freedom, and Monsieur Dumont was right—there was no future unless there was freedom. "Then it should be me."

≡CHAPTER 27≡

December 1943

Franz sat on the large stone, listening to the hush of the stream. The water glistened with oranges and blues as the sun reached for the horizon with the earliest rays of light. Just as it had yesterday, the day before that, and every day he'd been able to come in the past three weeks since leaving Rosalie to face her mother's wrath. It was their kiss he couldn't easily put from his mind. He needed to speak with her, know she was well.

"You're a fool." He closed his sketchbook and pushed to his feet to pace at the edge of the water. Nothing could come of his feelings for her, even if she returned them. A few stolen kisses. And then what? There was no happy ending, no marriage or family in their future, no matter which direction the war went. He needed to walk away now for both their sakes.

Yet he lingered, hoping to see her and speak with her again.

The sun rose high and began to melt the frost on the grass and naked trees, leaving Franz no choice but to start back toward the village. He detoured past her house where all sat silent and peaceful.

Back in his room, he changed into his uniform and polished his boots before appearing for duty. Franz smiled to himself as he strode past a wall painted with a cross nestled inside a V, no sign of a swastika hidden in the emblem of faith remaining. Bayerlein had sworn, and the major had grumbled, but the crosses were left. Not that they had acknowledged the defeat—merely that it was not worth the time to paint over the hundreds of crosses throughout the village. Besides, what harm could they cause? They were not a blatant symbol of victory. Franz wondered at that.

Outside of the major's headquarters, Hauptmann Meyer stood next to his car, paper in hand, scowl on his face. He waved Franz to join him. "Have you seen these?" He thrust the crude newsprint into Franz's hand. "One of our sources reports a new one each week, distributed on Sundays."

Franz glanced over the French headlines. A speech from Charles de Gaulle encouraging French citizens to be patient but hold on to hope. A report on the latest Allied advances. Highlights from the Resistance. "Dangerous," he said, returning the sheet to Meyer.

"Very. Especially with *Feldmarschall* Rommel expected."

"Feldmarschall Rommel? He is coming here?"

"The Führer has put him in command over the Atlantic Wall, building fortifications, preparing for invasion."

Franz's interest perked. "An Allied invasion is expected soon?"

"Ja. Though perhaps not until spring." Meyer smirked. "The Allies like fair weather. And short distances. Most likely they will strike at Cherbourg or farther west along the coast, closer to Calais or Dunkirk. Not Normandy. But we must still do our part to thwart any assistance from the inside." He waved the paper. "We must find the distributors, couriers, and source. It's no small operation, and its dismantling will be a great boon to crushing the Resistance in this area."

"Of course." Chances were Marcel and Rosalie were also involved. How long before they were discovered?

"What are you thinking, Leutnant? Do you have an idea on how to bring them to ground?"

"I wish I did. Let me think on it." And how he would keep them safe, hopefully until the Allies liberated them. He prayed an invasion would be met with success this time and wouldn't come too late.

"Feldmarschall Rommel has already sent word to Major Kaiser of his expectations," Hauptmann Meyer continued. "More fortifications must be built along the beaches. More obstacles, more wire."

"Before he arrives?" It was the middle of winter, and the wind blowing off the Channel would not be kind. "Or before spring?"

"Orders are to begin immediately. Tomorrow we will begin to gather laborers from the area."

"Most able-bodied men have already been sent to our factories and to keep roads open between here and Germany."

Meyer's eyes thinned ever so slightly as he watched Franz.

Franz focused on keeping his voice even when he spoke again. No emotion. "I only mean to suggest that the task of finding many laborers may be difficult."

"We're not picky. There are plenty of farms that are not being worked now that it is winter. And boys old enough to be useful. Once the fortifications are complete, they will be allowed to return to their land with plenty of time to prepare for seeding."

But only because the Nazi war machine had to be fed.

Franz took his orders and went about his mundane duties for the remainder of the day, his thoughts never far from Rosalie, Marcel, and what freedom would bring them if an Allied invasion were successful. He'd not consider what it meant for him with his own fate so intertwined with the Nazis. He was a simple cog, and their fate would be his own. Little that it mattered.

That night, he slept restlessly, tormented by dreams of Rosalie being searched and a bundle of the illegal newspapers found with her. He saw her beaten down, her broken, bloodied body tossed into a cell where she awaited her fate. In each dream he watched helpless from the sidelines, unable to speak or intercede.

A cold sweat drenched his face when Franz finally awoke. As he paced his room, images from the nightmare engraved themselves in his waking thoughts, becoming more real with each passing minute. Dumont's fate, which had been shared by so many others, could too easily become Rosalie's. He refused to let it fall to chance.

Franz dressed in the dark and trekked north from the village. The Barrieau home slept peacefully. All was well. He checked his watch in the moonlight. Four in the morning and frigid. Certain he was alone, he crept around the side of the house and ducked into the greenhouse which still retained heat from the day before. A stool at the far end provided a place to rest and he leaned his head into his palms, pain finding him in his exhaustion. He considered his options. Walk away and hope she wasn't involved with the newspapers, wake her somehow, or wait until morning to try warning her and her brother.

Ihr bruder.

Franz had almost forgotten his orders for today. Would Rosalie forgive him if he showed up later in the day with guards to haul Marcel away?

He groaned and massaged his aching temples. He couldn't leave— not without seeing her first. Getting comfortable, Franz settled in to wait. His eyes grew heavy by the time dawn glowed in the east.

A hand jostled him awake.

"What are you doing here?" Marcel demanded.

Franz jerked to his feet while still trying to clear his head. Dawn lit the sky. "I need to speak with Rosalie."

"Haven't you caused enough trouble?"

"That isn't my intent."

Marcel glowered. "Then what happened between you on your trip to Paris, and again a few weeks ago? I'm not blind."

"I care for your sister. I don't want to hurt her."

"What happened between you?"

"I kissed her." And he would take full responsibility for it.

Marcel glared at Franz but didn't make another attempt on his life, which could be considered a good sign. "It would never work. You must know that."

Franz wanted to argue, to suggest that they would find a way, but he knew the truth as well as Marcel. "Of course I know that. It was a mistake. We both know it, and it won't happen again."

"Good. But then why are you here?"

Franz sighed, not free of the desire to see Rosalie even for a moment. "We know about the newspaper the underground has been distributing in the area. I wanted to warn you in case either of you are involved. We will be seeking out the origin of the paper and all the couriers."

Marcel gave a single nod. "Very well." His tone held a dismissal.

"I need to know if she's involved," Franz insisted.

"Why?"

"Because I need to know she's safe. I need to be sure she's not taking any unnecessary risk."

"You're in love with her."

Franz froze, but it wasn't accusation in Marcel's voice. Just understanding. "Yes."

He nodded. "Wait here." He slipped from the greenhouse and made his way to the house. Minutes passed and Franz looked at his watch. It was almost six thirty, and he needed to be changed into his uniform and on duty by eight. He tapped his fist against his side, impatience gnawing as the minutes stretched on.

Finally, a figure hurried around the side of the house toward him. Rosalie wore a flowered robe over her nightgown and her hair was a rumpled mess around her shoulders. Her face was flushed from the cold air by the time she reached the greenhouse. Instinctively he rubbed her arms to warm them. "You should be wearing a coat."

"I'm fine." She stepped out of his reach. "Marcel said you had something important to tell me."

He tried to ignore her withdrawal and focused on what little time he had left. "Are you one of the couriers for the paper the Resistance has been spreading?"

She jerked in surprise. "Who else knows?"

"Hopefully no one. When do you do your route? What day and time, and what road? We know they aren't being published in Sainte-Mère-Église, so where are you bringing them in from?"

"I can't tell you that. There's too much at risk."

"You know you can trust me." Didn't she? Did she doubt him already?

"Yes, but why must you know all this?"

"Because I need to keep you safe." His words came with more fervency than he'd intended, but he had her attention now. "I want to help you, to make certain no one can suspect you."

"Oh." Rosalie's shoulders relaxed, as did her expression. "I have a travel permit for every Wednesday. I take my bicycle to Saint-Lô to clean for and see to the needs of a close friend of my father's. He is alone and has been ill. I return around three o'clock on the main road."

"So, you would be reaching the main checkpoint at the crossroads to Caen around four?"

"Closer to four thirty."

He blew out his breath. "I wish I could do the delivery for you, but I could never come up with a reason for a weekly trip to Saint-Lô."

Her lips curved. "Not even for your morale?"

He groaned. "Please, can we forget that?"

She shook her head.

"I will do my best to be at that checkpoint, to make certain your way goes as smoothly as possible." He gave her a tight smile, remembering his other purpose for coming. "I wish I could be as helpful to Marcel."

"What do you mean?"

"I will be returning today, but not alone. We have orders to collect laborers for fortifying the beaches."

She stiffened. "They're already death traps."

"Feldmarschall Rommel disagrees. He will be here soon to oversee the work is done properly."

"You can't take Marcel." She bit out the words between clenched teeth.

"I have no choice. Leaving him behind would be too obvious an oversight. I will do my best to keep him safe. If he keeps his head down and does as he's told, he shouldn't be in any danger."

"As he plants mines in the sand?" Her eyes flashed with anger but also fear.

"Rosalie—"

"And when they see that he is old enough and strong enough to be hauled away to a German work camp or factory?"

"I will do everything in my power to keep that from happening. You have to trust me."

She hugged herself, her face bearing all the conflict she felt.

He braced her shoulder. "I have to go. Talk to your brother, make sure he is ready." Franz dragged himself away, no other option in sight. He made it back to his room by quarter to eight but was a few minutes late changing into his uniform and joining his men. Bayerlein met him on the way, sneer in place.

"Sleeping in, Leutnant Kafka? Or were you not here last night? Perhaps that French girl kept you from getting any sleep. That would account for how tired you look."

Franz clenched his fist but refrained from smashing the man's jaw. Instead, he walked where his men waited and relayed their orders for the day. He sent Karl and another soldier for the truck they would need to round up their human cargo, all the while praying he would be able to keep Marcel safe.

⊱CHAPTER 28⊰

Franz purposefully avoided Rosalie's murderous glare as he collected Marcel that afternoon, having saved the Barrieau home for one of his final stops. He wished he had time to explain to her that he had convinced Hauptmann Meyer his men would be needed to guard the extra laborers, so he would be able to watch out for her brother.

But not her. Franz could only be at one location at a time, so for the next couple of weeks, he could not man the main checkpoint she would pass through every Wednesday.

Marcel came easily but almost seemed to be smirking. Maybe he knew Rosalie would never forgive this. One less problem for him.

For the next week Franz watched over the Frenchmen as they fortified their own beaches against their allies. The men were thin from winter months and slim rations, but they were strong, most of them farm workers, millers, and other essential laborers. Marcel worked as hard as any, but the glower in his eyes remained present. Occasionally, he would glance at Franz and raise a questioning brow.

After Feldmarschall Rommel's tour, the work moved inland in case the Allies made it past the initial fortifications. *Holzpfähle*, or wooden poles more affectionately nicknamed "Rommel's asparagus," were sharpened and planted in the surrounding fields to deter glider landings and parachutists. Low-lying river areas were flooded for the same purpose— anything that might hinder an invasion.

The rain last night had left the air heavy, and the morning's temperature dropped close to freezing. The shivering men worked to stay warm in the barren field of spiked poles—like a graveyard of trees.

"How are you holding up?" Franz whispered to Marcel as he dug holes for more *Rommelspargel*.

"Better than most." He emptied his spade inches from Franz's boot then shoved it back into the soggy soil. "How much longer do they expect us to keep going? Or do you have any answers?"

"Not many, I'm afraid."

"Just a book full of. . ." Marcel nodded to Franz's pack. "What have you been writing?"

"Not writing. I draw."

Marcel snorted. "What? This?" He motioned with his head to the bleakness on every side.

"I draw what I see, for whatever comes of it." Men laboring. Great crosses of iron across the sand. Branchless trees pointing toward the heavens.

Marcel took another spade full of dirt. "Can I see?"

Franz glanced around to see everyone busy with their own tasks. He shifted his body to shield his sketchbook as he slid it from his pack and opened to a picture of the beaches.

"Impressive details. Are they accurate?"

Franz nodded.

"Then keep drawing." Marcel pushed his spade back into the dirt. "I have friends who would probably like to see your art." His mouth twitched.

"I'll see what I can do."

That night, Franz looked at his sketches and added details he had not thought to include before but that might aid the Allies in knowing what awaited them if they landed in Normandy.

———— ≋ ————

"*Bonne année,*" Marcel said, raising his wineglass. After almost five weeks away, he was finally home.

"Happy New Year." Rosalie followed suit, the flicker of the lamp dancing on the little remaining in her glass. The electricity had been out for most of the week, but at least the soft light added to the mood of the evening. She sipped the sweet pear juice they had bottled and set aside for the feast of Saint Sylvestre. No champagne or wine, but they had also saved some cheese and a handful of clams they had traded for.

He set his glass aside and reached for her hand, pulling her from the sofa.

"What?"

"We should dance," he said towing her to the middle of the small parlor.

Rosalie raised a brow at her little brother, now so much a man at seventeen. "But it is so late, and Maman is already in bed. Perhaps we should do the same."

He shook his head and grinned as though he hadn't a care in the world, a look she'd not seen on him in so long. "It is a new year, and I feel it will be a good one. Freedom, Rosa, this year. It has to be this year."

She tried to smile but didn't feel it. Hadn't they hoped the same in years past? What would make this year any different? "How are you so confident?"

For a moment his smile faded, and she regretted her question. "Because I cannot keep living like this. I need to believe an end is near."

She squeezed his hands and forced her tone to lighten. "Of course, you are right. This year. We will be liberated next. Franz said it will be soon. Our allies will come, and we will be ready to do our part."

He started humming "Pretty Poppy," one of Papa's favorite songs, but Papa had always sung "rose" as they had danced or worked amongst their flowers.

"You are my very dearest flower of all," he would whisper to her. *"I love my rose."*

Marcel swung her around, forcing her to focus on her feet. How long had it been since she'd danced? Since they had danced? Memories returned with the sweetness of savory wines, celebrating New Year's as a family, Maman and Papa dancing with them, singing out loud their favorite tunes, kisses on cheeks before being tucked under warm covers and wished the very best of years.

A quiet tap on the door made both siblings freeze. Marcel raised a finger to his lips and motioned for her to lower the wick on the lamp. He stepped past her and cracked open the door. A shadowed form disappeared down the road, vanishing into the night, but on the step remained a red ribbon tied around flat sheets of cardboard. Marcel handed them to her, and she loosened the knot. Between the cardboards lay sketch after sketch of the Normandy fortifications.

"They're perfect," Marcel said beside her. "We will have to get them to our contacts in Saint-Lô."

She turned through the pages, wonder growing at both the detail and that Franz would do this for them.

"Your German has some talent."

"He's very talented. But he's not mine."

She turned to the next page, and Marcel chuckled. "Are you sure?"

The final sketch portrayed a rose, shades of gray bringing to life stunning detail.

Marcel closed the door and leaned against it. "I sometimes wonder what will be left for us on the other side of this war."

She tucked the sketches safely between the cardboard. "What do you mean?"

"First Lucas, then Papa. Maman hasn't been the same. . .maybe she never will be. Monsieur Dumont and Yvonne. So many others have left or been killed. I never really thought about it, always sort of held on to what life was like before. But there is no going back."

The fathomless sorrow in his eyes ripped her heart. "We can only go forward," she whispered, the words sounding so simple, but her soul bearing the grief of those being left behind. "And we will. Somehow." She clutched the sketches to her, seeing the charcoaled rose in her mind. Franz would be another one she'd have to let go.

⪉CHAPTER 29⪊

February 1944

Rosalie wrapped the stack of papers in brown paper and laid it in the bottom of her basket. A false bottom she had weaved to match laid over the dangerous cargo, followed by what remained of her meager lunch and her Bible. She carried the basket outside and fastened it to the back of her bicycle.

"*Je vous remercie, ma fille,*" Monsieur Dubois said, following her onto the street. He clasped her hand once more in his. "Thank your maman, again. She is an angel for sparing you to care for this old man." He released her and leaned heavier on his cane. "Your Papa would be proud, good man that he was."

"It is my pleasure to come." Rosalie leaned in and placed a kiss on each of his wrinkled cheeks. "Papa was so fond of you." Though he had never met her father, or her mother, the ruse had begun to feel real, as did her affection for Monsieur Dubois. He told her quite proudly when they first met that he would soon turn eighty-six, and he did not get around too well without his cane, but his vigor for freedom fed her own flame. "I'll see you next week. I wish I could come more often."

"I take what I can get, ma fille. Be safe."

She climbed onto her bicycle and caught the nod of approval from one of his neighbors. The woman had stopped Rosalie shortly after the New Year and praised her for her devotion to the old man. "My father, rest his soul, loved him like a father. I know this is what he would want."

Everyone in the neighborhood was convinced of their relationship, and hopefully that would be enough should the Nazis ever question her weekly trip to Saint-Lô.

Rosalie closed her eyes and offered a quick prayer before starting her journey home. She'd done this route over a dozen times successfully, yet each time her anxiety grew. How long before she ran out of luck—before they decided to search her basket more thoroughly?

Protect me, Father. Please, see me safely home.

Home. . .to a mother who still refused to look at her, let alone utter her name. She'd overheard Marcel trying to speak on her behalf, but it did little good. Maman would only believe what she saw and interpret it as she wished.

Turning from such sour thoughts, Rosalie pedaled toward the main road that would lead north from Saint-Lô. She had over an hour's ride before she reached the checkpoint, a main crossroads with vehicles queued in three different directions. She rolled to a stop behind a wagon, two trucks, and a car and braced her foot on the ground. The wagon pulled through, but there seemed to be a delay with the first truck, and her heart quickened its beat. She craned her neck to see the soldiers near the barricade. Was Franz there? She couldn't make him out, but he'd made sure he was posted here every Wednesday for the past month. With deep breaths, she practiced keeping her face neutral.

Traffic continued to trickle through in the other directions, while the soldiers searched the truck more thoroughly than usual, digging through the load of coal in the weathered wooden box. These days, most coal was shipped east for use in German homes and factories. Perhaps the driver did not have all the required documents.

One of the German guards shouted something about rifles. She focused to understand what was being said in the flurry of German words that followed. Under the coal. A box. No, *bundles*. Rifles. Where was the driver?

Rosalie followed the search with her gaze as the man raced toward the nearest outcropping of trees. So close. *Lord, only six more paces.* She jerked at the thunderous volley of bullets. The man arched his back then tumbled forward at the edge of the grove and what safety he might have found there. Rosalie's ribs clamped over her lungs, refusing them air. She no longer paid attention to what was said as two soldiers ran across the strip of field to the fallen man and dragged him back. Blood soaked his clothes and marred the path.

"Not pleasant," a soldier said from beside her, making her startle. "*Aber notwendig.*"

Necessary? Rosalie clenched her jaw to keep it from trembling. She would say nothing, as the man would likely only find amusement in her disgust and hate. Her whole body shook as she handed her documents to his outstretched hand. He took his time while sending amused glances to where the dead Frenchman lay near the side of the road. The truck's engine roared to life as another soldier moved the vehicle out of the way of traffic. The second truck and car pulled forward as directed, as though nothing had happened. Why was the soldier asking for her papers when two vehicles waited before her?

"You come much," the soldier said, examining the new travel visa Franz had provided her with. The rumble of a motorbike engine approaching the checkpoint made him look up. "As does he," he murmured in German. "You are a poorly kept secret."

Franz.

Franz's motorbike disappeared behind the line of traffic on the far side of the barricade. If the newsprint was found, she might not be the only one shot. She'd seen the soldier before. Always scowling, always angry about something. A memory resurfaced with a chill. The morning in the rain when Franz had been the one to demand her papers. This man had been there as well, and remembering his proposal clenched her stomach.

The soldier leered at her as he continued his mumbled rant in German. "He has everyone eating out of his hand—Kaiser, Meyer, and obviously you."

Rosalie schooled her expression, pretending she couldn't understand what he said. "May I go now?" she asked in French, holding out her hand for her documents.

"Nein, something's not good here." His French was as coarse as his mannerisms. He motioned to her travel permit.

"Everything is in perfect order. Please let me go home."

"Not yet." He waved her off her bicycle.

With no choice, she did as ordered, in a direct course past the man dead in the ditch. The soldier glanced back at her and smiled, seeming to enjoy her torment.

Where are you, Franz?

The soldier ordered her to wait near the small building where Franz had first kissed her, while he stepped inside and again turned through her documents. She glanced to Franz, but he appeared to be detained on the other side of the barricade, arguing with another soldier. Realization dawned with renewed dread. That's why the soldier delayed her—he was waiting for Franz to intercede.

"May I please go?" She attempted to smile at the man.

No response.

She shot a look at Franz, who seemed focused on the truck and its driver. Rosalie could not help another glance at the man who had lost his life.

Father, take him to Yourself. And bless his family wherever they are. She knew the pain they would feel, the questions they would have. *Grant them peace.* The thing she still sought.

Franz moved, and Rosalie caught his eye. He started around the barricade, headed in her direction. She shook her head and motioned to the building. Apparently, he had enemies too. Franz slowed, his frown deepening as the other soldier stepped out.

"Ah, Leutnant Kafka. I thought you had duties elsewhere today," he said in German.

"I did. But it appears you have had your hands full here. I need to speak with you about the incident with the coal truck driver. Give the woman her papers and let her be on her way."

The soldier chuckled. "Always coming to the rescue. But are you sure you have no unfinished business with her before she leaves? Such a pretty one." He reached out to touch Rosalie's cheek, but Franz struck his hand away.

"Don't touch her." Franz stepped between them and grabbed the documents from the man's other hand, looking them over quickly before handing them to her. "You have everything?" he asked her in French.

She glanced through the papers and tucked them away into the pocket of her coat. "Oui." A tremor quaked her voice. Her insides still trembled. "Merci."

"Go."

The single word was all she needed. She climbed onto her bicycle and pedaled toward home. Despite the cold air, sweat tickled her brow. The image of the dead man filled her thoughts, and her eyes burned. No, she refused to be so weak. There was no time for tears, but they tumbled down her cheeks all the same.

Franz wished he could go to Rosalie immediately, but it was dawn before he reached their spot at the stream with a prayer that she'd meet him.

In the morning light he could make out her figure. She hugged herself and peered into the icy water then pivoted toward him, and her breath turned white on the frozen air.

"How did you know?" she whispered as he drew near.

"Know what?"

"That I needed you." She stepped toward him, and he encircled her in his arms, pulling her to his chest. She shuddered, whether from the cold or emotions he wasn't sure.

"I'm so sorry," he said, not sure what else she needed to hear.

A moment passed, and she sniffled. "Am I so weak?"

Franz pulled back enough to see tears rolling down her reddened cheeks. "No. You can't think that."

Another sniffle. "Thousands and thousands of people have been killed in this war, and even more have watched others die. But I. . .I've never seen death before."

He took a breath and tried to imagine yesterday's shooting through her eyes. Watching a man gunned down in front of you. Franz had been frustrated by the event, even saddened by it—too many senseless killings. But even he had grown insensitive to death. He'd seen too much of it. He'd watched men beside him fall in the heat of battle. He'd killed.

"Lucas, Papa, Monsieur Dumont. I wasn't there. I never saw them at the end, never saw them fall, or saw the blank stare. And now I can't unsee them, each of them just like that man."

"I'm sorry." Again, he had no words. He should have been there when she needed him, should have protected her.

"Who will be next?" She looked at him, her eyes surprisingly clear despite the moisture hanging from her lashes. "Me? You? Marcel?"

He shook his head. "You don't need to keep doing this. We can find a way for your family out of France. You can have a new life in England or even America, far from all this."

"I can't run away. You know I can't."

"It's not the same as what I did. I joined them—you would just be escaping. You have done your part and given enough."

"Have I?" Rosalie pulled away from him and turned back toward the quiet rush of the stream. Thin ice laced the edge of the shore, glistening in the rising sun. A haze of mist rose from the surface. "I'm not afraid of death anymore."

The thought cemented Franz in place.

"Pain? Oui, I'm afraid of pain. But I don't think that man felt much pain. It was so sudden. Fear. A jolt of agony perhaps. . . His back arched as he was hit. And then death. A return to God."

She spoke so calmly, as though death was more fascinating than frightening. "But the man's family. Their pain is just beginning, and they will know no rest from it. Loss, not death, frightens me. To lose Marcel." She looked over her shoulder, and her brows pushed together. "Or you. I don't want that pain."

Franz swallowed hard against an emotion he hadn't expected. She cared for him that much? His eyes burned, and his voice cracked when he tried to speak. "Now you know why I wish you would leave France, why it scares me when you risk yourself. I couldn't forgive myself if anything happened to you."

"But you can't always be there. We have no guarantees any of us will make it through this alive." Moisture again shone in her eyes. "But we have to keep fighting. So more people will see their loved ones again. So someday there will be less pain."

Franz stood silently as her conviction sank through his reservations. It wasn't about him or her, but doing what was right. He'd spent too much time worrying about himself, his mother, his fears. . .and little on the needs of people around him, people he didn't know. No wonder he felt so unprepared to meet God.

" 'Greater love hath no man than this, that a man lay down his life for his friends,' " Rosalie quoted softly. Franz recognized the verse of scripture. His mother had quoted it when speaking of how his father had died. "I read those words again and again last night, trying to calm my mind enough to sleep. It's the love Christ had for us." Her eyes lit as though with new understanding. "And it doesn't matter if we live or die, does it? We are asked to give our *lives* for others, our friends. . .our neighbors."

"I wish I had your faith. Your goodness."

She looked at him strangely, then smiled. "I don't think you know yourself or see yourself very well, Franz Kafka." He wanted to argue, but she stepped closer to him and pressed a finger over his mouth. "I can't see a way for our story to end happily, at least not in this life. But I don't want to waste what time God has given us." She glanced past him. "I've made that mistake before."

Rosalie set her hand on his face, and he covered her chilled fingers with his own. "I love you," she whispered. Her lips pressed against his with a gentle caress.

Franz slid his hand to the back of her head, while his other encircled her shoulders, drawing her against him again. Maybe this would be their only moment. Tomorrow held no guarantees. He breathed in lavender and rosewater and felt spring come alive in him. Taking his time, he returned her kiss, exploring her lips. He would extend their moment for as long as possible, drinking in every second in her embrace and praising God for each second with her.

≡CHAPTER 30≡

May 1944

Where are they?

Rumors abounded that the Allies planned an invasion somewhere along the northern coast of France, and the Resistance had received messages to prepare, but still nothing.

Rosalie pressed small seedlings into the ground and said a prayer for each. France was starving and desperate for liberation, but she would do her best to stave off some of the deprivation in her small community until relief came. There were few greens and fruit trees producing yet, but another month of warmth and rain would work miracles in the gardens.

Miracles. She almost allowed herself to smile. Her life seemed filled with miracles, as small as they might be. The health of her family. Breath in her lungs despite her frequent dance with death. But mostly that Marcel and Franz remained safe.

How much longer can it last?

The question pestered, as it often did, but Rosalie tried not to entertain it. "Make the most of today," she whispered.

Her thoughts were broken by the roar of a truck along the road, pausing momentarily in front of the cottage. A door slammed. Rosalie stood and dusted the dirt from her knees. She abandoned the last of the seedlings for later and hurried past rows and rows of new plants reaching for the sun. Maman looked up from where she hoed between rows of lettuce, but she remained, silent and wary as always. The past few months had changed little in their relationship, despite

Marcel's attempts to intercede. They simply coexisted, few words passing between them.

Marcel met Rosalie at the arbor. He grabbed her arm and tugged her toward the front door of the cottage. "They've sent news."

"Of what?" She lowered her voice to match his. "Please say there is word of the invasion."

He nodded.

"Really?" She bit her lip to keep from squealing. As soon as they were inside, she turned to him. "What are they saying?"

"It will happen soon, but no date has been given. We are to prepare and listen." He motioned to the table and a small radio perched there.

"Oh, Marcel." Her eyes watered at seeing it there. No longer the isolation and wondering what happened in the world beyond their community.

"They will send more instructions and then coded messages when we're to act."

Rosalie smoothed her hand across the wood frame and small dials. "We must hide it."

They rolled the carpet back and set up a crate in the cellar as a table. "Monsieur Couture will come tonight. A load of explosives and ammunition is to be dropped near here for destroying the telephone lines between Sainte-Mère-Église and Caen. A location has already been arranged. We only have to wait for the signal." His eyes lit. "They have the two-way radio and are receiving more detailed instructions in preparation for the invasion. Every group has different tasks that only they will know—whether detonating railways and telephone lines or holding bridges and other transportation routes so the Nazis don't destroy them."

She looked at her brother. "But. . .do you mean to tell me they are coming here, to Normandy?"

"Unless we are a diversion."

She took a shaky breath. "Either way, it hardly matters. Only that they're coming. And soon."

They closed the cellar and made sure the rug was in place before returning to work outside. Rosalie looked over the rows of green, but her thoughts were on the radio. She ached to listen to the latest from England, the progress of the Allies, and the rebuttals from the Nazis. She wished she could share the progress with Franz, but no chances could be taken. The fewer who knew, the safer for everyone.

———— ≋ ————

Monsieur Couture never arrived as expected, and Marcel paced the parlor until midnight. They listened briefly to the radio, but unease hung in the air like an approaching storm. "I need to go to bed," Rosalie said just before two. "I have my trip to Saint-Lô in the morning." Not that sleep was possible.

She woke exhausted and dressed for her ride, applying more makeup than usual to hide the exhaustion. The first checkpoint went smoothly, the guards now used to her weekly routine. She smiled at them, and they smiled back, though there were times she wished she didn't understand German and the comments they often made to each other about her.

Monsieur Dubois met her at the door with his usual warm greeting, but as soon as the door closed his whole countenance darkened. "Follow me." He led her through a narrow corridor to his study.

"What's happened? Has anyone heard from Monsieur Couture?"

"He sent word this morning. He fears someone might be watching him and suggests no one contact him."

Rosalie's empty stomach turned. "My brother met with him yesterday."

Dubois leaned into his cane, his face grave. "Perhaps forgo today's delivery."

"No, I'm sure I'll be fine. I'll be careful." Still, uneasiness clouded her thoughts as she went about her work tidying his home and fixing his lunch as though this was the full purpose of her trip here every week. She would keep her usual schedule, make nothing appear out of the ordinary… just in case.

Rosalie bundled the papers as she always did and slid them into the false bottom of her basket. Today was different though. The tiny hairs on her neck prickled. Every soldier put her on high alert. Were they watching her? Did they suspect?

———— ≋ ————

Franz nodded at the guard to raise the bar for yet another wagon. Another car. Several pedestrians. One after another, their papers were checked and loads searched before they were allowed to pass to or from Sainte-Mère-Église, Saint-Lô, or Caen.

He glanced up, surveying the horizon. No sign of Rosalie. Where was she?

"You seem unsettled today," Karl observed. "Are you not expecting your French girl today?"

Franz's frown deepened. He had allowed the perception of his and Rosalie's relationship to continue but hated what it meant for her reputation.

"Did something happen between you two?"

"Of course not." Their true relationship, like their lives, sat in limbo. Secret kisses. Quick embraces. And too many goodbyes. What sat heaviest on his mind was the growing speculation about the Allied invasion. He, like Rosalie, wanted the Allies to be successful in pushing back the German army, but what would happen when they finally arrived? Should he surrender to the Allies or retreat with the remainder of the Wehrmacht?

"Are you concerned about Unteroffizier Bayerlein's interest in her?"

Franz jerked around to the younger man. "What?"

Karl raised a brow. "You haven't seen? He watches her. And her brother too, I believe."

Franz waved the next car through without bothering with papers. "Where is Unteroffizier Bayerlein today?"

"That's why I was asking. Everyone knows she travels to Saint-Lô every Wednesday, and you are always here. Unteroffizier Bayerlein gained permission to set up a temporary checkpoint at the crossroads to Thèreval."

Franz cursed under his breath. "Take over here. I'll be back." Anger and fear charged through him as he commandeered a nearby motorcycle. He revved the engine to life and sprayed gravel as he spun it southward toward Saint-Lô. The wind wiped his face and rushed in his ears while panic climbed in his throat. It wouldn't be the first time Bayerlein had interfered.

He pushed the bike to its limits and still took over twenty minutes to reach where the road branched between Thèreval and Saint-Lô. A truck pulled through the checkpoint and Rosalie came into view. She stood beside her bicycle, Bayerlein reaching for the basket fastened to the back. Another minute and all their secrets would be known. Franz hit the ditch, bypassing the barricade and traffic, and then swerved back onto the road. He skidded the motorbike to a stop mere feet from them.

"What are you doing?" Franz demanded.

Bayerlein glowered. "You're the one away from your post."

"That's none of your concern."

"And what concern is this of yours?" He waved toward Rosalie. "Oh. The woman. Of course."

Franz dismounted the motorbike. "Any quarrel you have is with me, not her."

"On the contrary. I feel certain things have been overlooked. Every week this woman rides all the way to Saint-Lô, and when she arrives at our checkpoints, we merely smile and send her on her way." He ripped open the basket.

Franz grabbed his wrist. "Get your hands off—"

"He's welcome to look," Rosalie said and caught Franz's eye. "I have nothing to hide."

Franz withdrew but didn't relax until Bayerlein had emptied the basket of the familiar Bible and an untouched lunch pail. The Unteroffizier's scowl deepened as he shoved everything but the Bible back into the basket. He flipped through the pages of the Bible, dislodging several papers. Rosalie jerked like she wanted to grab them but remained in place.

A smirk crept over Bayerlein's face as examined the papers. He smacked them against Franz's chest. "I believe you are getting far too involved, Leutnant."

Franz looked at the pages—the information he had given Rosalie concerning her father and the rose he had sketched. "I think you are far too interested, Unteroffizier."

Franz took Rosalie's elbow and the handlebars of her bicycle and led her through the barricade.

"You have an enemy," she whispered.

"I can handle him."

"He won't back down just because you outrank him."

"No. If anything, that's one of the reasons he hates me." Franz squeezed her arm. "Don't worry about him."

"How can I not?"

Franz held her bicycle while she climbed aboard. "What did you do with the papers?"

"I left them in Saint-Lô."

He sighed, and some of the tension fell from his shoulders. The day might have ended quite differently if she hadn't.

"It feels like everything is unraveling."

"Unraveling?" They'd had a close call but had made it through unscathed. He'd figure out how to get Bayerlein off his back. "Lay low for a while and don't make any more trips to Saint-Lô. Just for a few weeks. Tensions are high right now."

"But if I don't go, he will only suspect us more."

Unfortunately, true. "Let's discuss it later. I'll meet you in the morning?"

She nodded and pushed off.

Franz blew out his breath as he watched her ride away. When he looked back, Bayerlein had his arms folded across his chest, eyes narrowed. Rosalie was right. Something had to be done about the man before he discovered just how involved Franz had become.

≡ CHAPTER 31 ≡

June 1944

Rosalie awoke to darkness and the roll of thunder...or was it the pounding of antiaircraft fire? She looked at the clock on her bedside table. Eleven forty. She had only slept for an hour or so. With a groan, she tucked the covers to her chin and willed sleep to come. Instead, she became aware of the muffled voices downstairs.

Blinking away the need for rest, she climbed out of bed and wrapped a robe around her shoulders. The cellar door sat open, and the radio spilled messages—like verses of a poem, but none that fit the line before.

But where was Marcel? Why had he been so foolish to leave the radio unattended?

She jumped at the shuffle of boots behind her.

Her brother, dressed in black, appeared at the top of the stairs.

Rosalie suppressed the chill skittering down her spine and the desire to rebuke Marcel for frightening her. She turned off the radio and joined him above. "Where are you going?"

"The drop is being made tonight. I just received the message."

"You're going alone? What of Monsieur Couture?"

"The Germans are still watching his house. But I have all the information I need. I can do it."

Her heart raced at the possible dangers that might await. "Non."

"Rosa, I must. The lines between here and Caen have to be destroyed when the word is given. We need the explosives."

She brushed past him on the way back to her room. "I'm not stopping you. I'm coming. Give me a minute to dress."

Minutes later, she tied a dark blue scarf over her hair and followed Marcel into the field across from their cottage. A drizzle of rain gave the summer night an eerie foreboding. Silence hung between them. The rain broke by the time they arrived at the prearranged meadow. A couple of cows grazed with heads low, but otherwise all sat silent as they crouched at the edge to wait. Marcel turned on a torch and shone it heavenward.

Minutes turned to an hour, and Rosalie sat back and stretched her legs out in front of her, massaging the cramps in her muscles. "It's so peaceful right now, it's strange to think of what might be coming."

A popping of artillery miles away made Marcel chuckle. "You spoke too soon. But I wonder that a lot too. How bad will it be when the Allies arrive? I know what awaits them on those beaches. And if they get past all that? It's not as though the Nazis will throw up their hands and retreat without a fight. Artillery. Tanks. And thousands and thousands of soldiers marching through these fields."

"Makes you wonder what will be left when they have finally pushed the Nazis from their footings," Rosalie whispered into the night. Would Franz be caught up in the fight? How would he escape it?

"Will there be anything left?"

An ache pressed against her heart. "I don't know."

Marcel shifted his position. "Why didn't we stop them when we could? Why didn't we fight longer before letting them dig in and fortify themselves? How much harder will the fight be now?"

The low hum of an approaching aircraft spurred them both to their feet. Marcel waved his torch as the plane pulled low enough for them to see the open door at the side and a man push out a large duffel with a small chute. Rosalie pictured Robert at the controls and smiled.

Marcel switched off the light and raced across the field toward the duffel, Rosalie fast on his heels. They located the bag and began to untangle the chute. Something moved at the other side of the meadow. They both dropped onto their stomachs.

"Get out of here," Marcel whispered. "Stay low and go home."

She shook her head. "Not unless you're with me."

Boots crushed through the undergrowth of the treed area, growing louder and closer with each step.

"We have to leave it." She grabbed his sleeve. "Come on."

A quick nod and they started running, crouched low. Gunfire rang out as they reached the grove.

"Halt!"

Rosalie ran faster, trying her best to keep up with Marcel who led the way, fear clutching her throat. Branches clawed at their clothing, slowing their retreat. Her foot caught on a root or fallen log and she went down hard, ankle rolling. Lightning shot up her leg. She clamped her teeth against the pain and scrambled to get up. Footsteps behind her closed in quickly. Ducking down, she crawled into thicker brush. Thorns scratched her arms and snagged her hair.

A light shone ahead, and Rosalie peered up to see Marcel through the dense branches. He hesitated at the edge of the grove and his hands raised to his head. The white of a Nazi torch lit his face.

Her heart seized. *Father, please don't let them shoot him. Please don't shoot.*

She flinched when one of the soldiers yanked Marcel forward, almost pulling him off his feet. "I thought there were two. Who else is out there?"

A grunt of pain broke from Marcel, and Rosalie clamped her eyes closed. Should she give herself up? How would that protect him? No, she needed Franz. There had to be a way to save her brother.

She kept silent, ignoring the bite in her knee and the piercing throb of her ankle. From her hiding place, she watched the soldiers search the area and drag out the duffel heavy with supplies meant for the Resistance. Her eyes burned, but she blinked back the moisture. She couldn't allow weakness or hopelessness to overcome her.

Darkness again surrounded her, the night becoming as still and silent as before. Only her heart continued to thunder in her ears. She waited awhile before she dared move. Her left ankle protested, but she ignored the discomfort and crept as silently as possible, staying low until she knew she was safe.

Her legs were numb and spent by the time she reached home. She paused and took in her surroundings, each sense on high alert. All seemed as it should, but part of her expected the soldiers to appear at any moment. She let herself inside and hobbled up the stairs to change her clothes. She tossed dress after dress on the bed, not sure of what to wear. Something plain to not draw attention? Something flattering to turn their minds to other things when she asked for Franz? Though maybe he'd already heard and would meet her in their usual spot in the morning so they could plan. Could she wait that long?

"What are you doing?" Her mother's voice came from the hallway. She pushed into Rosalie's bedroom. "Where is Marcel?"

Rosalie dropped onto the edge of the bed, letting her exhaustion take her for a moment. How much dare she tell her mother? She'd wasted away over the past few years, though Rosalie had never seen it as acutely as now in the lamplight from her bedside table. Maman hugged a thin robe around her frame, not much more than skin and bone. Her cheeks were sunken, and her eyes seemed too large. What had become of her sweet mother and her subtle smile? The woman standing there was almost a stranger.

"Where is Marcel?" she demanded.

Rosalie wanted to protect her, shield her from the worry, but her mother needed to know the truth. "Soldiers took him."

"This is your doing." The venom in her mother's tone stung. "You have been carrying on with that German."

"This has nothing to do with him. Marcel has been working with the Resistance—we both have. We are fighting for France."

"There is nothing left to fight for," she wailed. "You've killed him."

"No! I'll find a way to save him. I will. And this wasn't my fault. I was trying to help him. He would have gone anyway."

"It's that German officer you've sold yourself to. It's because of him." Maman backed into the hall. "Can't be trusted. They take, take, take."

"Franz is a good man who is trying to help us. He has nothing to do with this. Please, Maman, you must listen to me." Rosalie stepped toward her mother, but she pulled away.

"They're dead. They are all dead."

Tears blurred Rosalie's vision as her mother shrank away. Her brothers, her husband, and now her only son. How could anyone fault her hate for the Germans? Or the brokenness of her heart. "I won't let them hurt him." But as she spoke the words dread rose up in Rosalie. It might already be too late. What if there wasn't a way to save Marcel? Even Franz hadn't been able to rescue Monsieur Dumont.

Maman looked back, and for a brief moment her eyes cleared. Only the pain remained. "You were the mistake. You've always been one of them."

Rosalie stared after her retreat. "There has to be a way." She pushed past her mother's words and the doom attempting to swallow her and hurried to change into a simple skirt and a cream blouse. She could loosen it around the collar if there was no other option. Red lipstick and a little eye makeup were a little more difficult to apply with her quaking hands.

The stream trickled peacefully over stone and through young reeds while Rosalie watched the sun rise above the tops of the trees, fighting to break through the thick clouds, but to little avail. Rain drizzled down on her. Her mother's last words haunted.

"You were the mistake."

Not that she'd made a mistake. She *was* the mistake.

"You've always been one of them."

A memory rose from years faded with time. Rosalie had sat on the stairs listening, waiting, anxious to meet her new brother. The midwife opened the door to the bedroom and called for Papa to go in. She had stood, but the midwife had waved her back down.

"Give your maman a few minutes, child," she said before stepping outside with a basket of soiled laundry.

Rosalie waited a moment to make sure she wasn't returning, then tiptoed to the bedroom door. Inside Maman lay in bed, blankets surrounding her, her hair pulled back into a braid that had mostly fallen loose. Against her chest huddled the baby. Papa lowered onto the edge of the bed.

"Look at this fine boy," he whispered, something different about his voice.

"Your child. Your very own."

Papa touched her face. "Oh, Julie, mon amour, they are both mine. I've told you that. I love Rosalie just as much as this child or any we will have together."

A rooster crowed from a nearby barn, and Rosalie stood. The ankle she'd twisted protested, but it was more stiff than sore, and agitation overpowered the need to rest. She wanted to bury the past and the tiny seed that had been planted in her young heart, but questions had splashed upon it her whole life, causing doubt to root within her soul. Maman's words only nourished the seedling to the point Rosalie could no longer ignore it.

"It doesn't matter." Not with her brother in the hands of the Nazis. She paced the shoreline, anxiety giving way to raw fear as images of her brother suffering, perhaps being tortured, for any information he might have flashed in her mind. She would almost rather he give it for his own sake. They would come for her, but that hardly mattered anymore.

She faced south toward Sainte-Mère-Église. No sign of Franz. Why had she waited? What was happening to Marcel while she stood here doing nothing? She hugged herself against a cool breeze. The clouds hung low and gray, weeping over her. What if it was already too late?

Rosalie sank to her knees on the wet grass and clasped her hands. "Father, help my brother. Help me save him. Let him live."

In her mind she could see the man at the checkpoint, running away as the Nazis shot him. His back arching in pain as the bullets struck his body. The blood pouring from his wounds. The blank look in his eyes. Death.

She lifted her gaze heavenward as the rain briefly subsided. Morning of the fifth of June. Another day. Another breath. Soon the Allies would invade, making freedom a possibility. That's what she wanted for her brother. "God, take me instead. If someone has to die, let it be me."

≡CHAPTER 32≡

"They will cross at Cherbourg," Hauptmann Meyer said, tapping the northern pinnacle of Normandy on the map of Europe pinned to the wall. "Von Schlieben has a garrison of nearly fifty thousand, and Feldmarschall Rommel has nearly doubled the fortifications and artillery power there."

"Unless they choose a weaker point because of that," the major replied. "We've received our fair share of bombardment the past month."

"But we are too far away."

"Our Normandy coast is still within range of smaller bombers. Close enough to be the target."

"But the focus has been farther north and to the east, closer to England. It allows them to deliver with more strength." Meyer looked to Franz. "Don't you agree, Leutnant?"

Franz cleared his throat, but the last thing he wanted was to be caught in the crossfire. "It seems even the Führer's generals and staff struggle with the same arguments. And the timing? Most thought the invasion would come in May."

"The weather was perfect for it." The major looked out to the darkened clouds. "Now the winds are changing, and the rains will be blowing in. The last weather report forecasts more of the same for June, and worse over the Channel. We'll be able to rest easy for a couple weeks."

"Did I hear correctly that Feldmarschall Rommel is traveling home while the weather is poor?" Meyer folded his arms, straining his uniform across his shoulders.

"Yes. Since there is little to worry about for the time being, he has gone to celebrate his wife's birthday with her."

"Ah, the privilege of rank," Meyer said.

"The privilege of having a wife," another officer murmured.

Everyone chuckled. Even Franz managed a short laugh, his thoughts on Rosalie. Meyer had reported arresting a man with the underground and capturing a shipment of ammunitions and explosives, thus beginning the discussion of a possible invasion coming soon. But not here. Unlikely. Franz hardly heard most of the conversation buzzing around the room. Who had been arrested? Were Rosalie and her brother safe?

The officers were dismissed, and Franz beelined toward the door. Just outside, he glanced at his watch. It was too late to meet with Rosalie this morning without going directly to her home, something he'd rather not do.

"In a hurry, are you, Leutnant?"

Franz turned to Meyer and offered a half smile. "Plenty to do with the preparations we've been asked to make."

"Hardly an immediate concern, as noted this morning." He swatted at a smudge of dust on his sleeve. "And I have a feeling you are more concerned with your personal affairs."

Franz stopped.

"Do you know of a Jean Couture? He is from Bayux, but we have been watching him closely the past few weeks."

"I don't know the name. Why the interest?" And what did this have to do with him?

"We have been informed he is involved with the underground."

"Informed?" Franz stiffened as understanding dawned. "Is Unteroffizier Bayerlein involved?"

Meyer's mouth turned up, though with no pleasure in his expression. "He has taken interest in this investigation and has provided useful information, but no. A citizen of Sainte-Mère-Église brought his suspicions to our attentions, a Claude Fournier."

The name sparked recognition in Franz's brain. Had Rosalie mentioned the man? "Interesting. Is all this somehow linked to the man you arrested last night?"

"Ja, Fournier knows the man and has seen him with Couture."

"And the man you arrested?"

"His name is Marcel Barrieau."

Not Marcel. Franz's stomach dropped, and it was all he could do to keep his expression flat.

"I've also been informed Barrieau has a sister." Meyer's face turned hard as he circled. "What have you told that woman you have been carrying on with? Strategies? Strongholds? Has she traded herself to you for information to then pass on to the underground?"

"Nein." Franz gritted out the word. "I do not speak of logistics and army secrets while wooing women. If that is what she's been after, she's been wasting her time."

"A relief to hear." But Meyer's eyes held doubt. "After we've questioned the brother, we will take her into custody also."

Franz's blood ran cold. He had to think fast—there had to be a way to buy time. "What are your plans with the brother?"

"He will be executed of course. Once we're convinced he's told us all he knows."

"Ja, of course." Franz's brain churned through scenarios and any way to save Marcel from the torture that awaited. Time. He needed time. "I would like to question him. One day. Give me one day to get the information you want."

Meyer narrowed his eyes. "How exactly?"

"His sister. He will try to protect her. I will convince him I am her only hope." The truth of his words crushed down on him.

"Very well. You have until eighteen hundred hours. No longer."

"Thank you, Hauptmann Meyer." Franz raised a salute, but the man didn't move.

"But beware, Leutnant Kafka. Some would also place you under suspicion."

He glanced over his shoulder to see Bayerlein leaning against a nearby building, cigarette tucked in the corner of his mouth. Perhaps he had underestimated the man's influence. "I believe those who suggest such have a personal quarrel with me that has no bearing on this investigation."

After leaving Meyer, Franz started toward the barracks. He needed a moment to think, to plan. He had to get Rosalie out of France. And Marcel. . .what was he going to do about Marcel?

"Leutnant."

Franz turned as Brenner approached at a jog. "What is it?"

"I've been waiting for you. Or I should say, *she's* been waiting for you." He motioned across the street to where Rosalie stood like a porcelain statue against a background of gray stone. "I've been keeping an eye on her, making sure no one gives her any trouble."

Franz clapped the boy on the shoulder. "I owe you." He crossed to her, not caring who watched or what they thought. There was no time.

"They have Marcel," she said as soon as he reached her.

"I know." He took her arm and led her toward her home. Before long, they drew the gazes of everyone they passed. Not just Germans but the French who waited in queues at the shops or hurried about their business—her people. They looked at her with both revulsion and anger, as though she had betrayed them. Because of him.

Franz dropped her arm. "I can't do this to you. Meet me at your house."

Her eyes widened. "I can't go home. I can't face Maman. Not without Marcel."

He had no time to argue. "Meet me at the stream then."

She nodded, and Franz turned away, putting distance between them, though it might already be too late.

Despite taking separate routes, they arrived at the same time. The stream ran high from the recent rains, and the wind blew chill. Rosalie sank onto the rock. "They came in the night while we were collecting a drop of supplies. It was like they knew where to find us."

"Maybe they did."

Her eyes widened. "But how? Have they also arrested Monsieur Couture?"

"I don't believe so. Not yet, anyway." He looked at her, feeling the raw fear mirrored in her eyes. "You are also on their list. We need to get you away from here."

"Not without Marcel. There must be something we can do to save him. Please, Franz." She gripped his hand. "I have to save my brother, but I don't know how to do it without you. I need you."

He pulled away, feeling as though he'd already failed her. "There's nothing I can do. They already suspect me, questioning how much information you were able to seduce from me. I may have bought us a little time, but I can't think of a way to get both of you safely away from here."

"You don't have to keep me safe, Franz. That isn't what I'm asking. Just Marcel. Maybe they'll make a trade, me for him."

"Nazis don't make trades."

She raised her chin, eyes flashing. "So, it's the same as it was with Monsieur Dumont? Stand back while they shoot my brother, saving our own skins?"

He felt the accusation slash across him. "No. I'll think of something. But not until you are away from here. Because the chance of me succeeding..." Franz swallowed hard. Who was he fooling? There was little, if any, chance of surviving a plot to help her brother escape. Even if he managed to free Marcel, they would never make it out of France alive.

————— ≈ —————

Rosalie went home, but only because there was no other option. She didn't want to face her mother again. Maman sat in her rocking chair, her movements slow but steady, still wearing her nightgown though the day was half spent. Rosalie said nothing, slipping past her and up the stairs, first to her room where she threw a few things into a small suitcase. She picked up the old Bible last and sank to her knees.

"We need a miracle, Father. Please give us a miracle."

When she finished baring her heart to God, she placed the Bible in her suitcase and closed the lid. She glanced over her room one last time for anything she might need, wondering if she would ever return. In Marcel's room, she collected a change of clothes and then dug through every drawer, every box, every corner, and under his mattress. She'd seen his revolver, knew he had one. But where?

With every hiding place searched, Rosalie collected the luggage and steeled herself for returning downstairs. Maman looked up as she approached.

"I think it would be best if you went to the village and stayed with the Fourniers for a while," Rosalie said before pulling back the rug to search the cellar. She left the suitcase at the top of the steep stairs.

"Where are you going?"

Rosalie paused and glanced back. "If we are successful in freeing Marcel, we can't come back here. It won't be safe." Not until France was free—if that day ever came.

"How will I know?" Her voice was weak, broken.

Oh, Maman. . . "I'll find a way to send word." Emotions gaining a foothold, Rosalie ducked into the cellar and searched every conceivable place for her brother's hidden gun. Was it possible he'd had it on him last night?

The radio sat silent on the stool in the center of the cellar. She sighed and turned the dial, keeping the volume barely above a whisper. She sat down and rested her head in her hands while she listened to the reports of the Allies in England, waiting, just as they were.

"A Frenchman speaking to his countrymen."

Rosalie's head came up as the voice continued, but this time it was different, one poem, three lines from the middle.

"My heart is drowned
In the slow sound
Languorous and long"

An almost giddy panic skittered through her.
Impossible.

The signal for the invasion. It was about to happen. What had Marcel told her about their mission? The telephone lines running between Sainte-Mère-Église and Cean were supposed to be destroyed. But how? Monsieur Couture was under surveillance if not already arrested, Marcel was a prisoner, and the explosives had been captured by the Germans. She switched off the radio and bolted up the stairs.

Franz said he would meet her in a couple of hours to explain how he intended to free Marcel and where they would go from there, but she would have to change their plans. If he could get her explosives... The task was hers now. Franz would save Marcel...and she would help save France.

≡CHAPTER 33≡

"That is not an option. I can't let you do it. Not alone."

Rosalie fought the urge to grab Franz's shoulders and shake him. "There is no one else. The other members of the Resistance have their own tasks, and there is no way to even contact them in time. Marcel needs you. This task is mine. Get me the explosives. That is all I ask."

He stared at her, the concern in his blue eyes piercing through her resolve. What did she know about explosives or detonating them? What if she failed?

"Rosalie. . ." He released a breath and shook his head. "I'll see what I can find and leave them under our tree." He took her arms and tugged her to him. "Please, be careful."

She pressed a kiss to his mouth. "You too."

His arms tightened around her, and she tucked her face against his neck and inhaled deeply, an attempt to memorize his scent, the feel of his lips against her head, the warmth radiating from him. Their time drew to an end. Even if everything went perfectly tonight, their story was almost over. The chances they would all survive until tomorrow were slimmer than she wanted to dwell on. Instead, she closed her eyes and pleaded with God for a miracle.

Franz kissed her one last time before squeezing her hand and turning away. She watched him stride to the motorbike he had left in the tall grass beside the road. Full uniform, so very German, and yet rooted so deeply in her heart, he threatened to crack it apart. What if she were wrong to ask him to risk himself to save her brother? She loved them both. . .and now she might lose them both.

"Don't give up hope," she whispered. That was the one thing the

Nazis could not take from her unless she allowed them. She would not surrender it again. Not with the chance of liberation on the horizon.

Knowing soldiers could arrive any moment to arrest her, she hurried home on her sore ankle to pack a few things for herself and her mother. Maman, now dressed, slowly swayed in the rocking chair. So many questions and so much hurt stood between them. "Come. It's time to go."

Maman shook her head, but Rosalie took her hand and pulled her to her feet. "You must, Maman. I will try to send word when Marcel is safe, but he would not rest well knowing you were still here alone."

"I can't lose him too."

"I know." Rosalie led her mother to the door, pausing to make sure all the lights were switched off. Not that it made much difference anymore with how frequent power outages had become.

They made their way across the fields toward the village, every step nagging Rosalie to ask the one question burning the strongest. She pushed down the angst wedging in her throat and let the words tumble from her lips before she changed her mind. "Who was my father?"

Maman stiffened but kept her gaze fixed ahead.

The silence between them spoke louder than any words her mother could utter. "It wasn't Charles Barrieau, was it?" Rosalie whispered.

Maman gave a tight shake of her head.

"Then who am I?"

Maman shook her head again and walked away. Rosalie let her go. There were too many soldiers in Sainte-Mère-Église. It was better if she kept her distance. Maman would be safe—for now.

Is anyone safe?

Probably not.

She would have to trust her family and Franz to God.

The remaining hours until sunset dragged on in slow procession. Rosalie hid in a nearby orchard and stared upward at the small green fruit that blended so well with the leaves, making them almost invisible. She focused her thoughts on all that needed to happen once evening came and did her best to forget the subtle shake of her mother's head that so fully tipped her world on end.

"Who am I?" *If not the daughter of Charles Barrieau?*

"Well done, my Rosa."

She heard his voice in her head as clearly as though he had just left them. He was showing Marcel how to throw a line in the creek, and Rosalie had pulled up a fish on hers.

"Well done."

Rosalie grinned up at Papa, though the carp dangling from her line was the smallest she had ever seen. *Probably the smallest he'd seen too.*

"I want one!" six-year-old Marcel had shouted, his wide eyes admiring his sister's catch.

"We all want one." Papa clapped his son on the back and directed him toward the edge of the shore. *"Best we let our Rosa show us how it is done."*

He'd smiled at her, and she'd never forget that look in his eyes or the pure love that flowed from him to herself and Marcel.

"But I wasn't yours," Rosalie whispered.

Marcel was though. His only son. His only child. She could not give up hope in her brother so long as there was a chance of saving him.

Finally, the sun slipped below the horizon. Rosalie grabbed her luggage and hurried across the fields toward her meeting spot with Franz. Under the tree, nestled deep in the high grass, was a leather satchel filled with explosive charges, lines, and a small detonator. On top was a note with step-by-step directions in Franz's handwriting.

Be careful, mon amour, he wrote.

"I'll do my best." She left her luggage there and hung the satchel over her shoulder. Her ankle still ached from the night before, tempting her to take her bicycle for speed, but then she would have to travel on the road, a risk she couldn't take. Instead, she set off cross-country on foot. The way was slow as she crossed through hedges and over stone fences, and heavy clouds hung in the sky, blocking much of the light from an otherwise full moon. The telephone line was supposed to be cut far enough outside the village that it would be difficult to locate and repair. She walked for more an hour, her ankle growing sorer with each step before she was satisfied with the location. Here, the telephone lines were set a little farther from the road, allowing more seclusion.

She placed the charges at the base of four poles, a line running from each. Her hands shook as she laid out the wire through the grass and down the slope. Headlights flashed from an approaching vehicle. She ducked out of sight while the car rolled past. Her heart raced, drowning out the purr of the engine. It was probably midnight by now. If all went well, Marcel would be free soon and he and Franz would be on their way to meet her. She couldn't wait any longer.

Rosalie connected the detonator and crouched down behind an old stump. With a prayer on her lips, she plunged the small lever.

Like fireworks, four explosions popped one after another down the line. The poles lurched then fell sideways, ripping wires loose and snapping them. Dirt and splinters showered over her. Rosalie shielded her head with her arms. Ignoring the sting, she found her feet and scurried back the way she'd come, adrenaline spurring her on.

———— ≈ ————

Shortly after midnight, Franz hung the bag with an extra uniform over his shoulder, loaded his pistol, and started across the street to the town hall where Marcel was imprisoned in the basement. Memories flashed of his visit almost a year earlier, when he hadn't been able to intervene, and a man had been shot. The last moments with Dumont still haunted him.

There is nothing I can do for you. . .

Not without risking his own skin.

Seemed to hardly matter anymore, so long as Rosalie and her brother were saved.

The church bell rang, halting his steps. There was no special mass or holiday that would give cause for the ringing growing in the night, waking villagers and soldiers alike.

"Fire!" a man shouted at the end of the block, hands waving.

Franz squinted into the darkness. Smoke wafted on a gust of wind, and a glow grew within a distant building.

"What's happened?" a voice demanded from behind.

Franz turned to see Meyer among a group of other men hurrying from their barracks onto the street. The Hauptmann fought with the buttons of his uniform. Franz saw his moment slipping through his fingers.

"Just a fire." Franz cut him off. "I have a much more urgent matter to discuss with you."

"Oh, what have you found out?"

Franz motioned to the town hall. "Best we step inside."

Meyer glanced again in the direction of the fire and gathering crowd, then nodded. "Very well."

Franz followed Hauptmann Meyer inside and down the hall to the man's office. Meyer crossed to his desk before looking back. "What do you have for me?"

Franz drew his gun while he shoved the door closed behind him.

"What is this?"

"Keep your voice down or neither of us will be walking out of this room alive. I've made my peace with that."

Meyers stiffened, fear flashing in his eyes. "What is it you want?" He splayed his hands on the desk.

"Order of release, Marcel Barrieau into my custody. And travel documents, orders for me to deliver the prisoner to Paris." Franz crossed behind the desk and relieved Meyer of his revolver.

"What do you hope to accomplish by that?" His chin shot up. "You've entrapped yourself with the sister, deceived yourself into thinking you love her."

"That is none of your concern. Now start writing."

Franz stood over him, watching every movement, every twitch, while Hauptman Meyer completed the two forms and slid them across the desk. "Unteroffizier Bayerlein was right after all. You are a traitor."

Franz tried not to flinch. He wasn't the one who betrayed his people or his country. The Nazis were who he fought.

Meyer folded his arms across his chest. "Now what?"

Franz kept his aim steady while pulling a rope from his satchel, only setting his gun aside a moment to tie Hauptmann Meyer's hands. Meyer jerked as though to struggle free, but Franz jabbed his revolver in the man's ribs. "I still have it here."

With a grumble, Meyer relaxed back into his chair and allowed Franz to finish securing him. Next came a wad of cloth in the mouth and a gag.

"Now you sit quietly and wait until someone finds you. Hopefully not until morning." Franz gathered the signed documents and locked the door as he went.

Phase One complete.

Adrenaline surging with renewed intensity, Franz jogged down the stairs as the church bell continued its frantic peal, a blessed distraction as he made his way to the same room Dumont had been held.

The guards shoved to their feet as he came near. "What is going on out there?"

Franz shrugged. "A fire. Perhaps set by the Resistance." He handed the first guard the freshly signed order. "I have been instructed to move the prisoner."

"Tonight?"

Franz glared. "Are you questioning Hauptmann Meyer?"

The soldier flushed and shoved the paper at Franz. "Of course not."

"Good. Bring him out." Franz waited while the guards disappeared into the room. The shuffle of feet. A grunt of pain. Finally, Marcel appeared, shirt ripped, nose bloody, but otherwise seemingly in one piece. Franz prayed it was so for the sake of their escape.

He grabbed Marcel's arm and shoved him down the hall, hopefully not hurting him too much. Who knew what he'd endured since the six p.m. deadline. "We have a tight schedule to make it to Paris in time where you will wish you had kept your head down and done as you were told."

Phase Two complete.

They reached the outside door and stepped into the breezy night air. The church bell continued ringing while flames climbed the walls of a building, which blessedly drew most everyone's attention.

"Look," Marcel said, staring heavenward.

Franz followed his gaze and blinked, not sure what he was seeing. White clouds? Smoke from the fire, perhaps. No, they were too small and too white. And circular.

"What are you doing with the prisoner?"

Marcel jerked, and Franz spun to where Bayerlein stood with pistol in hand. "I have orders," Franz bit out.

"Let me see them." Bayerlein held out his hand, the gun never wavering.

Franz yanked the forms from his pocket, but he doubted Bayerlein would permit him to leave without word from Meyer himself. "Let's step back inside so you have the light you need to read every last detail of my orders."

He followed the Unteroffizier past the heavy doors, one hand gripping Marcel, the other clutching the travel documents. Bayerlein lowered his gun to take the papers.

Franz lunged and cracked the butt of his own weapon into the man's head. Bayerlein dropped like a piece of lead, hitting the floor with hardly a grunt. Franz shoved Bayerlein's revolver into Marcel's hands while holstering his own, then took hold of the Unteroffizier's arms to drag him into a nearby room. Franz fumbled with the lock when the echoing of machine gun and rifle fire broke through the gong of the church bells.

"Franz!" Marcel's warning pulled him around to where another soldier hurried down the hall toward them. Marcel raised the revolver toward Karl's position.

"Non!" Franz knocked Marcel's aim while again reaching for his own gun.

Karl trained his rife on them. "What have you done to Unteroffizier Bayerlein? Did you kill him?" His gaze darted to Marcel and the weapon in his lowered hand. "Where are you taking the prisoner?"

Franz maneuvered in front of Marcel. Would he have to kill one friend to save the other? "Nein. Unteroffizier Bayerlein is just taking a nap. He'll be fine. I don't want to hurt anyone. Not him. Not you."

Karl's aim wavered ever so slightly. His wide eyes held uncertainty. "What's going on? There are paratroopers landing in the village. Are you with them? Have you betrayed us?"

"Nein. Not you. Not the Fatherland. Forget what they have been telling you, Karl. All the propaganda and lies they've rammed into that head of yours. You're smarter than that—think for yourself for one minute. These people, the French, the Poles, the Dutch, have done nothing against us. They just want their freedom. Safety for their families. We've taken that from them. And for what? Because a few power-hungry men in Berlin decided they should rule all of Europe? All the world? It's not even for the glory of Germany. They've destroyed our Fatherland. They have murdered hundreds, maybe thousands of our own people. We are on the wrong side of this war. You must see that."

⣿CHAPTER 34⣿

Rosalie's pulse kept a healthy pace as she hurried back to rendezvous with Franz and Marcel. The pain in her ankle stabbed deeper with each step. She prayed they had success in obtaining a vehicle, as she wasn't sure how much farther she could go. A couple miles to the south, in Sainte-Mère-Église, church bells rang, and she wished she knew the cause. Had Franz and Marcel made it away safely? Had something terrible happened? She quickened her pace, praying they would already be waiting for her.

Boots pounded the road ahead of her, and Rosalie ducked down behind a hedge. As they passed by, she raised up enough to see the German patrol disappear around the next bend in the road. A few more minutes passed before she dared continue as quietly as she could. Rosalie only made it a short way when a whooshing thud dropped her back down. A scramble of footsteps through the brush. She glanced up in time to see a white cloud descend several hedgerows over. Chickens squawked.

She waited and listened.

Click.

Click-click.

"Man, am I glad to see you guys!" The words were English. The invasion! Or was this part of the distraction? Excitement and nervousness ignited her nerves as she inched closer.

"Have any idea where we are?"

"France," someone said drolly.

"Not where we are supposed to be," someone else muttered. They were coming closer.

With a breath and a prayer, she stood and stepped into sight, hands held so they could be seen. "I can help you."

Three paratroopers jerked their rifles in her direction. They seemed to release a collective sigh, which she shared with them. "Who are you?" one asked, a sergeant's insignia on his shoulder along with a double-A badge.

"I am from here, but with *la Resistance*." She motioned to their uniforms. "You are *Américain, oui?*"

"Yes." He glanced at his companions. "How did we get so lucky?"

They all chuckled, but there was a nervousness about it.

"Can you tell us where the Nazis are?"

"A patrol just passed by, going. . ." She pointed south. "*Sud.*"

"What is down that way? The bells? What town is that?"

"*Sainte-Mère-Église. Peut être.* . .three, maybe four, miles from here."

The sergeant groaned. "We're way off our drop zone."

"Saves us the walk," another said, straightening his helmet.

"If we can find more of our company. Rather not storm Sainte-Mère-Église on our own." The sergeant grunted and then nodded to Rosalie. "You mind pointing us in the right direction, miss? We'll see who else we can find on our way there."

Rosalie nodded and waved for them to follow her while trying to catch her breath. Was this possible? Had the invasion finally come? She led them through the maze of hedges and stone fences, refusing to show the pain shooting up her leg or her anxiousness to slip away and find Franz and Marcel. As they came close to her home, the shattering of glass seized her heart. Not Papa's greenhouse.

"Wait here." She jogged across the road, her limp becoming more pronounced with each step. The roof of the greenhouse gapped with jagged glass, and a form moved within, struggling free of his chute.

She stood and waved to the Americans behind her. They came quickly and followed her to the newcomer who still worked to untangle himself and step past the broken glass. While the men congregated outside, Rosalie glanced over the destruction. Two large panes broken out of the roof, an overturned table, broken pottery, and a revolver buried in the rubble and spilled soil. Marcel's gun! Why hadn't she considered the greenhouse? She tucked the weapon into the back of her skirt and rejoined the paratroopers. There were somehow five of them now, another having joined minutes before.

"Come." She motioned for them to follow. They hadn't made it far when the hum of an engine dropped them behind a low hedge. The clouds were breaking, allowing the full moon to glint down on a jeep headed toward them. Rosalie squinted, but it was impossible to make out the identity of the two soldiers as they approached.

"Krauts!" the sergeant whispered.

She caught a motion out of the corner of her eye and glanced to see one of the Americans pull a grenade from his pouch. He tugged the pin free to throw it into the oncoming jeep before she could react.

"Non!" She lunged at the man, and the grenade fell short, striking the back tire of the jeep. They sheltered their heads while the vehicle jumped then swerved into the low ditch and stone fence, jerking to a stop while angling onto the passenger side.

The Americans brought their rifles up, ready to finish off anyone who moved.

"Wait," Rosalie begged, voice hoarse.

"What are you doing?" The sergeant grabbed for her.

Beside them, one of the rifles discharged, and she heard a pained grunt from the other side of the jeep.

"S'il te plaît, arête!" Marcel's voice came from the jeep.

Rosalie jerked away. "It is mon frère, my brother. Please! He's with the Resistance." She scampered toward the jeep.

The Americans stood back, rifles still at the ready as she fell against the side of the jeep. Marcel, in German uniform, had his hands raised. Franz sagged over the steering wheel, blood spreading across his back.

"Rosalie? What are you doing here?" Marcel questioned.

"I'm with American paratroopers. They thought you were the Germans."

Marcel swore and ripped the helmet from his head. He pulled the officer's cap from Franz and pushed him upright in the seat. Franz groaned, and Rosalie found her breath. He was alive! *Thank you, Father.*

"What is this?" an American demanded from behind her as they gathered in.

Marcel tossed a gun into the back seat and began to rip off the uniform Franz had given him.

Rosalie opened Franz's door. "This is our friend, and my brother," she said in English, kneeling on the edge of the seat. "My brother was a prisoner."

"This is their escape?"

"Oui." She pulled the scarf from her head and pressed it over the wound.

Franz rolled his head to look at her.

"Don't speak," she whispered. The Americans couldn't know who he really was.

"Here, move aside." The American sergeant pulled her out of the way. "Let's get him out of there."

She gritted her teeth, feeling Franz's pain as they carried him from the jeep and out of sight of the road. They set him down, and someone shone a torch down on him.

"I don't like this, Sarg," one of the soldiers grumbled. "He looks too German for my liking. And it's not just the uniform."

The sergeant leaned close. "Who exactly are you?"

Rosalie pushed her way back to Franz's side. "I told you. He is a friend. He's been helping us."

"Why won't he answer me? He is German, isn't he?"

"Yes," Franz said, before Rosalie could answer. Now there was no denying it. Even in the single English word, his accent was undeniable.

The sergeant narrowed his eyes at Rosalie as he brought his revolver up. "What exactly is your story? How can we trust you?"

"You must believe me. My brother and I are with the Resistance. And this man, he has helped us. He saved my brother from the Nazis."

"Sarg? What do you want us to do?" All the men waited, rifles trained on Franz and Marcel.

"Please," Rosalie said. "Let my brother take our friend back to our home and tend him. I will come with you and help you find your way."

"Non," Marcel broke in, speaking in French, "he needs you." He nodded to Franz. "I will help the Americans."

She wanted to agree, to be with Franz and see he was looked after, but Marcel held the side of his body as though cradling his ribs, and his face was battered. Franz was not the only one who needed care. "Non, this is my task. Please see to Franz and yourself until I return."

His eyes pleaded. "The village is not safe."

"Is anywhere?"

"Speak so we can understand you," the sergeant ordered, uneasiness in his voice.

"I am sorry. If someone can help them back to our home, I will show you the way to Sainte-Mère-Église."

"Very well." The sergeant nodded to his men. "Search them for weapons."

Rosalie surrendered the revolver she'd found and stood back as the soldiers relieved Franz of his gun. They returned the short way to the

Barrieau cottage. After quickly wrapping her ankle with a thin scarf, Rosalie dropped to Franz's side where they had deposited him just inside the door. "How are any of us still alive?" she whispered.

"Your God is one of miracles, it seems."

"I don't even have the Bible with me this time to keep us safe."

He raised his good arm and tapped two fingers over her heart. "Yes, you do."

The hovering presence of one of the Americans kept her from kissing Franz. Instead, she squeezed his fingers.

I love you.

He nodded as though he read her thoughts.

"I'll be back." She let his hand fall away, following the paratroopers again into the night.

The going was slow, thankfully, for the sake of her ankle. The group made their way along hedges and stone fences as they inched closer to the village, adding additional paratroopers to their numbers as they went. Gunfire broke out here and there in the distance, putting her on edge. She quickly came to appreciate the small "crickets" they carried. One click was answered by two.

There were sixteen men by the time they reached the outskirts of the village. Orange glowed above the center of Sainte-Mère-Église, and smoke hung on the air.

"Maybe we should wait until there are more of us," one of the men suggested.

Rifle fire broke out to the east, and they all hunched down.

"Seems like more are on the way."

The sergeant crouched down beside Rosalie and touched her arm. "You best get along home. This won't be any place for you."

She nodded, wishing she had more to offer them. They risked so much for her and her people. "I will pray for you. All of you."

His mouth turned up a little "You be careful, and. . ." He shook his head. "I still don't know what to think about your German friend, or any of that, but you did what you said you would, and we're grateful for that."

"Not as grateful as I." Her vision blurred. "You came."

Rosalie left them but paused, the glow of the village still within sight. A battle would soon run in the streets. Should she find her mother and bring her home? Uncertainty made her hesitate. The battle had already started between hedgerows and fields. Surely Maman was safer behind locked doors with the Fourniers. Rosalie prayed it was so.

She hurried through the night, every rustle of leaves or breaking twig bringing thoughts of the paratroopers making their way to the village and the German troops patrolling the dark roads. When she arrived home, she found Franz asleep on the kitchen floor, his shirt gone and his wound bandaged with one of their bedsheets. Marcel sat at the table, also shirtless, but with his torso wrapped. The radio sat in front of him, a low murmur.

"Anything?"

He shook his head.

She lowered into the chair beside him, surveying his battered face in the low light. "Are you all right?"

Marcel looked at her, and she glimpsed the agony in his eyes. "Ribs hurt, but I don't think anything's broken. Not like if Franz hadn't come." His mouth opened, but for a moment he didn't speak. "I kept telling myself it wouldn't matter what they did. I wouldn't say anything." He blinked, and moisture trickled down his bruised cheek. "You. Franz. Monsieur Couture. So many lives depending on me. And my silence."

Rosalie brushed his shaggy hair from the side of his face and pressed a kiss there. "You feel chilled." She slipped away for an armful of blankets. She laid one over her brother's shoulders and another across Franz's prone body before sitting beside him and pulling his head onto her lap. She leaned against the wall, blanket around her shoulders, throbbing ankle stretched out. She closed her eyes for a moment and felt herself drift.

The ground trembled.

"What was that?"

"The Allies," Marcel said. A gust of air broke between his chapped lips. "This wasn't a distraction or decoy. They're striking Normandy."

The thunder of distant artillery roared in the east as dawn glowed in the window. Not just a drill or antiaircraft fire. A bombardment that seemed to intensify with each passing minute.

Rosalie felt a hand on her knee and glanced to Franz as he pulled himself up. He slid his good arm around her and pressed a kiss to her head as they listened to the distant onslaught from the Allies firing upon her homeland with hopes to dislodge the Germans from their fortifications. Freedom was on their doorstep. . .but would anything be left of France when they finished?

⊰CHAPTER 35⊱

Franz leaned against the hard wall while Rosalie slept on his good shoulder. His back ached, and agony radiated from his wound, but he resisted disturbing her from the few hours of sleep she'd finally allowed herself—or succumbed to. Instead, he listened to the bombardment that thundered on every side and memorized the scent of her hair and the rhythm of her breathing. Goodbye hung like a storm cloud on the horizon.

The door slammed open, and midday sun streamed through the house. Rosalie jerked awake as Marcel appeared around the corner. He'd slipped out shortly after she'd fallen asleep. "They have taken Sainte-Mère-Église!" he panted. Despite the excitement in his eyes, one arm hugged his ribs, and the bruising on his face was even more pronounced in the daylight with shades of purple and yellow.

"The Americans?" Franz asked. For the past few hours, he had argued with himself about the safety of remaining here with Rosalie. He had listened and waited, trying not to succumb to the growing exhaustion made more acute by his body's need to heal—or at least cope with the shock of a bullet ripping through his shoulder.

"Yes." Marcel glanced away and shook his head. "Some came down in the village last night. A massacre. The Nazis shot them before their feet even touched soil. Bodies still hung from light poles and even the church steeple until an American commander ordered them cut down."

Franz's gut twisted. He'd heard the machine gun fire and had seen a glimpse of the white chutes lowering into the town. At the time he had been grateful for the distraction that had allowed Marcel and him to escape. There had been no time to consider the cost of life.

"Sounds like the Germans are retreating toward Caen," Marcel continued.

Was Karl among them? He'd probably joined the others after he had lowered his weapon and Franz had left him. Or Brenner? A seventeen-year-old should be home finishing school, not in the middle of a battle.

"I heard more Americans, British, and Canadians have landed on the beaches," Marcel went on. "From here to the Orne River. The soldiers that landed near here have already broken through German defenses and have met up with the paratroopers. This area is mostly secured."

Had his friends survived?

Rosalie stood but strongly favored her left ankle while crossing to her brother and wrapping him in a hug and kissing him on both cheeks. She turned to Franz with a smile, and he did his best to return it. "It doesn't seem possible after so long," she said.

Marcel smiled too, but Franz recognized the deeper shadows in his eyes. He'd seen what remained after battle. The destruction, the carnage.

"What of Maman?" Rosalie's smile slipped away.

"I went there first. She is well. But Sainte-Mère-Église. . . A lot of damage has been done. Mayor Renaud has called upon all who can help."

Rosalie nodded her understanding. "Are you sure you should return? Your injuries. . ."

"Not immediately and not to Sainte-Mère-Église. Our French troops, what is left of them, will be reforming as we drive the Nazis back, and I plan to fight with them."

Franz remained silent while Rosalie gently embraced her brother. For Franz, the war was over. No more fighting. No more pretending. When she drew away, Franz pushed to his feet, blinking against a wave of darkness threatening to pull him back down. "You will take me with you, Marcel? Turn me over to the Americans as a prisoner."

She spun. "No, Franz."

"What else is there to do?" He leaned his good shoulder against the wall, weaker than he'd realized. "I will be a danger to you so long as I am here. If I am found out, your own people will hate you for protecting me. If all goes well, Germany will surrender, and someday I will be allowed to return home." Though he wasn't sure he still had a home there.

Rosalie's eyes watered. Perhaps she realized the finality of this moment. "But your shoulder. You need more time. Heal awhile first."

"She's right." Marcel spoke up. "There is too much chaos right now; it's a mess out there. Wait awhile longer and get some rest. You look barely able to stand."

Franz submitted with a nod and attempted to cross to the closest chair before he ended up on the floor again. His legs quaked under him.

"There has to be another way." Rosalie met him halfway and assisted him onto a chair beside the table, her own limp more obvious with each step. "Somehow convince them that he helped the Resistance, that he—"

"Convince them what? That I'm not a German soldier?" He managed a rueful smile. "I am." He drew her onto the chair next to his. "Convince them that I have never fought against them? I have. You think they could let me remain here?" Franz closed his eyes, wishing he hadn't stood in the first place. His head hurt almost as much his shoulder. "I have been stationed here over a year, and there are orders I followed which did not endear me to the locals. Or do you convince them to ship me to England and rent me an apartment? That would take some convincing, and my English is significantly worse than my French."

"If we could find Robert, he could help," she said to her brother, obviously ignoring him.

"Find him how?" Marcel questioned. "Every pilot will be in the middle of the invasion, and then the continued offensive. It might be months before we can get word to him. Franz is right. As a prisoner of war, he will hopefully receive the care he needs and will someday be returned to Germany where he belongs."

Belongs.

Such a fickle word—one that deepened the pain in his chest beyond the physical torment of his wound. Did he belong anywhere?

The conversation wasn't getting them anywhere. "Let me see that ankle." Franz directed Rosalie to put her foot on his knee. He unwrapped the blue scarf and grimaced on her behalf. Dark bruising suggested extensive damage. "What have you done to yourself?"

Rosalie nodded to his shoulder. "You're one to talk." She reached for his hand. Their fingers entwined, and belonging found new meaning. He belonged with her. Her eyes spoke the same.

———— ≈ ————

"D-day has come. Allied troops were landed under strong Naval and air cover on the coast of Normandy early this morning."

Rosalie turned up the volume. Finally, news of what was happening around her. She'd been listening to the BBC most of the afternoon, hoping they would have more concise details of the invasion.

"The Prime Minister has told the Commons that the commanding officers have reported everything going to plan so far, with beach landings still going on at midday and mass airborne landings successfully made behind enemy lines."

Success. Words she had prayed to hear. With the bombardment still heard on the beaches and sounds of battle from every other direction, it was hard to imagine what might be going on out there.

"More than four thousand ships, with several thousand smaller craft, have crossed the Channel, and some eleven thousand first-line aircraft can be drawn upon for battle."

She pictured Robert and offered a prayer for his protection.

"His Majesty the King will broadcast at nine o'clock tonight."

With that, the report ended. Rosalie settled into the nearest kitchen chair and lowered the volume. Hopefully Franz still slept, having moved as far as the sofa. She'd pestered him about relocating to the cellar, but he'd refused to hide.

"In the end, it changes nothing," he'd said.

"It buys us more time." Maybe even months, just as when they'd hid Robert.

But then what?

"Won't make goodbye any easier," he'd whispered.

I don't want goodbye.

Rosalie stepped to the parlor and leaned against the wall to watch Franz sleep. Discomfort pinched between his eyes and a lock of blond hair lay across his forehead. She fought the desire to brush it back, remaining in place instead, waiting for an idea or plan that allowed him to stay.

You can only delay. She groaned at the pesky voice of reason. She didn't want logic to play a role, to dictate an end.

"What are you doing there?" Franz asked sleepily. He started to sit up.

"Don't move." She hurried to his side but was too late to stop the motion. He opened his good arm to her, and she slipped onto the sofa beside him. He hummed and sank lower, resting his head against the back, and again closed his eyes.

"I'm sorry if I woke you."

"You didn't." The corner of his mouth turned up. "And this is good."

"You need rest, not—"

"I need you." His arm tightened around her. He leaned in and nuzzled her neck with a kiss. "Just you."

She turned her head so he could kiss her lips, the sensation igniting every fiber of her. "There has to be a way," she murmured against his mouth.

"I wish there were any way. I'm so. . ." He kissed her again. "Not." Long and slow against the side of her mouth. "Ready." He deepened the kiss. "To say *auf Wiedersehen*." He sat up to face her more fully. His good hand came to her cheek, then slipped to the nape of her neck.

A fist hammered on the door. Rosalie drew back but wasn't ready to pull away. The knocking thundered through the cottage again.

"Go." Franz slid his hand back.

She pushed to her feet and hobbled to the door. "Who's there?"

No answer, just more pounding.

She glanced at Franz. He forced himself to his feet and lifted the revolver Marcel had left with them. He still wore half of his uniform, had insisted on not changing. He nodded, and she eased the door open a crack. Americans, but not paratroopers. They must have made it inland from the beaches.

"Are you alone, ma'am?"

She opened her mouth and felt her breath quicken. Fear spiked through her. It was too soon.

"Do you understand?"

"Oui, I understand. Everything is fine here." But her voice still trembled.

The soldier in front gave a nod, and the other two brought up their rifles. "Can you step outside, ma'am?"

"I. . ."

Franz touched her arm. "*Laisse-moi partir*," he whispered. "You must let me go." He pressed his lips to her fingers behind the door.

Not like this. She wasn't ready. But the American already reached for her other arm. His companions stepped forward with rifles ready. She glanced at Franz to see he'd set the revolver aside and his hands were rising despite the pain of the movement.

The American clutched her wrist and tugged her from the doorway. "He's unarmed!" She jerked away, trying to step sideways to block Franz from them. Her ankle protested with a bolt of pain. "He's already hurt."

One of the soldiers again yanked her out of the way, and they pushed past. Thankfully, they held their fire, instead motioning with their weapons for Franz to step outside. One soldier glanced at her out of the corner of his eye and spat on the floor.

"He's not like them," she tried to interject. "He's not one of them anymore." She wanted to explain what he had done for the Resistance, for Robert and Marcel, but they shook their heads as they led Franz away, a prisoner of war. Her stomach churned with fear for his sake. This wasn't right. How had they known where to come, where to find him? Had the paratroopers or a neighbor betrayed them?

Only when they were out of sight did Rosalie turn back inside the cottage. The revolver remained on the edge of the sofa where Franz had left it. His stained jacket hung over the arm. Her lips tingled with the sensation of his kisses.

You must let me go.

She wasn't sure she could.

‎CHAPTER 36‎

Rosalie walked toward the village, relying heavily on a cane she'd found that had belonged to her Grandfather Barrieau. If she could still claim him as her grandfather. All ties to family and heritage seemed frayed or severed completely, setting her adrift and leaving her heart aching. Despite liberation, her whole world seemed shaken.

She stayed to the side of the road as tanks and transports rolled toward Sainte-Mère-Église and onward in pursuit of the retreating Germans. A meadow on the outskirts was strewn with parachutes billowing in the breeze. The village bustled with activity. American forces organized their regiments and supplies while villagers watched and celebrated their liberation. Rosalie's heart warred between jubilation and a deep-set sorrow. And loneliness.

The Fournier home stood with shuttered windows, silent and dark. In the past she would have felt welcome to enter with a call out to anyone home. She pictured Lucas with his big smile and dark eyes. He would have been one of the loudest in his celebrations of the day. She rapped her knuckles on the door and waited.

Aline Fournier appeared and frowned, looking Rosalie up and down. "What are you doing here?"

"I need to see my mother. Just for a moment."

"If she will see you." She said nothing else as she turned back inside the house and closed the door.

Rosalie waited on the doorstep, hoping her mother would come, but almost fearful that she would. Her mother's shunning would cut so much deeper. She hoped knowledge of Marcel's freedom would entice Maman to listen to what had happened and forgive her.

You've done nothing wrong.

And yet it felt like a great crime to love a German, even one who had done so much for her family and country.

"Rosalie Barrieau, how dare you show your face here?" a man said from behind her. She spun to see Claude Fournier stalking toward her. "We've seen you carrying on with that German officer. Do you think we will so easily forget?"

She stared at him, a knot roiling in her stomach. Had Marcel said anything about Franz with the Fourniers present? Was that how the Americans found him?

Claude continued his railing, his booming voice calling others to attention. Several started in their direction.

"You don't know what you saw." She turned from him but couldn't shut out his taunts or the gathering crowd, like vultures around their prey.

"You betrayed my son and his memory with a Nazi. You've betrayed your own people!"

The accusation cut, and Rosalie tightened her jaw against the surge of emotion choking her. She glanced back at the door to confirm that her mother had no intention of seeing her, then stepped to leave.

Claude and his neighbors blocked her path.

"Please let me pass." She cleared her throat and raised her voice. "I betrayed no one. I fought the Germans just as fervently as any of you. If Monsieur Dumont were here, he'd—"

"Dumont was denounced to the Nazis," someone accused. "He is dead, and his daughter missing. Had you anything to do with that?"

Everything to do with it, but not how they must think. "I—"

"We don't need to hear her excuses." Claude grabbed her arm and shouted for someone to hold her steady. He'd been as dear as a father to her once upon a time, but now his fingers bit her skin. And his eyes. . . It wasn't anger she saw there, but fear.

Had he anything to do with Dumont's death?

The thought was drowned out by the accusations and curses that rained down upon her. Two men held her firmly, offering no chance for retreat. Someone yanked on her hair. Steel scraped against steel next to her ear. A handful of dark hair fell across her shoulders and to the dirt under her feet. Large shears, more fit for sheeps' wool, hovered over her scalp, removing handful after handful of her hair until she was shoved aside.

Like the tide against the shore, the crowd released and rolled back, the deed done. She dropped to her knees amongst the dark locks littering the street.

"You don't belong here anymore," Claude spat, his voice wheezing. He was the last to leave.

Rosalie knelt numb, her mind trying to grasp what had happened. A shuffle of feet drew her gaze to the doorway and her mother. "Maman. . ."

Her mother wore no expression but the glassy sheen in her eyes.

Rosalie found her cane and pushed to her feet. No tears. She forced her chin up but took the shortest route away from the village, cutting across the fields toward home.

Despite the backdrop of air raids and distant battle, the cottage cradled her in silence. She made her way up the stairs to her room where curiosity compelled her to glance at her reflection in the mirror. She stared at the ragged mess on top of her head and ran her fingers though what was left of her dark brown locks, not sure what to feel or what to do. Curl up in her bed and cry? Find her Bible and read until the pain diminished enough to think clearly?

Downstairs, a door opened and clicked closed. Rosalie stood in place, waiting as she mentally followed the footsteps into the kitchen, and then up the stairs. She closed her eyes and pictured Papa coming through the door as he had so often done throughout her life, whether to tuck her into bed or discuss something that had upset her. If only he were there now. He'd wrap her in an embrace while she wept, then wipe her tears away with his large thumbs.

"You are the most precious rose of all."

Then why do I feel as though I'm wilting, my petals falling away, my color fading to nothing. "I have nothing. I'm not even yours."

"Of course you are mine."

Rosalie turned to her mother, her breath in her throat. "Maman?"

She seemed to hesitate at the bedroom threshold. Rosalie remained in place as her mother crossed the floor to stand behind her. She touched the jagged locks. Without a word said, she pulled a chair over and guided Rosalie to sit. Gentle fingers slid against her scalp, and moisture pooled in her eyes. With a fine pair of scissors, Maman began to trim away the uneven ends of her hair.

"I thought. . ." Rosalie started, unable to voice her fears that her mother hated her and wanted nothing to do with her.

"I have despised myself for so long," Maman breathed, her words barely audible.

"Not me?"

"You were a reminder. Of what I did. What I thought I had to do. To survive."

The door banged open downstairs and heavy feet hammered up the stairs. Marcel appeared in the doorway to her bedroom, fresh blood smeared from his nose. "I heard what happened." He waved at his face. "The man who told me looks worse."

"Oh, Marcel," Rosalie squeaked.

He leaned against the doorframe, his hand cradling his bruised ribs. "Don't worry about what they think. We know the truth. And I'll set every last one of them straight." His mouth tipped up in a rueful smile. "Forcefully if needed."

Maman guided Marcel to the bed to lie down before returning to Rosalie.

When her hair was tamed, Rosalie took a breath and analyzed herself in the mirror. Not perfect, and much shorter than she had ever worn her hair or was fashionable, but cooler for the summer she supposed. She had no plans to go anywhere. Despite her brother's efforts, she would never be fully welcome in the village. Even Maman had disappeared again as quietly as she had come, but Rosalie would hold those moments with her mother and the knowledge that she was loved.

The beaches of Normandy provided a much-needed resting place after hours of marching. Franz sank to the sand and lay flat on his back. His old injuries ached from the excursion but seemed nothing to the agony ripping through his shoulder with every motion. Almost enough to distract him from his thirst.

He listened to the waves crashing onto the shore and dreamed of lying within reach, cool water rushing over him. The beaches were so different from last he'd seen them—fortifications left in shambles, craters in the sand where it had been struck by artillery shells. He wondered if his sketches had ever reached the Allies, and if they had helped.

"You want a drink, Leutnant?"

Franz opened his eyes to Brenner, who crouched beside him, brow pinched with concern. He held a pail with a ladle.

"Bitte." Franz forced himself into a sitting position and reached his good hand for the ladle. It shook as he took a long draw of the tepid water.

"They are shipping us to England, aren't they?" Brenner cast a glance at their American guards.

"From the little I've heard, that seems the plan." Far away from the war. Farther away from Rosalie. He tried to focus on the present. "Did you see what happened to Karl?"

Brenner shook his head. "He was still alive when I surrendered, but I think he pulled back with the major and the others."

In the far distance the sounds of war continued. "They are probably still fighting." Battling for every mile.

Brenner returned the ladle to the pail but lingered beside him. "Are you glad it's over for us?"

"Ja," Franz offered honestly. "If we don't make any trouble, we'll hopefully be treated fairly. We'll wait out the war in England or wherever they send us." He wiped the back of his wrist over the sweat on his forehead. Thankfully the sky was overcast and didn't add to his discomfort.

"Simple enough for you." Another voice joined, and Franz swung his head to see Bayerlein making his way around other men. Dirt and dried blood soiled his usually impeccable uniform, and he wore no hat, but otherwise he looked like he had fared well before being captured. "Are you here to spy on us, Kafka? Are you still working for them?"

"Nein," he answered shortly, every muscle tensing.

Bayerlein lunged, hands finding Franz's throat and pressing him into the sand. "You're one of them. You knew what was coming and took advantage of it. You traitor!"

Franz choked against the pressure on his windpipe. He slammed his good arm against the side of Bayerlein's head, but he didn't budge. A cough tore at the back of Franz's throat, unable to release. Black blotches infiltrated his vision. Franz pressed his hand into the other man's face and wedged his knee between them. The pressure on his throat eased. He gulped a breath while knuckles slammed into his jaw.

Someone yanked Bayerlein from behind, dragging him back.

A rifle discharged only feet away as three stockade guards hurried toward them. Bayerlein jerked away from Brenner's grasp and spat at Franz. "Here are your friends, come to rescue you."

The Americans shouted something in English Franz didn't quite understand but was easy enough to guess. Other German prisoners dispersed, leaving Franz to sink back into the sand.

One of the guards hovered over Franz, and he followed the American's gaze to the scarlet soaking the bandages that wrapped his shoulder. He blinked at the large drop of sweat rolling into his eyes.

"Medic" was the only word Franz recognized, but someone was soon at his side. A shot of morphine brought blessed relief while they cut his bandage free and doused his inflamed shoulder with alcohol. Exhaustion and nausea pummeled him with equal fervency, and Franz closed his eyes.

He woke up some time later, his body prone on a stretcher. British soldiers deposited him among a group of other wounded aboard one of their transport ships. The vessel rocked as it crossed the Channel, adding to the nausea still brewing within him. He ignored it as best he could when food was brought—the first he'd tasted in a couple of days. A serving of mashed potatoes, sausage, white bread, and coffee did little to fill the empty pit of his stomach. Although others returned again and again to fill their plates, Franz didn't dare eat more.

Despite the uncertainty of their future, most of the men seemed in good spirits. Young men, many not yet twenty, joked and laughed with each other. Franz sighted Brenner among them and caught his gaze. The youth made his way around the others and crouched near Franz.

"Can I get you anything, Leutnant?"

He shook his head.

"The sausage is not bad."

"Not great either. Just better than anything we have had in months." He shook his head and fought another wave of nausea. "Honestly, I'm still trying to hold it down."

The younger man's eyes showed concern. "You don't look well."

Franz didn't doubt it. But he wouldn't rest easy without knowing one last thing. "What happened to Hauptmann Meyer? Do you know?"

"Hauptmann Meyer is dead. He was upset about something when he joined us during the first night of the invasion, and then we fell back. His car was struck by one of the American bombers."

Franz sighed. While he'd been prepared to kill the man for Marcel's sake, he hadn't wanted him dead. "I'm sorry to hear it."

"Is it true, Leutnant Kafka?" Brenner lowered his voice. "What Unteroffizier Bayerlein said about you?"

Franz thought again of his sketches and the other information he had fed Rosalie and Marcel over the past few months. "I don't know if what I did helped the Allies, but I am tired of this war, and of innocent people being hurt."

The boy seemed to digest that. "I'm glad we don't have to fight anymore," he finally whispered. He looked up at the others surrounding them. The ship rocked on a wave. "But I wonder where they will take us."

So much still unknown, and Franz had control over none of it. He allowed his eyes to close, his body growing weary, as though a great weight pressed down. His shoulder burned. A chill moved through him, and he realized he hadn't felt warm for a while. Was it the clamminess of the room or the fever's effect on him? His war was far from over, but he could do nothing but turn his fate over to God. He focused his thoughts on memories of a charred Bible and the faith of the woman who carried it.

⅀CHAPTER 37⅀

Normandy, France – March 1946

Rosalie jerked her hand back from the dead thorn that had caught her finger. *"Aie-aie-aie."* She wiped the drop of blood and maneuvered her shears more carefully to snip the offending branch from the rosebush. It fell away. Neglect had left its toll on the bush, but new growth would come, and more blossoms. How she yearned for fields and arbors of flowers again, to return the gardens to how Papa had left them.

Papa.

Maman never would tell her who her real father was, and Rosalie was coming to accept that she might never know whether he was French or German, never mind his name. All she knew was that Charles Barrieau had found Julie Martin after the war as he'd journeyed home. She'd never understood why he'd taken compassion on her, with so many others destitute, but he had offered a home in Normandy for her and her baby.

Not just a home but love.

Rosalie closed her eyes and pictured her papa's face, imagined his embrace. The sun warmed her face, and she could almost remember his hand cupping her chin as he pressed a kiss to her head. *"My Rosa."*

No matter what was in her family's past, she was *his*.

She looked up at the pale blue sky, and the warmth penetrated deeper.

You are also mine.

She didn't hear the words, but they seeped into her thoughts and heart. A smile touched her lips.

Rosalie finished with the rosebush and threw the dead stems into the pile in the back field that she would later burn. She examined the black earth and imagined row after row of flowers nodding in the breeze, just as they had been before the war. Not this year, as food was still scarce and vegetables were more vital than tulips, but someday. . .

"Bonjour!"

Rosalie turned to see Yvonne at the arbor, hand waving. She started in that direction.

"Has Marcel returned?" Yvonne questioned. "He told me he has a surprise for you, and I wanted to be here for it." She grinned, her eyes mischievous. What were the two of them up to? Yvonne had returned to her home in the fall, shortly after VE day, but she might as well have moved in with them for how often she visited, mostly to be with Marcel.

"I haven't seen him since morning, but I have the feeling you already know where he has been all day."

Yvonne merely smiled and led the way to the front of the house. "Why don't you step in and wash up."

Rosalie hesitated. There was still so much to do before planting, and she'd already spent more time than she should have in the flower beds. But if Marcel was on his way with a "surprise," then she might as well humor them.

As soon as she had washed her hands, Yvonne looked her up and down, head wagging. "You should probably change into something a little nicer."

"Why does my dress matter?" She dusted at the brown skirt and noticed a snag in the blouse.

"You'll see."

Suspicions rising, Rosalie trudged upstairs and began digging through her clothes for something acceptable to wear. It was a more difficult task than she would have had though, as Yvonne shook her head at each suggested skirt or dress. Finally, the younger woman pushed past her and withdrew the deep blue dress she had worn to Paris with Franz. She'd worn it again for the celebrations when Germany surrendered, officially ending the war in Europe, but not since.

"This one. Trust me." Yvonne practically skipped out of the room, closing the door behind her.

"What on earth?" Did Marcel's surprise include a visitor? As she turned through possibilities, one person clung to her mind and refused to be pushed aside, no matter how impossible. She donned the dress and looked in the mirror. All she could think about was Franz's intense gaze when he had seen her in this dress. She closed her eyes with memories of their night in Paris and their attempt to pretend the war away. She'd be much more successful now.

If only she could pretend she'd see him again.

Voices at the front of the cottage pulled her to the bedroom window, but whoever had come was already near the door and blocked from her sight. Rosalie quickly ran a brush through her hair, trying to tame the waves tumbling to her shoulders. She wrapped it up in a bun, thinking that better. But no, not as flattering. If only she knew who was now downstairs. With her hair down again, Rosalie gave up on the mirror. She made it halfway down the stairs before pulling to a stop.

A man in British uniform spoke with Marcel and Yvonne, who stood arm in arm. Maman lingered near the kitchen entry, likely not understanding everything said in English.

"I would have liked to return months ago, but there's always been something standing in the way," the man said.

Rosalie tested her voice. "Robert?"

He turned and grinned up at her. "There she is, and as beautiful as ever a rose was." He opened his arms, and she hurried down to him, stopping just short of his embrace.

"You did come."

He gripped her arms. "I told you I would, though every time I wrote, it seemed I had nothing but another reason I had to stay away."

"It doesn't matter. Not anymore."

Marcel stepped to her side, saving her from the awkward space between them. "I just got home in the New Year."

Robert glanced at him but still held her arms. "Ah yes, Rosalie wrote you had joined the French forces." They spoke a moment more about shared experiences with the last year of the war and everything that followed.

Rosalie barely followed their conversation, her mind spinning with Robert's presence in their home and the arm he wrapped around her. They'd been corresponding by letters over the past year, but little of consequence had been exchanged. He asked about her health and her family, and what had happened to the German who had saved his life, but nothing of feelings that might still exist between them.

Robert glanced at her. "Some German prisoners of war have been sent home. Though many are being detained to help rebuild roads and buildings throughout the rest of Europe."

"Did you ever find him?" Hope bubbled up through her. "I know you said you hadn't, but that was months ago."

"Him?" Yvonne sounded confused.

Marcel frowned at Rosalie, obviously not approving of her interest, but how did they expect her to forget him, to not keep wondering and praying?

"I did track down a Lieutenant Franz Kafka who was sent with a group of prisoners to the United States."

"America. . ." So far away. "And?"

"I had some American friends on their way home, so I asked them to look into it more. There is a Camp Patrick Henry near Warwick, Virginia."

She hung on his every word. After almost two years without news, it was like rain to thirsty roots. "And Franz was sent there?"

"Yes." He watched her closely, as though gauging her reaction.

She managed a half smile. "It's good to finally know."

He nodded, seeming to consider that.

"Is he still there? You said some prisoners are being sent home."

"Yes. But he won't be returning to Germany."

Rosalie stared. Had she not heard correctly? "I thought. . . I do not understand."

"My friends not only found him but helped me secure his release. We pestered some higher officials until someone listened and decided that in saving my life, and given the assistance he rendered the French Resistance, he would be allowed his freedom."

"But he's not returning to Germany?" She still didn't understand.

"He requested to remain in the United States."

"Oh." She tried to smile. She was happy for Franz. Free. With a new home. Hopefully his English had improved during his time there. . .but so far away. "That is good."

Robert glanced at the others. "I'm going to steal Rosalie away for a few minutes if that's all right." He took her hand and led her from the house. She allowed him to guide her, but her thoughts remained in America. How had Franz coped with being a prisoner? Did he like his new home? Had he met a woman there, and had that influenced his decision to stay?

"I have a letter for you," Robert said as they walked. "But I wanted to see you first and get a feel for where things stand between us." He pulled her around to face him. The side of his mouth turned up, and he touched her face. Slowly, he leaned in and pressed his lips to hers. She didn't pull away, but neither could she find it in herself to return his kiss. Yes, his attention had once moved her, but she'd been so young when it came to relationships and love. She'd been flattered and infatuated with Robert, but she *loved* Franz.

He withdrew, but his hand lingered at her chin. "I thought as much. As soon as I mentioned him, your eyes lit far more than when you saw me. You are in love with him, aren't you?"

"Yes." And two years had done nothing to loosen his hold on her heart.

Robert nodded with a rueful smile and withdrew an envelope from the front pocket of his coat. "This is for you." He passed her the letter and turned back to the house.

"You won't leave already?" Though her feelings were not as he wished, she did care.

"Take a few minutes with your letter. I'll be here." He walked back to the cottage.

Rosalie watched him go, then looked at the envelope addressed from America. She held it close and walked toward the stream where she'd rendezvoused with Franz so many times. She still came often to read the Bible, pray, and wonder what the future would hold for her.

Seated on her stone beside the rush of water, she unfolded the single sheet of paper to the French words scripted at the top.

My Rosalie,

As a free man, I sit here staring at the paper, so much to say. Words do not often come easily for me. It is not how my mind works once pencil meets paper.

His words ended there, but below, shades of gray brought to life the face of a woman with warm eyes and a sad smile. Against her cheek, she held a rose.

The sketch disappeared behind a sheen of moisture. She closed her eyes, though the image remained vivid in her mind.

"What is this about you going to America?" Marcel questioned, closing the distance between them.

She wiped at her moist face and turned. "Who said I was leaving?"

"Robert. He told us he would pay for your journey to Virginia if you wished?" Her brother searched her eyes. "You will leave?"

"Robert will help me?" She couldn't hold the wonder from her voice. Until this moment she had not considered going to America, of leaving her family behind. There was so little money, nothing to be wasted on a journey across the ocean to be reunited with the man she still yearned for. Being together was impossible, wasn't it? And yet now here it sat, within her grasp.

"You are going to him," Marcel said somberly. "I can see it in your eyes. You will go."

"Is it wrong if I do? I feel as though I would be abandoning you and Maman. And Papa. All we worked for and fought for."

"We fought for freedom." Marcel cracked a rueful smile. "Freedom to stay or to leave. Freedom to love who we wish, and to map out our own lives."

Rosalie looked out over Papa's fields, nervous anticipation mingling with sudden loneliness. "I think I do know what I want for my life."

Virginia, USA – July 1946

Franz leaned his head back on the seat of the bus, allowing his eyes to close for a few minutes while it wound its way to the other side of Richmond where an evening of study awaited him. He covered a yawn with the back of his hand, his palms still stained with a day's work filling potholes. He'd gotten a job repairing roads after his release and squirreled away every extra cent with hopes of school, a house, and maybe someday sending for Rosalie—at least asking if she would consider joining him here.

Why haven't you?

He'd had the chance when Robert's friends had tracked him down. But he wasn't ready. He had nothing but a hole-in-the-wall apartment, beans, and potatoes. His English was still horrible, giving him few other options for employment for now. He needed time.

And if it's too late by then?

Then he'd have to figure out some way to get her out of his head. He'd have more than one sketchbook to burn.

"*Gott*, give me direction." His frequent prayer, but unfortunately direction was only half the battle. He needed a miracle.

The bus jerked to a stop, and Franz pried open his eyes to see how far they'd come. Two stops remained. As they rolled forward again, he calculated what he'd earned, what he'd be able to save, and how much he would send to his mother. With Ernst in prison for his role in war crimes, Franz tried to make sure she had enough and often wished he could bring her here as well, but for now it was impossible. She wouldn't agree to it anyway. She had lived in Berlin her whole life, she'd written, and had no intention of ever leaving.

Another stop, and three more people boarded the bus. One man dropped onto the seat beside Franz. "You don't mind, do you?"

"Of course not."

The man raised a brow. "Quite the accent you have." He narrowed his eyes as though considering its origin as they always did, suspicion in his gaze. Most recognized where Franz was from quick enough, he could see it in their eyes, but they always asked about Switzerland or somewhere similar. Or maybe he had come to America before the war or was a refugee from Nazi oppression. Thankfully, this man settled back in his seat and said nothing more.

Franz allowed the tension to slip from his shoulders. Few wanted to hear his story, and he had no desire to share it.

The bus began to slow once more, and Franz stood and excused himself. He made his way to the front of the bus to wait for it to stop. Summer hung on the air, hot and moist, an overcast sky threatening an evening shower.

Across the street, a group of boys kicked a ball between them, not a worry in the world.

A woman stood from a nearby bench, small suitcase clutched in her hands. "Franz."

He froze in place, not daring to move or blink for fear she might disappear.

She stared back, biting her bottom lip as a grin spread across her face. "Bonjour."

"Bonjour," he managed. How was this possible? Wow, she looked amazing—so much more beautiful than his memory. Perhaps it was the blush in her cheeks and the vibrancy of her eyes.

She took a step toward him. "That is all you have to say to me?"

A laugh broke from him. Oh, the things he wanted to say, to tell her. "You're here."

"I am."

"You're really here."

A sheen of moisture glistened in her eyes. "I really am."

"Oh, my Rosa..." He opened his arms, and she dropped her luggage and ran into them. He crushed her against him, to feel her, to see her alive, safe... He pressed a kiss into the side of her head, burying it in her thick hair. Just to hold her again. "You're here."

"I am," she whispered against his collar. "I'm here."

"And you'll stay?"

She pulled away just enough to gaze into his eyes. Her hands cupped either side of his face. "Of course I will."

He tasted her lips and breathed her deep, still not sure how this was possible and not able to let go. Only enough to whisper, "Be my wife."

"Oui," she said against his lips, then smiled. "How is that for your morale?"

His groan mingled with a chuckle. "My morale has never been better."

AUTHOR'S NOTE

Thank you so much for joining me for Rosalie and Franz's story. Though fictional, these characters have come to mean a lot to me because of the people whose lives and experiences they represent. Franz was my very first character in a novel I started writing as a teenager. Though much of that early work will never see the light of day, I am glad I can finally share him with you.

Every November 11th since I was a child, I would sit with my dad and watch WWII documentaries and movies like *A Bridge Too Far* or *The Longest Day* which featured Sainte-Mère-Église during the D-day landings. So many of those stories beg to be remembered, and I tried to include as much as I could in this novel, even in passing. Stories such as John Steele of the 505th Parachute Infantry Regiment, who dropped into the war zone of Sainte-Mère-Église that night and had his chute catch on the spire of the church. He hung limply for hours, pretending to be dead, before the Germans took him prisoner. John later escaped and rejoined his division. Or Henry Langrehr who landed five miles from his drop zone, crashing through a greenhouse on the way down. He was unharmed from the fall but was later wounded and captured. He lived into his nineties to tell the tale.

Many of the events and deeds of the Resistance in the novel are also pulled from history. The French citizens willingly risked their lives to transport weapons and information and to staunchly resist the brutal German occupation. It is estimated that approximately 90,000 men and women—and children—were killed, tortured, or deported by the Germans for their efforts.

Though many of the characters in this story are fictional, there are so many men and women who truly did live through the horrors of this war in Europe and, more importantly, risked or sacrificed their all for the freedom and lives of others.

I pray we never forget.

To keep from freezing in the Great White North, **Angela K. Couch** cuddles under quilts with her laptop. Winning short story contests, being a semi-finalist in ACFW's Genesis Contest, and being a finalist in the 2016 International Digital Awards also helped warm her up. As a passionate believer in Christ, her faith permeates the stories she tells. Her martial arts training, experience with horses, and appreciation for good romance sneak in as well. When not writing, she stays fit (and toasty warm) by chasing after five munchkins.

⚊ HEROINES OF WWII ⚊

They went above the call of duty and expectations to aid the Allies war efforts and save the oppressed. Full of intrigue, adventure, and romance, this new series celebrates the unsung heroes—the heroines of WWII.

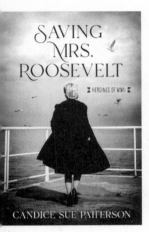

Saving Mrs. Roosevelt
BY CANDICE SUE PATTERSON

Shirley Davenport is as much a patriot as her four brothers. She too wants to aid her country in the war efforts and joins a new branch of the Coast Guard for single women called SPARs. At the end of basic training, Captain Webber commissions her back home in Maine under the ruse of a dishonorable discharge to help uncover a plot against the First Lady. Shirley soon discovers nothing is as it seems. Why do the people she loves want to harm the First Lady?

Paperback / 978-1-63609-089-4 / $14.99

Mrs. Witherspoon Goes to War
BY MARY DAVIS

Peggy Witherspoon, a widow, mother, and pilot flying for the Women's Airforce Service in 1944 clashes with her new reporting officer. Army Air Corp Major Howie Berg was injured in combat and is now stationed at Bolling Field in Washington D.C. Most of Peggy's jobs are safe, predictable, and she can be home each night with her three daughters—until a cargo run to Cuba alerts her to three American soldiers being held captive there, despite Cuba being an "ally." Will Peggy go against orders to help the men—even risk her own life?

Paperback / 978-1-63609-156-3 / $14.99